Praise for Allie Boniface

"Allie Boniface's *Summer's Song* is an engrossing story about hidden pasts, lost memories, and finding love despite everything else. Summer is a complex character who you will grow to care about...Damian, the protector, is compelling... I thoroughly enjoyed this book, a wonderful read."

—Ecataromance

"The descriptions of the scenery, the buildings and the animals are so vivid I feel that I am there... Boniface is a new to me author and I look forward to reading more of her books if this is her caliber of writing."

—4 Blue Ribbons, Romance Junkies on *Winter's Wonder*

"*Winter's Wonder* is a heart melting pick me up from the heart whisperer Allie Boniface...she creates the most beautiful characters that are down on their luck or wallowing in disappointment and self-doubt and then supplies the exact guidance and encouragement needed from the most unlikely source."

—Hopeless Romantic Review Blog

"Thrilling action and suspense complement a budding romance in this touching story of two people finding new beginnings. Appealing secondary characters add depth to an engaging plot."

—RT Book Reviews on *One Night in Memphis*

Look for these titles by Allie Boniface

Now Available:

Pine Point series
Summer's Song
Winter's Wonder

Spring Secrets

Allie Boniface

Samhain Publishing, Ltd.
11821 Mason Montgomery Road, 4B
Cincinnati, OH 45249
www.samhainpublishing.com

Spring Secrets

Print ISBN: 978-1-61923-491-8
Digital ISBN: 978-1-61923-490-1

Editing by Heidi Moore
Cover by Syd Gill Designs

First Samhain Publishing, Ltd. electronic publication: May 2016
First Samhain Publishing, Ltd. print publication: May 2016

Dedication

For everyone who's started over…

Chapter One

Sienna tightened her hands around the steering wheel as she left the interstate and turned onto Main Street. *I can't believe I'm back in Pine Point.* She hadn't meant to return, but life had a funny way of spinning her around and shoving her into situations she'd never dreamed possible. She hadn't meant to sleep on friends' couches all through high school either, or pay her way through college by working two jobs and living in her car. But she was this close to being the first in her family to finish an advanced college degree, and if that meant returning to her childhood hometown for a few months, then so be it.

She slowed as she passed the Feed 'n Seed, the Beauty Barn, a strip mall with a Chinese food place, and cheap apartments she remembered too well. Her eyes burned with unshed tears, and she blinked to keep them from falling. *"You're going home?"* her friends at graduate school had asked when she'd told them. *"Sounds like fun. I haven't been home in ages."* But a knot had tightened in the middle of her chest. Going home for Sienna meant heartache and loneliness, not reuniting with high school friends or visiting favorite childhood hangouts. She cut her speed from fifty to forty to thirty-five, as if slowing her arrival would make it more bearable.

"You were here just last month," she said aloud. "It wasn't any big deal back then. It won't be any big deal now."

But last month had been a reconnaissance trip, a whim to see if the Pine Point of her youth would turn out to be a place she could research. She'd come only at the urging of the professor advising her dissertation. *"You want to write about the psychology of small towns? You grew up in one. Start there."*

Sienna turned her head almost involuntarily as she passed the brightly lit parking lot of the Pine Point Medical Center. That shouldn't be the last place her fifteen-year-old self remembered with any detail. And at twenty-six years old, she should have put those details out of her mind by now.

Except hearing a white-faced doctor try to explain her mother had died of a heart attack was something a girl tended to remember.

Sienna turned up the radio. She didn't recognize the song, but that didn't matter. Maybe the incessant bass would drive out all other thoughts. The sleeves of her coat slipped up, and the faint white scar on her left wrist stood out as she drove under the streetlights already on in the growing shadows. A few cars passed her going in the opposite direction, but traffic was light this Sunday afternoon. She'd waited until the last possible minute to make the ten-hour drive from North Carolina, and even now she wondered if she'd made a mistake.

"Tomorrow I'll be an elementary school teacher," she said aloud. Teacher by day, researcher by night. That was the plan. Six months from now, she'd ideally have everything she needed to prove that small towns like Pine Point really did simmer with secrets and scandal. The Peyton Place syndrome was oh so real. Even picturesque Main Streets like this one held mysteries behind their storefronts. People smiled to their neighbors and then went home and hit the bottle a little too hard, or doctored the Little League financial records to skim a little off the top, or told themselves online cheating wasn't the same as actually sleeping with someone else. Then they went to church on Sundays and put an extra ten in the offering plate to atone.

"It's not that I think big cities are any better," she once told a classmate. *"It's just that from what I've seen, small towns pride themselves on being safe and conservative and good, wholesome places to raise a family, when they're hiding just as much dirty laundry as anywhere else."*

She braked outside Springer Fitness. The one-story gray building sat on the south end of town, with a bright red sign above the door and steamed-up front windows. At the desk inside stood the owner, a broad-shouldered guy with a blond crew cut and blazing blue eyes. She'd gone out with him a couple of times last month, also on a whim, because he'd asked her with a sideways grin that had sent squiggles into her stomach. It hadn't amounted to much, and they hadn't slept together. She hadn't told him she was coming back. She hadn't told anyone at all, except the landlord of a third-floor apartment on Main Street and the elementary school principal.

Sienna pulled to the curb and parked. It was too early for a drink. It was certainly too early to climb under the covers and go to sleep. But it was the perfect time for a kick-ass workout with a guy who knew how to bench three hundred pounds and then kiss a girl until her knees buckled. She checked her reflection in the rearview mirror, grabbed her workout gear, and headed inside.

Mike Springer grunted and shoved up the chest-press bar one last time. His arms shook and sweat ran down his face, but he got it all the way up.

"Hell, man, two ninety-five." Zane Andrews, Mike's best friend, took the bar and set it back on the rack. "Nice job."

Mike sat up and mopped his face. "Thanks." He drank deeply from the bottle of water beside him and then draped the towel around his neck. "You got a shift this afternoon?"

"Nope. Day off." Zane, who'd already finished his reps, leaned against the rack of free weights and surveyed the gym, half full at four o'clock on a Sunday afternoon. "Looks good in here."

Mike stood, legs still a little wobbly from the squats they'd done earlier. "Yep. New Year's resolutions brought a bunch of new people in." He hoped they wouldn't stop coming by the time February rolled around. "I got three new classes set up starting next week. Pilates on Saturday mornings, and kickboxing Tuesday and Thursday nights."

Only one year into the gym-owning business, he was still trying to see what appealed to Pine Point residents. For now, he kept the place open seven days a week, with shorter hours on the weekends. He experimented with the classes he offered, and slowly, his membership was growing. He'd be lying if he said he wasn't damn proud of that. He'd come back to Pine Point with nothing but twenty bucks in his wallet and a dream of leaving the last six years behind him. Eighteen months after leaving California, he was making a go of it. He owed his sanity and his livelihood to Pine Point and the people who lived here. This town had saved him.

"How are things with Becca?" he asked as they wiped down the equipment and wrapped up their workout.

"Awesome." Zane grinned. "Think she might be the real deal, man."

"Good for you." Mike still couldn't believe his buddy had settled down with one of the smartest, most grounded women in town. He couldn't believe Zane had settled down, period. Mike himself had no intention of going down that road again. *Once is more than enough.* He scanned his arms, trying to decide on his next tattoo. Already inked from both elbows up, and from both ankles to knees, he chose more carefully now. No more impulsive decisions, not like in his late teens or early twenties, when everything he did stemmed from late nights of too much drinking or the wrong woman in his bed.

Zane wiped his face, finished his water, and headed for the door as Mike turned for the locker room. "Have a good one, man. See you tomorrow."

"Yep. Likewise." A few minutes later, Mike walked to the front of the gym, dressed in a clean pair of workout pants and a red-collared shirt with *Springer Fitness* embroidered over the pocket. "How's things?" he asked Hans, the twenty-year-old kid manning the desk.

"Good. One new sign-up, and two women came in for a tour."

Mike flipped through paperwork and glanced outside. Yesterday's snow had finally stopped, but he could tell by the white streams coming from pedestrians' mouths that the frigid temperatures remained.

"Days like this, don't you miss L.A.?" Hans asked.

"Nah."

"Seriously?" The kid rested his arms on the desk. "I'd be out there in a minute if I could afford it. Warm weather, palm trees, beaches…shit, and all those women in bikinis." He grinned. "Is it true? Is everything out there silicone and Botox?"

Mike pulled up last month's spreadsheets. "Most of it."

"I don't think I'd care. Fake or real, if I can put my hands on it, it's good enough for me."

"It gets old after a while," Mike said, eyes still on his computer screen.

"How long were you out there?"

"Too long."

Hans elbowed him. "C'mon, man."

"Six years on the West Coast. Only three of 'em in L.A., though." The three worst years of his life.

"All right, I'm heading out," Hans said as he pulled on his ski jacket and hat. "See you tomorrow at nine."

"Have a good one."

"I will." Hans winked. "Remember Liesel, the exchange student from Norway who's staying with the Humphreys?"

Mike vaguely recalled a tall blond with a lilting accent who'd shown up a few times last month. "Yeah. How old is she?"

"Eighteen. Don't worry, Dad. I won't get myself in trouble."

Mike flipped the kid the bird as he left. *Dad.* That was the last thing he needed anyone to call him. *I can barely take care of my own life, let alone anyone else's.* Still, with all the shit he'd been through, he saw it as his civic duty to pass along warnings to other men when it came to getting involved with women.

He focused his attention back on the spreadsheets. Outside, daylight waned as the sun set and clouds crawled over the sky. This far north in New York State, winter lasted forever. Mike didn't care. He'd still rather be here in Pine Point, where people had your back instead of trying to stab you in it.

The door opened with a rush of cold air, and he looked up. He hoped it might be another newcomer looking for a year-long membership, or at least someone interested in a month's trial run. But his fingers froze on the keyboard. His dick immediately went hard. Not a newcomer. Not even close. He knew the dark-haired, dark-eyed woman who stood on the other side of the desk. Not well, certainly not as well as he'd once wanted to, but enough that when she parted her lips in hello, his traitorous heart did a backflip inside his chest.

"Hey, Mike." Sienna Cruz, gorgeous, brilliant, and sexy as hell, tossed her curly black ponytail over one shoulder and flashed him a stunning smile. "Want to box?"

Chapter Two

Sienna began to sweat ten minutes into the workout. Didn't help that Mike had changed into navy shorts and a black tank top that showed off every muscle in his gorgeous body. *Why didn't we ever sleep together?* she wondered as they went through a series of punches, kicks, and a few rounds of sparring. She blew her hair from her forehead and backpedaled as he took a drink of water.

"You're looking good," she said.

He grinned. His gaze raked her from head to toe and turned her hotter than she already was. He adjusted his gloves and approached again, moving toward her on his toes and letting her take a few practice swings as he did. On the last swing, he ducked, moved in, and wrapped one strong arm around her waist, pulling her tight against his chest. Sienna's breath hitched. He grinned again for a second before letting her go. "Gotta protect against that," he said.

But she wasn't sure she wanted to. His torso had felt pretty damn nice pressed against hers. "Give me another chance?"

He took a few steps back and spread his arms wide. Tattoos covered his skin, and their intricate designs distracted her for a moment. He had ink on both legs too, which made for one heck of a piece of artwork standing across from her.

"I'm ready," he said.

She blinked, surprised at the desire surging through her. *So am I. You have no idea.*

* * * * *

One hour later, flushed with adrenaline and good old-fashioned lust, Mike poured two high-protein smoothies into tall glasses. He slid one across the desk to Sienna.

"Thanks." She wrapped her lips around the straw and sucked, which did nothing to cool his desire. She loosened her damp hair from its ponytail and combed it out with her fingers. "And thanks for the workout. I needed it."

They'd spent the better part of an hour sparring, nothing crazy, just footwork and punches, but it hadn't taken long for Mike to remember she had the form of someone who'd been doing martial arts for a long time. She also had the form of someone he'd like to take to bed.

He took a long swallow of his own smoothie. "You're welcome." *Look away. Don't go there. Don't ask where she's been.* But the warnings echoed hollowly inside his head. "So, you gonna tell me why you're back in town?"

He hadn't heard a word from her since she'd left Pine Point before the holidays. He'd called once, texted twice, then left it alone. He'd been a little hurt, sure, especially after three dates and two hot-as-hell make-out sessions. But her silence had spoken volumes, and he'd finally written her off after spending New Year's Eve solo. He sure hadn't expected her to walk back into his gym almost a month later like they'd said goodbye the day before.

She draped a towel around her neck and didn't meet his gaze. A narrow scar stood out on the dark brown skin of her left wrist, and though he remembered seeing it before, he'd never asked her about it.

"You want the long or short version?" she asked.

"Which do you feel like giving me?"

Something like a shadow crossed her face, and he almost expected her to say neither one. The few times they'd gone out, she'd spoken little of herself. He knew nothing except she'd once lived in Pine Point, she'd left town in high school, and she was getting her PhD in some field way beyond his realm of understanding.

"Well, I'm finishing up some research for my dissertation."

"Ah, right. What's that about again?"

"Personality psychology."

He frowned. "Meaning…"

"Meaning a fancy way of saying that people are shaped by the places they grow up. Small towns, like this one, affect people differently than big cities."

"Guess that makes sense."

"I also got a job teaching at Pine Point Elementary. Just until June," she added. "The regular teacher's on maternity leave."

If Mike hadn't been sitting down, he probably would have fallen over. "Teaching? Really?"

Sienna arched a brow. "Really. Surprised?"

"Ah, yeah. I didn't know you could—" He stopped as two of his buddies walked through the front door. "Hey, guys." He lifted his chin in greeting and turned back to Sienna. "You remember Mac Herbert from high school? Think he might've been ahead of you a few years."

She studied the stocky guy with the thick neck and gap between his two front teeth. "Sorry, no."

Mac reached over and shook her hand. "Hi, there. I don't remember you either, so we're even."

"Sienna Cruz. I only went to Pine Point High through tenth grade."

"Oh, yeah? Where'd you go after that?"

She pushed her hair from her face. "Down south to live with my father and stepbrother. I graduated from a high school in North Carolina. I've been attending UNC on and off since then."

Mac whistled and glanced at Mike. "A smarty pants, huh? What's she's doin' here at your place? Slumming?"

Mike gave him a jab on the shoulder. "Watch it." He gestured at the other man. "Damian Knight," he said to Sienna. "Moved to town—what? Three, four years ago? These guys work construction."

"Not in this shitty weather," Mac grumbled.

"It's nice to meet you." Damian smiled at Sienna. "What are you studying at UNC?"

"Psychology. But I got my undergrad in special education. I'm actually here because I'm taking over a class at the elementary school until June."

Mac nodded. "Lucy Foster's class, right? She just had twins," he said to Mike. "I'm not into babies, but those two kids are cute as hell."

"Oh, yeah." Mike still couldn't believe Sienna was about to spend her days at Pine Point Elementary. He'd never pegged her as the teacher type. Tall, gorgeous, exotic, almond-eyed, dressed to kill, with wit and intelligence to boot? Yeah. Not someone who was about to plant seeds in egg cartons or read picture books to kids sitting on a carpet.

Mac yanked Damian's sleeve and groaned. "C'mon. Let's get this hell over with. Nice meeting you," he said over his shoulder as they walked toward the locker room.

"You too." Sienna finished her smoothie and slid the glass back across the counter. "I guess I should go," she said. "I still have to unpack. I haven't even been to my apartment yet."

"Sure. Thanks for stopping in." He cleared his throat. "Good to see you again."

She bit her lip. "Listen, about before," she said. "When I was in town before, I mean. I'm sorry I didn't call or text you after I left. I thought…"

"You thought you wouldn't see me again," he finished for her. "You didn't plan on coming back to Pine Point." He got off his stool and walked behind the counter to rinse their glasses.

"You have to admit, the long-distance thing doesn't usually work," she said. "And we only went out a couple of times."

"True." He busied himself with the faucet and with soaping up and rinsing out the glasses twice more than they needed.

"I just wanted to clear the air. And apologize."

"Apology accepted." He set the glasses in the drainer to dry. Then, against his better judgment, he said, "Let me walk you to your car."

She smiled, and her cheeks pinked.

He held up her coat and waited as she slipped first one slender arm and then the other inside. A touch closer and he could wrap her in his arms. He bit the inside of his cheek to keep himself from growing hard again. Then he pulled on his own coat and followed Sienna to the door. Their breath came in long white streams the moment they stepped outside.

"I forgot how miserable this weather can be." She unlocked her car, shivering.

He glanced up. "But take a look at that view." Above them, a few stars studded the early evening sky.

"It's pretty, I'll give you that." She blinked and looked upward as well, and her long lashes fell to her cheeks before rising again. Everything in Mike turned white-hot with desire. "I guess I'll see you around."

This was the moment she would turn and say goodbye, duck into her car, and leave him standing in the falling snow. Except she didn't. She stood with her back against her cute little sports car, not moving, her chest lifting and falling, the breath still streaming from between her cherry lips, until on impulse, he leaned forward and kissed her.

He meant to kiss her once, fast and hard, but the moment he tasted her again, his hands went to her waist and pulled her tightly against him. His tongue teased her lips open, and she wound her arms around his neck and kissed him back. She smelled like something spicy and forbidden, and despite the cold, she was fire under his touch. Her cheeks and neck and every place he could feel sizzled with sexuality.

I want you. Now. Naked. Anywhere. Here. The crazy thoughts flashed in and out of his head, and suddenly he was twenty-three again and kissing someone else who'd turned him head over heels with lust.

Mike stopped. He dropped his hands from Sienna's face and stepped back. "Ah, sorry."

"Don't be." She touched his cheek with the gloved fingers of one hand. "It's really good to see you again."

He didn't answer. He couldn't.

This time, she did leave. She slipped inside the car, buckled her seat belt, and drove toward the center of town. Mike laced his hands behind his head and watched her go. She hadn't told him where she was renting an apartment. She hadn't told him much of anything.

Damn mistake. He had no intention of falling for a woman. He would not, could not, let a woman mess up his head or his heart again. He'd kissed her, okay, but that was the last time. He shook his head and forced himself to turn away from Sienna's vanishing taillights. He'd vowed eighteen months ago to focus on his mom, then his business, then his friends, in that order. Not women. Not relationships. Sienna Cruz was only in town until June anyway. They had absolutely no reason to get involved.

The next time he saw her, he'd tell her exactly that.

Chapter Three

Sienna thought about that kiss the entire way to her new apartment on the opposite end of town. She thought about it as she carried boxes and luggage up three flights of stairs and when she finally peeled off her clothes and took a long, hot shower. She could still feel Mike's mouth on hers, his hands pulling her close in the biting winter air. All muscle. All confidence. She had no intention of getting seriously involved with anyone while she was in town, but *damn.* A guy like that might almost make her change her mind.

As she wrapped a towel around her head and pulled on a robe and fuzzy socks, she surveyed her new living room. Couch in one corner, recliner across from it, and a brand new flat-screen TV hanging on the wall. A fireplace with a gas insert burned brightly and did a decent job of keeping the January chill at bay. Small kitchen to her left, bathroom and two small bedrooms down the hall. All furnished as well. A place like this, even unfurnished, would cost well over a thousand dollars back in Chapel Hill. Here, two floors above a diner, she'd be paying six-fifty a month. Including all utilities.

Sienna walked to the wide window that overlooked Main Street. From here, she could see one long block in each direction. Two floors below her sat Zeb's Diner, a fixture in town for as long as she could remember. Directly across the street was Bernie's Barber Shop, with what looked like apartments on its second and third floor. She could see a pet store, some kind of clothing boutique, and a hardware store to the left. St. Mary's Church sat on her right. Beyond that, if she remembered correctly, was the entrance to a small local park. A few streetlights twinkled in the dark. A car, then two pickup trucks, then a snowmobile, drove down the street and north toward County Route 78 and Red Barn Road, which eventually led out of town and over the hills to Silver Valley.

Sienna sank into the recliner and tucked her feet beneath her. Three bulging boxes of books and papers sat under the front window. For the first time, a squiggle of doubt moved through her. Was it wrong not to tell anyone the real reason she'd come to Pine Point? Did someone besides her dissertation advisor need to know she was analyzing the behavior of the people who lived here? She loosened the towel, raked her fingers through her long curls, and shook her head. She wouldn't use identifying information. It would all be kept confidential and anonymous.

She reached into a brown leather backpack and pulled out a new, sealed stack of yellow notepads. Twenty-first-century technology might be great in a lot of ways, but she still preferred taking notes longhand and then transferring them to her computer. *Map out Main Street*, she jotted on the top page of her notepad She needed to get a feel for the town again, see who spent time where and what they did. As a kid, even as a teenager, she hadn't paid attention to much of that. Their rundown apartment, the school, and the streets and shops between them had been all she knew until the day she left.

Local residents, she wrote below her Main Street note. She thought a minute, then added *blue-collar workers* in parentheses.

Mac Herbert

Damian Knight

Mike Springer

She stopped. Small-business owners weren't really considered blue-collar workers, were they? She drew a line through Mike's name and flipped to the next page. *Local professionals*, she wrote instead.

A car horn beeped outside, and Sienna leaned over to see a bulky black SUV pull into the parking spot behind her car. Matching blond twenty-somethings emerged from the vehicle, one dressed in a red parka, jeans, and work boots, the other in a slimming blue ski jacket and what looked like black leggings and stiletto heels.

Sienna added the names of Ella and Becca Ericksen to her second list. They must have been out for a late supper at Zeb's. But to her surprise, they unlocked the door beside the diner entrance. A moment later, she heard footsteps on the stairs and then the door below her open and shut. She scrawled *sisters sharing an apartment?* next to their names and wondered how difficult it was to have a social life when your sister slept in the bedroom next to you. She knew Becca was dating Zane Andrews. From what she recalled, Ella was dating half of Pine Point.

She stared at the notepad. Ella had been one grade above Sienna back in high school, one of the Queen Bees and the center of everything social. Sienna knew because she'd watched from far outside the center. Tears stung her eyes, and though she did her best to wipe them away, they slipped down her cheeks. *Things have changed since you were fifteen. You're not a lost, lonely teenager with a name and a face that doesn't fit in.*

True. She'd chalked up eleven years of living somewhere else, three years of therapy, a wide circle of friends, two serious boyfriends, a slew of jobs, and two college degrees. *You've done okay since leaving Pine Point.* She pinched the bridge of her nose. She'd done better than okay, her therapist would tell her, though she didn't always believe him. The scar on her wrist served as evidence of that. So did the scars inside, cut more deeply into her soul and impossible to see. Returning to a place where she'd never felt at ease, and where she'd lost the one person she loved in life, set all those old wounds to aching again.

Finally, she blew her nose and ran a hand over her face. Time for bed. Time for a fresh start in the morning. Sienna hadn't come back to Pine Point to mourn her mother or relive her childhood. She'd come back to finish her dissertation. Prove to the world she could do it, she could earn the highest college degree despite all the shit she'd lived through. If she had to do it by watching and recording the lives of the people who still lived here, then so be it.

* * * * *

Long after nightfall, Mike headed for the parking lot behind the gym and climbed into his jacked-up red pickup truck.

Zane had asked him once why he didn't put the name of his business on his truck. But which business? The gym, or towing and plowing? He figured it didn't matter either way.

Everyone in Pine Point knew where to find him when they needed him. He kept some business cards for the gym over in his towing garage outside of town, and he kept some business cards for the garage on the front desk of his gym, but other than that, he didn't do much advertising.

He passed the entrance to the interstate and then a few residential streets. Finally, he turned onto Cornwall Road and followed it out of town. Here on the south side of Pine Point, squat one-story homes alternated with rundown trailers and empty lots. After a mile, he turned into the driveway of the only two-story house on the road and parked in front of the garage. A single light burned in the living room.

He didn't bother to lock his truck. He never left anything inside it. He climbed the front steps and opened the door. Inside, his mother slept in front of the television tuned to a reality show. She wore a blue bathrobe and matching slippers and snored softly.

"Ma." He shook her shoulder. "Ma? I'm home."

Loretta Springer's eyes opened, and she blinked in confusion. "Mikey?" She sat up. "What time is it?"

"Almost eight thirty."

She yawned. "Oh." She reached for the half-empty cup of tea on the coffee table. "Did you have a good day at work?"

She always asked him the same thing, and he always answered the same way. "I did, yes. How was your day?"

"Busy." She turned off the television. "Martha came over for lunch." She gestured around the room. "I'm thinking about repainting in here. Maybe blue. It's been green for too long."

Mike dug a beer out of the fridge and joined her on the couch. "I think blue sounds nice. I can do it next weekend if you want. I'll ask Mac or Damian to come over and help."

"You don't have to. Martha's twin nephews are looking for some extra money. I told her I'd hire them."

Mike leaned his head against the couch and closed his eyes. *Good ol' Ma.* "That's nice of you."

"Nice, schmice," she said. "It's what you do for other people."

He patted her leg and let the cool beer slide down his throat. "You'll never believe who came into the gym tonight."

"No? Who?"

He sat up and opened his eyes. "Sienna Cruz."

She paused, not long enough to make him worry, but long enough to make him wonder. "Oh?"

He hadn't bothered to tell his mother he'd gone out with Sienna before. He didn't now. "She's filling in over at the school. Teaching Lucy Foster's class."

"Well, good for her. She was a smart girl." Loretta looked into the darkness. "I always wondered what happened to her after she left Pine Point."

"You remember when she lived here as a kid? And her mother?"

"Of course." Loretta finished her tea and set the cup aside. "Elenita and I worked together that summer cleaning houses." She stood and reached for his empty bottle. "Terrible, terrible thing when she passed. No child should lose a mother that young."

The tone of her voice struck Mike as odd, but before he could ask her about it, she walked into the kitchen. "Think I'll go to bed and read for a bit," she said over her shoulder.

Mike followed her to the small bedroom at the back of the tidy house. The only other bedroom, long since turned into her sewing room, still had pencil marks on one wall measuring his height, scratched there each September from first to twelfth grade. He'd had to make the marks himself when he'd outgrown her at fourteen.

He turned on the bedside light and illuminated a large crucifix on the wall above her bed. A Bible lay on the table next to her reading glasses. "Need anything?"

"No." She pressed a kiss to his cheek and patted his arm as if he were still a boy. "You be nice to Sienna. She's had a hard life."

And he hadn't? "Of course, Ma. I'm nice to everyone."

"Get some sleep tonight," she added. "You work hard. All the time. Too hard."

"I don't. But, yes, I'll get some sleep. And I'll see you in the morning." Although he had no idea how he might find sleep easily tonight, with the smell of Sienna still in his mind and the feel of her skin still on his hands. He climbed the back stairs to his apartment over the garage and wondered what she'd think if she knew he still lived at home. Of course, lots of people did in Pine Point, for various reasons. He hadn't thought twice about moving back in after returning from California. He'd needed a place to stay, his mother had needed a helping hand, and it had worked out well all the way around

Mike turned on the light over his small kitchen table and went to the bathroom to run a hot shower. Be nice to Sienna? He wondered what his mother would say if he told her he'd kissed Sienna. If he told her he'd spent the rest of tonight trying not to think about her and failing. He dropped his clothes to the floor. One tattoo above his right elbow stood out in stark contrast to the others, with a single date and the words *Never Again* inked above it.

He stared at the letters and the numbers until they were burned into his mind's eye. The memory of Edie mocked him all these years later, and his stomach clenched. He'd thought she'd had a hard life too, when they'd first met. He thought that was the reason fate had brought them together, so they could ease each other's hurt and build a life together. He'd realized only too late that Edie was more interested in setting him up and stealing every last dime to ease her own hurt and build her life with someone else.

Mike tightened his hand into a fist. *You put that tattoo there for a reason. Don't let a woman mess up your head again.* With that, he stepped under the spray and let the hot water ease the tension from his muscles and drive all thoughts of Sienna from his mind.

Chapter Four

"Who is that?" A thin boy with brown hair pointed at Sienna, his dark brows drawn together in concern. "Mrs. James, that is not our substitute teacher. Nor is it Mrs. Foster." His words, prim and proper, sounded funny coming from the lips of an eight-year-old.

"You're right, Caleb, this is someone brand new." Jenny James, the principal of Pine Point Elementary School, smiled at the boy. She and Sienna stood in the doorway of Room Eighteen. Jenny dropped her voice. "I didn't tell the class they might have a new teacher until I was sure you'd take the job. They were with a substitute last week." She gestured across the room. "Loni is one of our floating aides. She's available first thing in the morning and then after lunch, if you need an extra pair of hands."

Sienna nodded and looked around the classroom. Two wide-eyed boys with chubby cheeks sat on the rug while Loni, a matronly woman with a double chin, read them a book. Another boy, with the telltale upward eye slant of Down syndrome, rocked in a chair near the window. The only girl in the room, her hair pulled into two tight braids, walked a careful circle around the rug. Heel touched toe in careful, mincing steps, and her fingers tapped together in a rhythmic cadence. She kept her eyes on the floor.

"Dawn has OCD, anxiety, and selective mutism," the principal said as the girl walked by. "Billy and Bailey are twins and both developmentally delayed." She nodded at the aide, who continued to read. "Eight years old but at kindergarten levels for reading." She pointed at the boy standing in the middle of the room. "Caleb is on the autistic spectrum, as far as we can tell. Asperger's,

I suspect, but his parents refuse to have him formally tested."

"At all?"

"At all." Finally, Jenny walked to the child in the chair and patted his head. "And Silas is the lover boy of the class." As if on cue, he jumped from the chair and ran to Sienna. He wrapped his arms around her legs and grinned up at her. Sienna grinned back and tried not to lose her balance.

Jenny clapped her hands together three times. "Room Eighteen, all eyes on me, please. This is Miss Cruz." Jenny waited until they gathered around her in a haphazard semi-circle. "She's going to be your teacher for the rest of the year."

All the boys stared. Dawn continued to circle the room. "The whole year?" one of the twins asked.

"Yes. The whole year." Jenny patted Silas on the head. He turned and looked at Sienna with a wide grin.

"She's pretty," he said.

"Yes, she is," Jenny answered. She brushed her hands on the blue skirt of her business suit. The James family was one of the few old-money families in Pine Point. Most of them had ended up in law or real estate or business, and Sienna wondered what had brought Jenny, the baby of the family, to education instead.

Jenny motioned at the teacher's desk in the corner. "There are lesson plans in the top drawer, but of course you'll want to design your own once you get a feel for the class. The children's Individualized Education Plans are all in that file cabinet in the corner, top drawer, locked up." She produced a ring of keys from the pocket of her blazer. "The large one is for the classroom, the silver one for the closet in the corner, and the small gold one for the two file cabinets."

"Thank you." Sienna palmed them. Yes, she'd taught a special-needs class before. Once. Three years ago. During her interview for this position, it had seemed like the perfect qualification, along with her education and the fact she'd grown up in Pine Point. The superintendent and principal had obviously agreed. Now she wondered if they were all off their rockers.

"The schedule for the day is posted by the door," Jenny went on. She turned and pointed. As she did, Caleb walked over to the blue banner.

"Nine o'clock is arrival time," he began in his thin, high-pitched voice. "At nine-fifteen, you have to call the main office and tell them if anyone is absent. And if we are each having hot or cold lunch today." He paused. "I am having hot lunch. My mother gave me one dollar and fifty cents for it."

Jenny leaned close and whispered to Sienna, "He'll be your best resource."

Caleb dragged his finger down the banner and the explanations went on. "We leave for lunch at eleven-thirty. Every other day we have special, like Art, or Music…"

Jenny tiptoed her way around Caleb, mouthing, *"Call me if you need anything."* Loni stood and followed her with a smile and a bob of her chins. Sienna nodded at them both, and then it was just her alone with the students.

"At twelve o'clock, we go outside when the weather is nice," Caleb was explaining, "but not if the temperature is below freezing. That is thirty-two degrees Fahrenheit or zero degrees Celsius."

"Yes, it is," she said, but he didn't slow down or stop to respond.

"And at quarter to three, we have to pick up everything and walk out to the buses when the bell rings at three o'clock." He finished and folded his hands in front of him, like a public debater who'd finished his formal presentation.

"Well, thank you for all of that," Sienna said. She tried to give him a smile, but Caleb looked over her shoulder, avoiding eye contact. She didn't touch him. Instead, she walked over to the bookcase, selected two books, and sank into the chair at the edge of the rug. "How about a story or two to start the day?"

Billy and Bailey were squirming where they sat, but they looked up expectantly, which she took as a positive sign. Silas had returned to the chair under the window and was rocking it furiously. His cheeks had turned bright red, but he waved at her and grinned as if he was having the time of his life, so she left him there.

Caleb walked across the room, pulled out a chair, and sat at the small table near the teacher's desk. He folded his hands again and waited, his gaze still focused somewhere over Sienna's head. In the only other chair at the table sat Dawn, the lone girl in the class. She had wide blue eyes and beautiful blond hair pulled into neat braids. She wore what looked like designer clothes, a long maroon sweater over patterned leggings and cute black shoes with bows on the toes. But her cuticles were chewed to the quick, and as Sienna looked at her, she pulled her knees up to her chin and dropped her gaze to the floor.

A flash of memory swept over Sienna. The Pine Point playground in bleak winter, kids playing, Sienna standing near the swings and waiting for her turn.

"Her mother talks funny," one of the boys said in a low voice. He inspected his bright red ski jacket and tugged on the ski lift tag attached to the zipper.

Sienna dug her bare hands as far as they would go into the pockets of her secondhand coat.

"My mother says she's a *gringo*," said another boy with a glance at Sienna. "That means a dirty Mexican."

Eight-year-old Sienna turned, cheeks burning, and stumbled in the direction of the slide instead.

"I know the schedule says math at nine-thirty," she said as she banished the memory, "but I think since we're all getting to know each other today, we'll start with a story and then do math a little later on." She glanced at Caleb, but he continued to stare at the wall. Billy and Bailey were slapping each other's knees. Sienna reached down to put a hand between them and spread her fingers wide on the carpet. "One, two, three, four, five," she said, wiggling each finger in turn. "That's how much space I want here, okay?"

They blinked and frowned, but they stopped slapping each other and moved apart a few inches. One of the twins had a small scar on the bridge of his nose, and his hair was a shade darker brown than his brother's. *That's how I'll tell them apart. I'll figure this out.* She opened the book and began to read. *One step at a time.*

* * * * *

"You're teaching the special-ed class now, right? Lucy Foster's class?"

The voice came from behind Sienna as she stood in the doorway to the cafeteria and watched her students walk to their table. "Yes," she said and turned. A short, young woman with a dark blond bob and frosted-pink lipstick smiled up at her.

"I'm Polly Preston," the woman said. "Second grade." She pointed to the woman beside her, a taller version of Polly with the same haircut, only in light brown. "Harmony Donaldson. Third grade." They both dressed in long tunic tops and leggings, with identical black boots on their feet.

"Sienna Cruz. Nice to meet you."

Polly shook her hand. "You too." She looked and sounded exactly like a second grade teacher should, cute and sparkly and full of energy. "Are you from the area?"

"I was. Left when I was fifteen and moved to North Carolina."

"Oh, you must be freezing!" Polly said and rubbed her arms as if a winter wind had swept down the hall. "North Carolina must be a lot warmer than Pine Point in January."

Sienna couldn't help smiling. "It is." She glanced at Harmony, who hadn't stopped studying Sienna's clothes, her hair, her ringless left hand. "So…have you two worked here long?"

"Four years," Polly said.

"We've been best friends since second grade," Harmony added.

"You're from Pine Point?"

Polly shook her head. "Silver Valley."

Sienna mentally took a few notes. "And you both always wanted to be elementary school teachers?"

Harmony shrugged. "Not always. But it's a good job. Reliable. With benefits and summers off."

"It's good until we find husbands," Polly said. Her cheeks pinked, and she looked around as if to make sure no one else had heard her. "I mean…I want to have a family. I like kids and everything, but this is just until I have my own."

Sienna filed that information away with the rest of the stereotype beginning to emerge. She tried to give a conspiratorial smile. "I hear you."

But Harmony lifted a brow as if in doubt. "You're not married, right? I heard you were working on your PhD." She said the words as if getting a PhD precluded any chance of settling down with a husband and kids.

"Well, I am. But that doesn't mean I don't want a social life too."

"Harmony said she thought she saw you at Mike Springer's gym yesterday afternoon," Polly said. "Was that you?"

Harmony gave Sienna another quick up-and-down glance. "You work out, don't you?" She pinched at some imaginary fat on her belly. "I should. I just can't find the time."

"No kidding," Polly agreed. "Although I'm sure having Mike as a trainer is a pretty good incentive. Are you, you know, like, friends with him?" she asked Sienna.

Ah, so the real reason Polly and Harmony had stopped to chat. Sienna shrugged. "We've hung out a few times."

"He seems like a nice guy," Polly said. Five or six silver bracelets dangled on her wrist, and she played with them as she talked. "I don't really know him that well. He hasn't gone out much since he came back."

"Back from where?" Sienna asked. She'd always assumed Mike Springer was a local boy, born and raised. She remembered him vaguely from high school, three years ahead of her. His senior year, he'd sat with his buddies on the long stone wall outside Pine Point High's main entrance and whistled as the cute upperclassmen walked by.

A long look passed between Polly and Harmony. "He lived in California for a while," Polly said. "He came back to Pine Point a couple years ago and opened the gym."

"Oh. That's cool." Sienna gave what she hoped was a noncommittal nod. *Interesting he never mentioned that.* How long had he lived on the West Coast? How had he ended up that far from home? And why had he left to return to Pine Point?

"Anyway, we just wanted to say hi and introduce ourselves," Polly said, the bubbly tone returning to her voice. "Good luck with everything. I'm sure you'll do fine." She glanced into the cafeteria. "That Silas is a cutie-pie."

They all are, Sienna thought as she watched her five students clustered at a table in the corner. With a glance at the clock on the cafeteria wall, she pulled her phone from her pocket. She wanted to see Mike again. She wanted to talk to him, spar with him, get worked up and sweaty and then watch his arms flex as he mixed her a smoothie and grinned from behind the front desk. Finding out any backstory about his time in California would just be a bonus.

"How about a workout tonight?" she typed. *"I'm gonna need one after today."*

Chapter Five

Mike eyed the clock beside his computer. Some days, the time flew. Others, it crawled. Went backwards even. Since the text from Sienna around noon, he'd stared at the clock a hundred times. *Stop thinking about her that way,* he tried telling himself. *You're going to be polite when she gets here. Tell her you're better off as friends.*

Yeah, right.

The second hand ticked at a snail's pace, mocking him. At a few minutes after six, people from the five o'clock yoga class began to dribble from the fitness room at the back of the gym. Some chatted quietly, while others walked with relaxed expressions and heavy eyes. A middle-aged redhead slowed at the desk. "Hey, Mike."

"Hi, Chantell. How was class?"

"Great." She sighed and rested her enormous chest on the desk. As usual, she wore a low-cut top that revealed the top half of her overly bronzed breasts. "Have you ever taken it?"

"Yoga? No. But I hear it's great for the mind."

"And the body." She gave him a suggestive smile. "It's definitely helped my flexibility."

Mike coughed. Just then, the front door opened and Sienna walked inside. She wore a red hat pulled over her dark hair and a black workout suit. Gym bag over her shoulder. Cheeks pink from the cold. Despite all his earlier advice to himself, all Mike could do was stare.

"Ah, hello?" Chantell waved a hand in front of his face. "So you'll think about it?"

"I'm sorry." He dragged his attention away from Sienna, who grinned and leaned against the counter. "Think about what?"

Chantell took one look at Sienna, heaved a dramatic sigh, and turned away. "Never mind." With a hurt expression, she stomped toward the door.

"Sorry," Sienna said. "Was I interrupting something?"

"God, no. I was about to tell Chantell to go home to her husband."

"She's married?"

"Yeah."

"Doesn't stop her from flirting with you though, does it?"

Mike shrugged. He'd discovered over the last year that harmless flirtation went with the territory. It didn't take much—friendly conversation, a smile, a compliment—to make the women who came to his gym feel good about themselves. He wasn't interested in any of them, which made the conversation and the compliments easy to dole out.

"So how was your first day?" he asked.

She pulled off her hat and unzipped her jacket. "Not terrible. Just a lot harder than I remembered."

"And those kids are even tougher than the normal ones."

She gave him a look. "Normal ones?"

"Sorry. That's not the right word. They're different, that's all. Right? They have special needs and learn slower and stuff." He cleared his throat. *Stop talking. Tell her you have to do paperwork. Or you have a personal training client coming in.* But he did neither. Instead, he let his gaze rest on her mouth, which was smiling at him.

"Yes," she said. "They are. And they do." She took a long drink from her water bottle. "I need a workout. Something quick and intense that'll get my mind off school and burn a few calories."

Mike resisted the urge to invite her back to his place and engage in a quick and intense horizontal, no-clothes-required workout. Instead, he gave a short nod. "Fitness room is free for the rest of the night. How about we do twenty minutes of Tabata and then a ten-minute meditation?"

"Meditation?"

He lifted one shoulder and let it fall. "Something I picked up when I was living in California. Helps clear the mind."

Her eyes lit up. "I heard you were out there for a while."

"Yeah?" He grabbed two towels from the clean pile behind him.

"From two teachers at school. They mentioned it." She slowed and gave him a sideways glance. "Didn't know that."

He shrugged. "Don't talk that much about it."

"Any reason?"

Because I made some shitty mistakes and don't want everyone in town knowing about them. He kept his eyes focused straight ahead. "It's in the past."

"I get that," she said as he pulled open the glass door to the fitness room. When he glanced over, those delicious lips curved upward. "Let's hit this workout."

"C'mon, just twenty seconds," Mike urged as Sienna dropped for push-ups.

She gave him a dirty look, her breath coming too hard for words. The neckline of her tank top was drenched, her ponytail too. Mike's own shirt stuck to his back, and he took a quick drink of water before finishing his own round of push-ups.

"Twenty seconds around the room," he said as they clambered back to their feet. "Top speed."

"You're killing me," she said as she panted for breath.

"When's the last time you thought about school?" he asked from behind, taking in the perfect view as she ran. *I can look*, he told himself. *Just no touching.*

She picked up the pace and pulled away from him. He sped up too.

"Okay," she said. "You're right. Not since we started sweating."

"Good." He pushed the pace, willing her to keep up. She did, elbows pumping. When they finally finished, she bent over and put both hands on her knees.

"Keep moving," he said. He tugged on her elbow. "Let's take three walking laps. Get your heart rate down."

She nodded, didn't say anything, but followed him. After the third lap, they stretched briefly. "Now comes the good stuff," he said.

"Terrific." She raised her arms above her head, revealing an inch of smooth, caramel-colored belly skin. Mike blew out a long breath and considered the Yankees' chances of making it back to the World Series this year to distract himself. *Think about baseball. Pitch counts. Cold showers. Anything.*

He picked up two yoga mats from the stack in the corner and unrolled them. Then he turned off all the lights but one and sank to the floor.

"You ready?" He gestured at the mat beside him.

"I guess," she said as she sat. "I'm not much for staying in one place for very long. Just so you know."

"Give it a try. It might surprise you." He inhaled and exhaled slowly. "It's a good way to wrap up a workout. Or a rough day." He looked over. Sienna had crossed her legs and rested her wrists on her knees.

"Do I have to chant or say *om* or something?" she asked.

"Not unless you want to. Just close your eyes."

She lifted one brow.

He raised his palms in innocent supplication. "I promise I won't try any funny business."

She cocked her head. "I like funny business."

Shit. She was flirting with him. His jaw twitched as he thought of about a hundred responses. *So do I. Although funny might turn to dirty in the blink of an eye. Or in the touch of a hand. Or a kiss. Or your legs wrapped around…*

He cleared his throat and stretched both arms overhead. *The Yankees. The Rangers. The Giants.* Any goddamn sports team at all.

"Fine," she said when he didn't answer. She closed her eyes, opened one, then closed it again. "I'm listening."

He cleared his throat and felt like a teenager going through puberty all over again. "Breathe in for a count of four, then out for four. Then breathe in for five, and out for five. Go up to eight if you can, or if you can't, stay wherever feels comfortable. Stay at the top number four times, then work your way back down to four."

"And that's it?"

"That's it. Well, try not to think about anything except your breath."

She opened one hazel eye again. "That might be harder said than done."

"I know," he admitted. "But give it a try."

Mike closed his eyes. For the next few minutes, the only sound in the room was the soft swish of inhalations and exhalations. He fought the urge to cheat and watch Sienna's chest rise and fall. Instead, he did his best to satisfy himself with the thought of her beside him. After a few moments, he opened his eyes, letting them adjust to the dim light before looking over.

"Wow." Sienna brushed stray hairs from her forehead "You were right. That was pretty relaxing."

"Yeah?"

"Yeah." She leaned over and planted both hands on his mat. "And strangely erotic."

He barely had time to register the words before she kissed him. She tasted like lemons and the tang of salty sweat, and hot, base desire rushed over him. All his earlier vows fled, and for a long few seconds, he leaned in and kissed her back. He took her shoulders in his hands, bracing himself so he didn't fall over on top of her. *Not like that would be a bad thing.*

Then he broke the kiss. What the hell was he thinking? Windows lined the fitness room, which meant anyone working out could peek in and see them. But he didn't care so much about that. He absolutely, positively could not let this happen again. Not with Sienna. Not with anyone.

"Sorry." He grunted as he jumped up. "It's just not…" He didn't know how to finish.

She sat back and looked at him. An injured expression crossed her face. Her hair dropped into her face, but he could still see the confusion and hurt in her eyes. She opened her mouth and then closed it again. She gave a short nod, stood, and rolled up her mat. "Thanks for the workout," she said. She didn't look at him. "I'll see you around."

"Yeah. See you." *Idiot.* Mike cursed himself as he watched Sienna go. Then he loaded a bar with the heaviest weights he could manage and lifted until his arms burned.

Zane walked into the gym a few minutes later. "Hey, how's it going?" He peered at Mike's face. "Whoa. You look pissed as all hell. What happened?"

Mike sat on the floor beside the incline bench. He'd just finished one hundred sit-ups. Now his abs burned along with every other muscle in his body. "Nothin'."

"Bullshit." Zane arranged his lanky frame on the bench and began to do crunches.

Mike drank some water. "You hear Sienna's back in town?"

Zane stopped and braced his hands under his knees. "No. Really?"

"She's taking over Lucy Foster's class."

Zane dropped back down. "Sounds like that should be good news."

Mike didn't answer. He mopped his face with the edge of his T-shirt. The peace he'd felt after meditating had long since fled. His heart beat raggedly, and his calves had started to cramp.

"So what's the deal?" Zane swung himself to a seat. "She doesn't want to see you? Is that why you're pissed off?"

Mike shook his head. "She's been in here twice."

"But?"

"She's only in town short-term. 'Til June."

"Isn't that what you're looking for? No strings? No commitment?"

Mike shrugged again.

"You gonna let that shit that happened out in L.A. eat away at you forever?" Zane lay back down and started another set of crunches. A pair of young blond women walked by. The shorter and prettier of the two smiled and waved at Mike. He waved back. He couldn't place her.

"It's not eating away at me," he said when the women wandered over to the treadmills. "I'm just taking it as a lesson learned." He should have kept that in mind from the moment he met Sienna the first time. Forget the kisses. Forget everything. "I can't spend any more time with her," he said abruptly. She was wreaking havoc on his mind and body, and he'd only spent a handful of hours with her.

Zane stopped again, out of breath. He ran a hand across his brow. "So tell her that. She can't blame you." He thumped Mike on the back and walked to the free weights, where he started doing biceps curls.

Mike chewed his bottom lip as he headed for the locker room. *So tell her that.* Simple answer. He'd end things with her right here and now, before they went any further and he found himself half in love with someone who had no intention of sticking around. *Been there, done that,* he thought as he ran a hot shower. Nope, his only interaction with Sienna Cruz from this point forward would be a hearty handshake across the desk of Springer Fitness. Period.

Chapter Six

"What the hell was that?" Sienna said aloud. She sat in her car outside the gym and turned the heat to high. She'd caught Mike checking out her ass more than once as they worked out. They'd dated a handful of times last month. And he'd kissed her back, both today and last night. No mistaking the heat between them, his tongue meeting hers as he wrapped those strong hands around her arms. Her belly and all parts south clenched with the memory.

But then he'd pulled away from her like he'd been stung, or like he'd suddenly realized she carried the Black Plague. *I thought we were getting along*, she thought as she turned on her headlights and checked Main Street before pulling out. *Thought we had some chemistry. Guess I read that wrong*. She frowned as she slowed at the single traffic light in the center of town. *You're not interested in anything long-term*, she reminded herself, but that didn't ease the sting of his reaction. She liked Mike. She admired his hard work and growing business. Besides that, he turned her thoughts upside down every time she saw him. To be pushed away in the middle of a kiss—well, it hurt.

She drove by Zeb's Diner and her apartment but didn't stop. Last thing she wanted right now was to sit alone in an empty room and think about her day. Instead, she took a loop down Park Place Run, a new block of shops and office buildings and restaurants. Fifteen years ago, it had been farmland. Now sidewalks with miniature fir trees strung in twinkling lights flanked her. Clothing boutiques, an organic food store, and an upscale salon lined one side of the street. Two sleek office buildings, a bank, and a couple of restaurants lined the right. As she reached the dead end, something scurried across the street, and two yellow eyes blinked up at her.

Sienna stomped on the brakes as a skinny-looking cat bolted into a copse of frozen bushes next to Diva Designs. *Poor thing.* On a night like this one, it would probably freeze before morning. She peered into the dark, but it had vanished. Gently, she toed the accelerator and continued out of town, following Main Street as it turned into County Route 78 and then Red Barn Road. A few stately homes lined both sides of this road on the north side of Pine Point, though most remained in disrepair. One notable one, a gorgeous three story with a wide front porch, looked recently renovated. *Thompson,* read the name on the mailbox, and Sienna had a vague memory of a brother and sister with that last name back in school. *So few people I remember.* Even fewer she'd kept in touch with.

She left the town limits of Pine Point behind her as she climbed the mountain that led to Silver Valley. She wasn't planning on going all the way to the next town, but if she remembered correctly, a secondary road up ahead cut across the mountain and looped back on the other side of Pine Point.

She slowed, made a left turn on the nameless road, and pulled to the shoulder. Below her lay all of Pine Point, from the new gated development to Main Street to the mobile homes that made up the town's south end. A set of railroad tracks, no longer used, ran parallel to the interstate. The run-down area near the interstate had been the only place her mother could afford a second-floor, one-bedroom apartment. Her throat tightened as she recalled the constant smell of Chinese food from the restaurant below. Hong Lee, the owner, sometimes took pity on them and gave them leftovers at the end of the night.

"What is this?" her mother used to say in a sad, accented voice. *"I should be making you empanadas and tortillas. Instead, we are eating fried rice and wonton soup."*

Sienna had never minded. Worse than the cold Chinese food had been the look of sadness on her mother's face and the furrows in her brow that cut deeper every year. Only the last few months, she'd seemed happy again.

"I am making a better life for you," she said one afternoon when Sienna came home from school. She danced around the tiny room and pretended to

sprinkle fairy dust on Sienna's shoulders. *"All this is for you."* She pointed to the shabby couch, the TV, the table in the kitchen, and the steaming plate of rice and beans in the middle of it. *"You will have a better life than I did."*

When she smiled, the years fell away, and she looked like she could be Sienna's older sister, dark-eyed and dark-haired and dancing as salsa music played on the radio.

It wouldn't be hard to have a better life than someone who had died in her early thirties. Sienna's eyes filled, and suddenly the tears leaked out, over the hand pressed to her mouth, and down the front of her coat. Her shoulders shook, and for a moment her grief swelled so big it filled the car, pressed against the doors and windows and took away all the air.

She gulped in oxygen, her eyes and lungs burning with the effort. *Not fair.* She hadn't allowed herself to think those words in years. No one's life was fair. Everyone had troubles. Her mother had died, yes, but Sienna had moved on. She'd found another place to live. She'd put herself through school. She'd found friends and delved into research and vowed never to let her loss define her.

But on that lonely stretch of road, with the winter wind howling around her car and the tears continuing to fall, Sienna let herself ache. She missed her mother. She missed a life she'd never known, the security of growing up with a family and good friends and knowing where she'd wake in the morning and where she'd go to sleep at night. For a long time, she sat there, until she ran out of tears and the memories faded and her stomach growled to remind her it was well past dinner.

Can only move forward. Can't go back. Her lips moved as she repeated the words. She descended the mountain, coming into Pine Point on its far south side. A dog trotted along the side of the road, its tongue lolling from its mouth. The few homes she passed had broken-down cars in the front yards and garbage strewn across the steps. A scrawny yellow cat crept under the body of a rusted truck in one driveway. A pot-bellied woman stood on the porch, smoking a cigarette and shivering.

I might have ended up here. Sienna slowed. If she'd stayed and graduated from Pine Point High, she might have taken a job waiting tables, or cleaning homes like her mother. After eight or ten years, if she was lucky, she might have saved up enough money for a down payment on one of these mobile homes. Everything happened for a reason. If her mother's death had been the horrible avenue by which she found her way to North Carolina and a life of academics, then Sienna would focus on that.

A few specks of snow dotted her windshield, and she turned on the wipers. Time to eat. She didn't have much in her refrigerator, but she didn't feel like sitting alone in a restaurant either. She stopped at the end of the road, pulled a tissue from her purse, and blew her nose. Just past the interstate sat a row of fast food places. A burger and fries might not be the best choice, but it would hold her over until morning.

Food, then a shower, then she'd crawl under the covers and wait for tomorrow to come. Things always looked brighter in the morning.

Didn't they?

*****

Mike bounded up the front steps and into his mother's house, bringing a swath of snow and cold air with him. "Hi, Ma."

"Mikey." His mother smiled from the kitchen. Plastic containers lined the counters, and she scraped the bottom of a pot on the stove. The aromas of beef stew and homemade rolls filled the house. "You're home late tonight. I was just putting this away. Hungry?"

"Yum. Yes." He kicked off his boots and hung his jacket by the door. He found a beer in the fridge and sat at the small, chipped kitchen table. "Need any help?"

"No. But thank you." She patted his arm. "How was work today?"

"Good, fine." *If you don't count my acting like an idiot around a gorgeous woman.* "How was yours?"

"Very nice. Martha picked me up for lunch with the girls, and then we swung by the library so I could get some books."

Mike glanced at the table in the narrow hallway. Five or six thick hardcovers sat atop it. "How long will it take you to read those?"

She laughed. "Oh, I don't know. A week? Maybe longer?"

Mike took a long pull on his beer. He hadn't gotten the book bug from his mother, that was for sure. As far as he knew, he got his looks and his stubbornness from her, and his dyslexia and business smarts from his father, who'd long since left Pine Point in search of greener pastures and younger women.

Abruptly, he stood. "Ma, I'll be right back. Gotta change."

"Of course, honey."

He trudged up the back stairs and into his apartment, shivering. No prediction of snow tonight, but the temperatures were supposed to hit the single digits. He nudged up the thermostat as he peeled off his shirt and jeans and tossed them in the general direction of a laundry pile near his bedroom. He grabbed a clean T-shirt and sweats and was about to pull them on when he caught sight of himself in the bathroom mirror. A streak of black grease covered his right cheek. His hair stood up on end. But that wasn't what surprised him. Tiny lines at the edges of his eyes stood out in the yellow light. He took a couple steps closer to the medicine cabinet. *Shit. Take a look at those.* When he pulled on the skin, the wrinkles smoothed for only a second before returning.

"Shit. I am gettin' old." And he didn't turn thirty until next year. Well, that was what eight years of drinking and eight months in jail did to you.

I should be one of those guest speakers at a school, he thought as he turned off the lights and headed back to his mother's beef stew. *This is how you don't want to end up.* He'd tell them what choices not to make and how to find friends and women who wouldn't betray them. A harsh laugh left his lips. "Imagine me in a school." He'd done enough to get by back in Pine Point High, and he'd seen his share of the principal's office. School was the last place he would ever spend time as an adult, no matter how much life advice he had to give.

He stopped outside on the stairs and took a deep inhalation. Stars covered the night sky, and something inside him twinged, a longing for something he wasn't sure he'd ever have. *Be nice to have someone to look at the sky with.* The thought, silly and dramatic, surprised him. He took another breath and let the frosty air burn his lungs.

He'd been screwed but good by his ex out in L.A. He hadn't dated anyone seriously since returning to Pine Point, and he wasn't about to start. You trusted someone, and eventually they let you down. That was the story of life. He'd seen it happen to more good guys than he could count. His breath ribboned out against the night sky as he trudged down the remaining stairs. As much as he liked talking to Sienna, fantasized about her naked, and thought about her when she wasn't around, getting any more involved with her would only lead to a letdown.

Zane was right. Tomorrow, Mike would tell Sienna exactly how he felt.

Chapter Seven

Tuesday morning in Room Eighteen went better than Monday, if only because Sienna arrived before the kids and was prepared when they walked in from the bus. They made it through morning meeting, math, and half of reading before the meltdowns began.

"I wanted peanut butter!" Billy shrieked at the top of his lungs. He threw himself onto the rug and began to beat his hands and feet against the floor.

Sienna laced both hands over her eyes. They'd been reading the monthly school field trip guide, then the after-school movie list, and then the lunch menu. Today's cold lunch was ham and cheese on wheat bread. Not peanut butter. Thus the tantrum.

Silas climbed into his chair and rocked so hard the books on the shelf nearby vibrated. Caleb sat at the table, head bent over his math sheets. Bailey watched his brother with wide eyes and red cheeks, probably about to join in the shrieking. Sienna glanced at Dawn, who was chewing at her fingernails and making them bleed.

"Silas, honey, let's take it down a notch." She reached for a wooden Jacob's Ladder toy and handed it to him. "Here." He clutched it in both hands and looked at her for a moment, confused. Then the rocking slowed as he began to flip the pieces of the toy over and back.

Billy's cries grew weaker, and she decided to risk letting him wear himself out. She patted Bailey on the back and handed him the alphabet coloring sheets he'd been working on earlier. "Bailey, please sit down here," she said as she pulled out a chair across from Caleb. Caleb looked up in alarm, but she pointed at his worksheet. "Continue." He blinked and then looked down without a word.

As Bailey climbed into the chair and took a red crayon in one fist, his brother looked over his shoulder, still prone in the middle of the room. "I wanted peanut butter," he said in a mournful voice.

"I know, honey," Sienna said, "but we don't always get what we want." *Boy, isn't that the truth?* "You'll have peanut butter another day." She walked over and pulled him onto her lap, cradling him in a hug before smoothing his mussed hair and handing him a tissue. He left tear streaks on her blue shirt and what looked like a black handprint as well.

Without making a sound, Dawn began to pace in a circle around the room, following the pattern of the rug and then the tiles of the floor when the rug ended. She didn't speak. She didn't look at anyone else. She pinched her fingers together in a rhythm that matched her footsteps. Sienna didn't follow her or stop her. Instead, she looked at her watch. Eleven o'clock. Thirty more minutes before Caleb informed her they had to go to lunch.

Sienna slipped her phone from her pocket. No calls or texts from Mike. She wasn't sure she'd expected any, not after yesterday's weird-as-hell kiss, but still. Silence was strange too. She put the phone away again.

The clock crawled its way to lunchtime, and she dropped off her class at the cafeteria and found her way to the faculty room. In her former school, the teacher faculty room had always featured some kind of food, either pastries dropped off by appreciative parents or leftover snacks from a fundraiser. She hoped the same held true for Pine Point Elementary. She still hadn't managed to get to a grocery store, and all she'd had for breakfast was a granola bar and a large cup of coffee from Zeb's.

"I'm thinking about trying one of those dating sites," Sienna heard as she walked inside.

"Really? I don't know if—"

As soon as she saw Sienna, Polly Preston's mouth snapped shut. She sat next to Harmony Donaldson on one of two couches in the room. Today the teachers both wore long tunic sweaters and corduroys in muted colors. *Do they plan their outfits each day?* Sienna chided herself for the catty thought. *Stop it.* Maybe being best friends from the time you could walk meant you ended up with not only the same job but the same fashion sense. Sienna wouldn't know.

"Oh, hey, Sienna," Harmony said. "How's it going?"

Sienna headed straight for the bagels and cream cheese on the table under the window. A coffee maker and microwave sat beside it, next to a copier and a bulletin board with various flyers pinned to it. "I'm good," she said after grabbing a bagel and pouring a cup of lukewarm coffee. She leaned against the table. "Little bit of a rough morning, but I think we're under control now."

"Think the weather's getting to everyone," Polly said. She nibbled at a croissant. "My kids were off the wall this morning too."

"Glad to hear it wasn't just mine."

Harmony crossed one slim leg over the other. "So how many hot guys work out at Springer Fitness?"

A lump of bagel lodged itself in Sienna's throat. "I'm sorry?"

The brunette ran her fingers through her hair. "I know Mike Springer's pretty good eye candy. I don't know about the others though. I'm trying to decide if it's worth it to go there."

"I guess it depends on whether you're going for the guys or the workout." She tried to ignore the disappointment that crept over her at the memory of last night's kiss gone wrong.

Harmony winked at Polly. "Can't it be both?"

"A gym is as good a place as any to meet someone," Sienna said. Or, apparently, turn off someone. She still didn't know what she'd done to make Mike turn tail and run. As if on cue, her cell phone buzzed with an incoming call. She glanced down and saw his name on the screen.

"But do professional guys go there, or is it mostly meatheads?" Harmony went on.

This is the first time I've ever been in a conversation about husband hunting. Sienna slid her thumb over her phone to silence the ringer and send Mike's call to voicemail. "Combination of both, I'd say. Pine Point is pretty blue collar, from what I remember. If you guys live in Silver Valley, why don't you work out there?"

Polly looked at Harmony and giggled. "Well, the owner isn't nearly as nice to look at, for one."

Harmony's lips curled up. "No, he's definitely not. Plus, my ex-boyfriend goes to the gym in Silver Valley a lot," she added. "And he's the last person I want to see."

"Oh." Sienna nodded. "I get that."

Polly brushed the crumbs from her fingers. "It's not super easy to meet someone around here." She played with her bracelets. "I'm getting older by the day."

Sienna couldn't imagine either of them to be pushing thirty, but then again, she'd gone to college with a few women who considered it a failure if they didn't graduate at twenty-two with rings on their fingers.

"I'm sure you'll meet someone," she said. She almost added something about online dating sites being a decent option too, but then she bit her tongue. *I don't think I was supposed to hear that.*

"Bye," Polly said. "Hope your afternoon goes better than your morning did."

"Me too," Sienna answered, but they were already gone. She pulled out her phone and listened to Mike's message.

"Hey, thought I might catch you at your lunch break. Sorry about yesterday. Give me a call when you can."

She frowned, played the message again and tried to gauge the tone behind his words. He sounded matter-of-fact, polite, and sincere. Nothing else. She sighed and put her phone back in her pocket. A return call would have to wait until after school. Even better, maybe she'd stop by the gym and see Mike in person.

The weather warmed up, so they marched outside for recess. Sienna stood at the edge of the playground and watched the twins chase each other around the swings. Caleb crouched next to the snow gauge, walking back to her every so often to report his measurements, and Silas was content to stand near the bottom of the slide and clap as the other children came down.

The only student she couldn't keep track of was Dawn. Sienna scanned the playground on a regular basis, but every so often Dawn's blond braids would vanish, and Sienna would have to hurry over to one of the monitors. "Have you seen her? Red plaid coat, blond hair?" She thought about adding that Dawn didn't speak, but that wasn't useful to anyone.

Dawn always turned up. One time she was standing behind a tree, pressing her fingers against the bark and counting the marks it made on her skin. Another time she'd ventured over to the older kids' side of the playground and was watching a snowball fight. Just before they came back inside, she walked around the corner of the school, where Sienna found her staring up at the fringe of icicles hanging from the roof.

"Honey, you can't just walk away like that," she said for the third time. She took Dawn's mittened hand, but the girl pulled away and ran ahead of her back into the building. By the time three o'clock rolled around, Sienna was exhausted.

"Bye, bye, see you tomorrow," she called, waving as each of her students walked to their buses at the circular drive in front of the school. Her neck ached, her head spun, and she needed a workout in the worst way. She wasn't keen on having whatever weird conversation might develop with Mike, but avoiding Springer Fitness was the last thing she wanted to do.

She walked to the office to check her mailbox. Two memos, one about next week's faculty meeting and one about new field-trip policies. Sienna tucked them under her arm and glanced at Jenny James's door.

"Is she around?" she asked Hillary, the secretary behind the desk. Hillary, who could've been anywhere between forty and seventy years old, wore a flowered dress and a heavy silver cross around her neck. Her gray hair crossed in two braids across the top of her head, and when she spoke, Sienna could hear a faint German accent.

"She is, but she is not to be disturbed."

Sienna blinked. The door with the *Principal, Mrs. James* placard in the center of it remained securely closed. "Okay. I'll catch up with her tomorrow. Just had a question about ordering supplies."

Hillary produced a catalog from the top drawer of her desk. "I have ordering forms. You can return them to me."

"Oh, thank you."

She wouldn't have given any of the conversation a second thought, except when she walked to her car a few minutes later, the blinds in the principal's office jerked up for a moment. Behind them, looking out into the bleak winter day, Sienna saw Jenny's face. It looked like she'd been crying.

Chapter Eight

"Hi, stranger."

For a second, Mike kept his head bent over his spreadsheet. He hadn't expected her to come to the gym. Part of him hadn't even expected her to return his call. Sienna's voice teased everything south of his waist and made him think things damn near unspeakable. He cleared his throat, hit Save, and finally looked up.

"Hi." Did she ever not look gorgeous? His gaze took in a simple ponytail, minimal makeup and no glamorous outfit today, but that didn't matter. Her light brown eyes sparkled above a green turtleneck sweater, and her smile grew when he said her name.

"Hi yourself."

"How's the teaching going?"

"Up and down. Harder than I thought it would be, but the kids are pretty cute. And smarter than people give 'em credit for." She paused. "I got your message earlier. Maybe we can talk after I'm done working out?"

"Sure."

"I'm gonna hit the weights until I can't stand up."

"That doesn't sound too smart." Except it would allow him to come to her rescue, sling an arm around her waist and help her to a stool at the smoothie bar while he rubbed her shoulders and—

No! Stop thinking that way.

Mike spent the next hour doing his damnedest not to watch Sienna as she moved between the free weights and the Nautilus machines and finally ended up on the elliptical. She wore sleek black workout pants that ended just below the knee, which meant if he looked—not like he was—he could see every inch of smooth, caramel-colored bare calves.

Her arms and legs pumped back and forth, and her ponytail swung from side to side. She had earbuds in and her iPod clipped to her arm. *Wonder what she listens to?* Mike forced himself to turn away yet again.

"Hey, good-looking."

For once, he was glad to see Chantell. Today, the forty-something-year-old wore a bright yellow tank top and matching yellow and black patterned tights. "Hello, yourself. Trying out the new kickboxing class later?"

"You know it." She ran one finger down her water bottle, collected condensation, then popped the finger in her mouth.

Mike pressed his lips together to keep from grinning inappropriately.

"I was wondering if I could get a quick hour in with you first," she went on. The finger went back to her water bottle, then back to her mouth.

"Ah, let me check my schedule." He turned to look at the white board calendar on the wall behind him. "I do have a client coming in at five forty-five."

"That gives us twenty minutes," she said with a wide smile. "Meet you in the fitness room? I really want to work on my core today." She patted her ample belly and sauntered off.

Her core. Good Lord.

"She certainly is one of your most faithful clients, isn't she?" Sienna materialized from the other side of the desk.

"That she is."

Sienna wiped her face and chest with a towel and then draped it around her neck. "Got a smoothie for me? Extra shot of protein?"

"Coming right up. Strawberry or mango?"

"Surprise me."

Hell. Why did everything she say have a double meaning? Mike squatted to dig out the ingredients from his mini fridge behind the counter.

He added ingredients, set the blender to high for thirty seconds, and then poured her smoothie into a tall glass.

"Thanks." She took a long sip and ended up with foam on her upper lip. She snaked her tongue out to lick it away, and Mike's groin stirred. "So about yesterday," she began.

"I'm sorry," he said in a rush. It always seemed best to apologize to women straight off.

"For what exactly? Kissing me? Or pushing me away like I had the plague?"

He cleared his throat. "Ah, the second part." Hell, he wasn't sorry at all for kissing her. He was only sorry he had too much goddamn baggage to enjoy it.

Another sip of smoothie. Another swipe of the tongue over her lip. "Any particular reason for that?"

Mike cracked his knuckles. Bad nervous habit he'd picked up ages ago, but he couldn't help it. "I'm just thinking it's better if we don't go down that road."

"No?" Her brow crooked as if to say they were already halfway down it.

"You're not staying in Pine Point any longer than a few months." He spread his hands wide. "And I've got a lot on my plate with the gym. Seems like commitment isn't in the cards for either one of us right now."

She set down her glass and folded her arms on the counter. "Fair enough. So how about dinner as friends?"

"Friends?" He couldn't recall ever doing that before, not with a woman anyway. "Don't you, ah, have friends at school?"

Her face darkened. "I don't really have any friends here at all." She ran her fingers through her ponytail. "That sounds pathetic. I just mean I didn't keep in touch with people when I left, and you're pretty much the only person I've had a normal conversation with since I got back into town."

He cracked his knuckles again. "Gotta be honest, I'm not sure I'll be any good at that. Friends, I mean." *Be nice.* His mother's words echoed in his mind.

"I like you," she went on. "You're smart, you're a workaholic like I am, and I think we get along. You're right. I'm not planning on staying in town. But there are a lot of months between now and June, and I could really use dinner and a drink every once in a while with someone who can hold his own while boxing."

He let out a sigh. He'd never had a friend like that, except for maybe Zane. He thought for a long moment. What the hell? He could give it a try. At the very least, it would make his mother happy.

"I close up here at five on Fridays," he finally said. "How about we meet at six o'clock at Marc's Grille?"

"Sounds perfect. See you then."

Chapter Nine

"Counter or booth?" asked the waitress that met Sienna at the door of Zeb's Diner the following night.

"Oh, counter is fine." She pulled off her gloves and tucked them inside her purse. After a faculty meeting that had run until almost five, she hadn't felt like either the gym or the grocery store, so here she stood. She chose a stool between a man eating solo and a woman sitting with her three- or four-year-old daughter. The woman had dark circles under her eyes, and the edge of a fresh bruise peeked from under her shirt sleeve.

"Something to drink?" asked the waitress. She gave Sienna a funny look, her gaze lingering a little longer than necessary.

"Decaf, please. I need to warm up," she told the woman with the dyed-orange hair tucked into a messy bun on her head. *Josephine,* read the name tag over her ample left breast.

The waitress handed her a full mug and pushed over a plastic sugar container and two non-dairy creamers.

"How long have you worked here?" Sienna asked. From what she recalled, Zeb's was the heart of Pine Point, both geographically and figuratively. It had to hold a secret or two. The people who worked here had to have borne witness to some kind of gossip.

The man sitting down the counter looked over and grinned. "Too long, right, Josie?"

Josie let out a long whistle. "About twenty-six years. Woo-whee. That's a long time, ain't it? Give or take. I left for a few months when I got married, but that didn't take, so here I am."

Twenty-six years, exactly Sienna's age. She didn't remember the woman, but then she and her mother had never stepped foot inside Zeb's. They'd never had a spare dime to eat out. "Did you grow up here?" she asked. She itched to take out her notepad.

"I did." She handed Sienna a menu. "I'm a Pine Point girl, born and raised." She pointed at the man. "Same's this fellow."

"Now, Josie, I wasn't born here," the man said. He was eating apple pie and had dots of whipped cream in his beard. He winked at Sienna. "Moved here when I was all of two years old."

"And you never lived anywhere else?"

"Nah." The man returned to his pie. "This is a good town with solid people. Sure, cities might have fancier places to shop or eat dinner, but no one knows you in cities. They'll steal from you any chance they get. Why would I want to live anywhere else?"

"Maybe the weather," Josie said. "If I can save up some money, I might look into one of those condos down in Myrtle Beach. Better place to pass January and February than this frozen tundra." She slapped her palm on the counter, and Sienna jumped. "Now I recognize you."

"I'm sorry?"

Josie leaned forward and rested her chin on one palm. "You're the Cruz girl. Lived here when you were younger, right?"

"Ah, yes." Her cheeks warmed. "Sienna."

Josie snapped her gum and shook her head. "Such a sad thing when your mama passed on." She looked at the man. "You remember that, Sam? Remember that pretty Spanish woman who used to stop in here sometimes?"

"Oh, no," Sienna said. "I think you must have her mistaken for someone else. My mom…" *never would have come in here*, she almost finished, but Josie nodded and snapped her gum with vigor.

"Sure she did. Used to come in on Friday afternoons when the owner was sellin' the day-old bread and pastries for seventy-five percent off." She stopped suddenly, as if aware she'd said something wrong. "Wasn't just your mama, of course. Lots of people came in. The price of bread in the grocery store always was a damn crime. Still is, the way they jack up those prices and…" She dropped her gaze and turned to make a fresh pot of coffee.

My mother shopped here? Sienna's face burned even hotter. It made sense, of course. Her mother had stretched every dollar.

"Where did you get that dress?" one of her classmates asked. *"It looks like one I had a long time ago."*

Seven-year old Sienna twisted her hands in the patchwork skirt. *"My mom gave it to me. For my birthday."*

The classmate, Stella something-or-other, studied her with beady eyes. *"Well, it looks a lot like one my mom took to the Salvation Army last month."* The girl took an extra brownie from the serving line and walked off to join her friends at the popular table in the center of the cafeteria.

Sienna left her tray sitting on the line and bolted to the closest bathroom she could find. She'd loved this dress from the moment her mother brought it home. Now she wanted to rip it off and throw it in the garbage.

"Honey?" Josie's gum popping brought her back to the diner. "You want some more time, or are you ready to order?" She moved down the counter and cleared plates in front of the woman and child. The little girl yawned, and her chin almost hit the counter as her eyes drooped in sleep.

Before Sienna could answer, the front door opened, and the Ericksen sisters walked inside. They peeled off matching red jackets and draped their scarves over the coat tree. "Hi, Josie." Ella waved. She was heavily made up and wore a skin-tight pink sweater, black jeans, and stiletto boots. In contrast, Becca wore a blue sweatshirt, cargo pants, and heavy work boots.

"Hi, yourself," Josie answered. "You two are late tonight."

Becca rolled her eyes. "Tell me about it. Beauty Queen here couldn't manage to pick me up until ten minutes ago." She jabbed a thumb at her sister, who tossed her long ponytail and shrugged.

"Something came up," Ella said.

"Something always comes up," Becca mouthed at Josie.

Sienna smiled and turned back to her menu. Becca ran the local animal shelter, evidenced by the sweatshirt, work boots, and no-nonsense ponytail. She couldn't remember what Ella did for a living. Something that involved glamour and fashion, from the looks of her. Sienna studied them from the corner of her eye. Becca bent over her menu while Ella twisted her ponytail around her fingers and scanned the room. Her gaze settled on Sienna.

"Hi," she called out before Sienna could look away. Ella folded her hands on the table as if she was holding court and gave Sienna a dazzling white smile. "You're our new upstairs neighbor, right? Come join us."

"Oh, no, that's okay. I'm fine."

Ella lifted one perfectly groomed brow. "You're sure? We're better company than Mr. Moriarty."

The man on Sienna's right glanced over.

"No offense," Ella added.

He grinned and pushed back his empty pie plate. "None taken, I suppose." He put on his coat, left a five-dollar tip for his pie and coffee, and walked out. A moment later, the woman and child followed him.

"Thanks, Josie," the woman said in a tired voice. She pulled on the little girl's coat and tugged a hat over her head.

"You're welcome, Chloe. Anytime. You know that." As the door closed behind them, Josie pulled a ticket from her pad, scribbled something on it, then took a ten dollar bill from her own pocket and put it into the drawer of the cash register. She gave Sienna a dark look. "Husband likes to hit the bottle, then likes to hit her." She scowled. "I tol' her a dozen times to leave him, but she says she ain't got no place to go." She scrubbed the counter with a bleached-white towel. "She could stay with me, she and Ellen. I tol' her that too. I got an extra bedroom."

"So why won't she?" Sienna wanted to ask Chloe's last name, but she didn't dare.

Josie looked up and scowled more fiercely. "'Cause her husband is a judge over in Silver Valley. She ever left him, he'd come after her. Probably take custody of Ellen. Chloe knows it too. So she just takes it." She tossed the towel aside and pointed at Sienna. "Don't you ever take shit like that from a man."

"Don't worry." Sienna thought of her workouts with Mike. Maybe she could convince Chloe to take a few boxing lessons at the gym. *Local judge beats and blackmails his wife.* It hadn't taken long for Pine Point to reveal its first ugly secret. But the thought saddened her, and she couldn't get the picture of the woman's bruised arm from her mind.

The front door opened and she looked over, glad for the distraction. The construction workers Sienna had met at the gym walked inside.

"Hey, Josie." Mac waved a giant arm.

"Hey, boys." She poured two cups of coffee without asking and hollered over her shoulder to the cook on the line, "Guys are here. Two medium-rare burgers with the works."

"Not like we're regulars or anything," Damian said as they joined Sienna at the counter. "It's Sienna, right?"

She nodded. "You know what, I'll take a burger with the works too. Sounds delicious."

"You got it." Josie refilled Sienna's coffee mug and folded her arms on the counter. "How's things, boys?"

"Shitty." Mac grinned. "I hate electrical work. I hate working inside, period. But it's a paycheck." He took a long, loud slurp of coffee.

She thought he might have played football at Pine Point High. A fuzzy memory from eighth grade slipped into Sienna's mind, going to a game and holding hands under the bleachers with a boy whose name she couldn't recall. *Her-bert, Her-bert*, the crowd had chanted above them.

Behind the counter, the burgers sizzled on the grill, filling the space with fragrant smoke and making Sienna's mouth water.

"How's Mike?" Mac asked. "He coming out tonight?"

Sienna shook. "Um, no. I don't think so."

"Oh. Thought he and you might—ah, never mind." Mac shook his head and took another slurp of coffee. "Open mouth, insert foot, that's me. Don't listen to a word I say."

The burgers arrived, preventing Sienna from having to respond. Instead, she listened to the conversations around her.

"So you gonna see her again?" Damian asked Mac after a few bites of hamburger.

Mac shrugged. "Dunno. She said she wants to keep things casual."

"Or she wants to keep her options open 'til something better comes along."

Josie grinned as Mac elbowed his friend. "What's better than all this?" he asked, looking down and patting a belly that had obviously enjoyed many burgers at Zeb's.

"All I'm sayin' is, when a woman doesn't want to be seen in public with you, it's a bad sign." Damian looked up. "Josie, you're a woman."

"Last time I checked." She replaced the gum in her mouth with a fresh stick.

"What do you think? Mac here's been seeing this chick for…" He turned to Mac. "What is it now? Couple months?"

Mac shrugged and continued to eat.

"She goes over to his place. He goes over to hers. But the minute he wants to take her out, dinner or a movie or anything like that, she puts on the brakes. Says she doesn't want to rush into anything."

"Huh." Josie leaned on the counter. "Hate to say it, but you might be right on this one. Sounds like a bad sign. Unless she's some kind of introvert with one of those phobias of public places." She turned to Sienna. "You know what I'm talking about? What's that called? When people are afraid to go outside their homes?"

"Agoraphobia?"

Josie snapped her fingers. "Yup. That's it. Saw a *20/20* show on it once." She shook her head as she took two sandwich platters from the line and carried them over to the Ericksen sisters. "Damn shame," she said without missing a beat when she returned. "Can't imagine being afraid of people."

"I don't think she has agoraphobia," Damian said. "Far as I know, she's got a job. So she leaves the house for that."

Mac belched loudly. "You all done discussing my personal business yet?"

Sienna bit her lip to keep from smiling too much. Josie disappeared into the kitchen, and the guys' conversation turned to the thought of more shitty work tomorrow, plumbing this time, from the sounds of it.

Sienna finished her burger and left a generous tip. Looked as though she wouldn't have to travel too far to discover some of Pine Point's secrets. She hurried upstairs and took a quick shower. Then she sank into the recliner, grabbed her yellow notepad, and spent the next two hours writing notes on all she'd seen and heard.

Chapter Ten

"Ma, what are you doing?" Mike came home from work the following night to find his mother balancing on a step stool in the middle of the kitchen. Two open cans of paint sat on the counter, along with a collection of brushes and newspapers. Loretta wore jeans and a paint-streaked sweatshirt, and her gray hair looked as though it had a few extra dabs of white in it.

"I'm doing the edging," she explained and waved a brush at the seam between the kitchen wall and ceiling.

"I can see that. And you're doing a very good job, by the way. But I thought you wanted to paint the living room."

"I do. That room's too big for me to handle it, so the twins are coming over this weekend." She looked up at her handiwork and rubbed her nose with the hand holding the paintbrush. A white streak appeared on her forehead. "But there isn't much surface area in here. I want to paint over this eighties' mint green and make it all black and white." She gestured at a magazine flipped open on the table. "Like that."

Mike glanced at the checkerboard pattern in the glossy pages. "It's nice. But don't you think you're a little—"

"Don't you even say what I think you're about to," she warned. She waved the brush near his face. "Or I might give you a little edging while I'm at it." She touched up the final corner and then climbed down. "I am certainly not too old to do a little painting." She cleaned the brush and set it aside. "Or too arthritic, or too whatever else you were going to say."

"I wasn't going to say anything at all." Mike dropped a kiss onto her head.

"Oh, dear." Loretta frowned as she looked around the room.

"What's wrong?"

"I don't have anything to make for dinner. And this mess…"

He had already begun clearing away the papers and recapping the paint cans. He flipped the magazine shut and set it next to the couch in the living room. "How about we go out for dinner? Just you and me? We haven't done that in a while."

Loretta smiled. "No, we haven't. And I'd love to."

They walked into Zeb's Diner less than an hour later. Mike looked around, half-expecting to see Sienna sitting in one of the booths. Pine Point wasn't that big, and he'd heard through the grapevine she lived in one of the apartments up above. He would rather have gone across town, to the Ponderosa or even the more upscale restaurant with three buffets, the Corner Lounge, but his mother loved Zeb's.

He kept his gaze down. What would he say if he did see Sienna here? What would he do? Before California, before Edie, before prison, before all those mistakes, he'd been a regular guy. Maybe, on his good days, a little bit of a charmer. A few of the guys out west had even called him Casanova, since he'd never had a problem talking to women or taking them home with him.

All that had changed.

"Hello, Josie," Loretta crowed as soon as they arrived. "Look who's taking me out on the town tonight." She squeezed Mike's arm.

"Most handsome boy in the place," Josie said as she led them to a table in the back.

"I heard that," a gray-haired man at the counter said.

"I'm sure you did." Josie swatted the man as she returned to the cash register.

"So now tell me," Loretta began. She unwound her scarf and took off her coat and gloves. "Have you met anyone? Any nice girl at the gym?"

The question caught him so off guard, his knee jerked and hit the underside of the table. "Ma…"

"What?"

Josie came over with two plastic cups of water. "Ready to order?" she asked, even though they'd just sat down.

"Uh, sure." Mike scanned the handwritten page of specials taped inside the front of the menu. "Open-face-turkey sandwich for me."

"I'll take a cup of the soup and a salad," Loretta said.

"That's it?"

She swatted the back of his hand. "Yes, that's it. I don't pump iron all day long like my handsome boy. I don't need all those calories."

Though his face burned at the words, they soothed him too, down deep where most of him felt like it had calloused over years ago.

Josie smacked her gum, collected their menus, and strolled away.

"No one?" Loretta continued, as if their conversation hadn't been interrupted. "I wish you would. I want you to be happy."

"I am happy." *And I have no interest in getting involved with anyone, nice girl or not.*

She waved away his words. "Well, I'd like some grandbabies before I'm too old to pick them up or play with them."

"Ma, geez." He glanced around, thankful for a light Tuesday dinner crowd.

"I'm just saying." She took a sip of water. "What about Sienna Cruz?"

Oh, my God. Maybe taking his mother to dinner had been a colossal mistake.

"What about her?"

"Have you seen her again? How's school going for her? Must be a challenge, coming into a class midway through the year."

"I guess. I haven't really seen her. Or talked to her." Little white lie. Just a little one.

"That's too bad," Loretta said as Josie returned with their meals. "She was a beautiful young girl, from what I remember. Elenita used to show me pictures of her. I'm sure she's grown into a gorgeous woman."

Mike bent over his sandwich. Yes, she had. If she'd turned into an ugly, overweight, toothless hag, he'd have no problem getting her out of his mind. As it was, she filled almost every waking hour.

"You be nice to her," Loretta said.

"I already told you I will. I'm nice to everyone."

She shook her head and blew on a spoonful of soup. "I mean be extra nice. You don't know what she's been through." She thought for a minute. "In fact, why don't you invite her over for dinner one night? I'd love to see her again and welcome her home."

Chapter Eleven

Friday morning, Sienna overslept. Exhausted from a week of heading off student meltdowns, keeping track of paperwork, and staying up past midnight to take notes on Pine Point secrets, she buried her face in her pillow when her alarm went off the first time. When she finally opened her eyes again, the clock read quarter past eight, fifteen minutes before she was supposed to sign in.

"Shit!" She leaped out of bed and pulled on the first thing she saw, an old green sweater with fraying sleeves and the same pair of jeans she'd worn the day before. She splashed water on her face, tied her hair into a ponytail, and grabbed her makeup bag on the way out the door. Outside, an inch of newly fallen snow covered her car. *Of course.* Sienna stood in the middle of the sidewalk, not sure whether to cry or rage or just turn around and go back to bed.

"Hey, Sienna."

She looked over her shoulder to see Ella Ericksen coming down the stairs behind her. Ella had a designer bag slung over one shoulder and a lumpy paper bag in the crook of the other arm. Despite the early hour, she looked impeccable and fully awake. Even back in high school, she'd bounce into classes with limitless energy and smiles for all the guys surrounding her. She was the last person Sienna wanted to see in her own sorry state right then.

"Hey." Sienna stared mournfully at her car and then began wiping the windshield with one mittened hand.

"Don't you have a snow brush?" Ella opened the back of her sturdy-looking SUV, parked as usual behind Sienna's car.

"Ah, no."

"Here." With two quick sweeps of a long brush, Ella had cleared Sienna's windshield. She walked around the car, clearing the rest of it without getting any snow on her long red jacket or in her perfectly coiffed hair. Then she handed the brush to Sienna. "Take it. I have another one upstairs."

"Really? You're sure?"

"Of course." Ella tossed her hair and beamed. "That's what neighbors are for."

Sienna stood there as the beauty queen climbed into her SUV, beeped the horn twice, and drove away. *Neighbors*. She supposed they were.

Sienna dashed into the school twenty minutes later. Loni, the double-chinned monitor, sat at Sienna's desk. She'd called the office, and Jenny had reassured her that the children would be taken care of, but by the time she reached her classroom, sweat drenched Sienna's back. *Please let everything be calm and peaceful.* Surely the twins wouldn't be awake enough to have started their tantrums. Caleb would be bent over his work, and Silas was probably rocking happily in his chair.

"Thank goodness you're here." Loni got up. "They've been about ready to throw tantrums, all of them."

"Really? I'm sorry." Sienna surveyed the room. Billy and Bailey sat red-faced in the corner by the new bookshelf. Silas was rocking, but in a manner so jerky and agitated, she was afraid he'd pitch forward out of the chair and knock himself silly. Caleb wasn't sitting in his usual chair, but instead stood in the corner under the window, blinking too fast. And Dawn was nowhere to be seen.

"Where's Dawn?"

"In the closet, last time I saw her." She gave a little nod to the corner as she walked out. "Good luck."

Sienna sank to the ground. Her legs gave out, and she simply folded into a pretzel on the rug. *I'm in over my head.* For a long few minutes, she sat there, unmoving and unspeaking. How did people do this year after year? She remembered why she'd left teaching. It was too damn hard. That, and too damn heartbreaking. She pressed her fingertips to her temples and told herself to breathe. *This isn't forever. This is temporary. You can do this.* And if she couldn't, what was the worst that would happen? They'd find someone else to teach the class, and she'd return to UNC and find another small town to study.

She took another few breaths. Finally, she pushed herself to a stand and walked over to Caleb. She didn't touch him. She didn't try to look at him. Instead, she pointed at the bookshelf and spoke over his left shoulder.

"Caleb, please pick out two books. Then you can sit at the table and read them to yourself, and we'll talk about them in thirty minutes."

His gaze shifted, and for a second—maybe a half second—his eyes met hers. Then he nodded and walked to the bookshelf.

Silas stopped rocking. He looked at her with tears in his eyes, and suddenly she realized the magnitude of her lateness. *They thought I wasn't coming back.* On impulse, she reached down and picked him up, a heavy mass of floppy arms and legs. Then she sat in the rocking chair and snuggled him to her chest. His body tensed, and she waited for him to leap up and stumble across the room. But he didn't. After a breath or two, he relaxed into her, and together they rocked in silence.

Sienna kept one eye on the twins and the other on the ajar closet door. She continued to rock. Caleb sat at the table and dragged his finger down the first page of his book. After a few minutes, Billy walked over to her, sniffling.

"Miss Cruz, are we gonna do math this morning?"

"Would you like to?"

He gave her a long, soulful look and nodded.

"Yes," Bailey said from the other side of the room. "I want to do math."

Well, that was a first. Sienna put Silas on the floor. She sat the twins at the table with worksheets and freshly sharpened pencils and walked over to the closet.

"Dawn?"

Nothing. She pushed the door open a few more inches. "Sweetheart, I know you want to stay in here." As her eyes adjusted, she made out the girl's tiny frame in the far corner. Sienna held out one hand. "But I need you to come out now." *Please.* "I promise you I will be here for you. I will not leave you, and I will make things as safe as I can inside this classroom."

As she spoke the words aloud, a memory flashed into Sienna's mind. Kids teasing her in the lunchroom for the funny food in her paper bag. Sienna waiting on the playground as other kids rushed by her to claim the swings. One boy elbowed her in the ribs, and when she cried out in pain, he turned and made a face. The monitors stood at the edge of the playground and kept their eyes averted, talking about soap operas and restaurants and summer vacation. She wondered if things might have been different if a teacher had said those words to her years ago. *I will keep you safe. I will protect you.*

"Dawn?"

This time, the figure moved in the shadows, and a moment later, Dawn reached out one sticky hand and placed it in Sienna's. The girl didn't speak. But she squeezed Sienna's fingers slightly, as if to say, "Okay, I'm here. But remember. You promised."

* * * * *

Later that night, Mike unlocked his apartment with a yawn. He debated watching the Knicks-Lakers game, but he'd already missed the first half. Instead, he tuned his iPod to a rap station and spooned vanilla ice cream into a bowl. Sure wasn't health food, but he spent enough time working out that he figured he could cheat every so often.

His phone buzzed on the kitchen table. *"Going to Jimmy's later,"* Zane texted. *"Stop by."*

Mike rubbed his eyes and yawned again. *"Long day. Gonna skip it. Thanks."*

"Pussy. Stop thinking about her."

Mike gave his phone the bird and kept eating his ice cream. Zane could call him a pussy all he wanted. The bar scene had lost its appeal long ago. His phone buzzed again, and he was about to send Zane a bunch of X-rated emojis when he checked the name on the screen.

"Hey, friend," Sienna had written. She put a winky face after friend. "*You still up?"*

He licked the last of the ice cream from his spoon and set it in the empty bowl. "*Yeah. How are you?"*

"Tired. Long day."

"Bad or good day?" he asked.

"Little bit of both. I overslept and was late to class. The kids flipped out."

Mike kicked off his shoes and carried his phone into the bedroom, where he stretched out on his bed.

"I'm sure they'll be okay."

"I'm sure they will too. Just started the day off wrong."

"In 24 hours it'll be better," Mike typed. Then he erased the words. Too corny.

"How was your day?" she asked.

Mike rested his head on one arm. Was this what friends did? Texted about their day? He'd rather talk to her in person. Of course, if she was actually here in person, he didn't think they'd talk for very long. He'd be too busy trying to figure out how to get her clothes off.

"Good day," he answered. He wriggled out of his workout pants and pulled his shirt over his head. "*You'll never guess what happened around lunch though."*

'What? Tell me." Another winky face.

"I got two clients I just found out are sleeping with the same guy. They were both telling me about him while I was training them. Shoulda seen the looks on their faces when they found out they were talking about the same guy." It took him almost a minute to type the message.

She sent back a bunch of exclamation points. *"No way! Guess that's a small town for you, huh?"*

"People cheat in big cities too." A lump rose into his throat as he typed. Boy, did they ever.

"True. But how likely are they to come into the same place at the same time? That could happen a dozen times a day here."

"I guess." He didn't want to talk about it anymore. Didn't matter. Didn't affect him.

"I'm looking forward to dinner," she wrote after a moment of silence.

Against his best efforts, his groin tightened with desire. *"Me too."*

"Guess I'll call it a night. Have a good one."

"You too." He dropped the phone on the bed and reached down to settle a hand on his growing cock. He still didn't think it was possible to be friends with a woman, especially a woman like Sienna, without wanting more. Here was proof. They could talk about their day, say goodnight, and all he'd think about was what she was wearing. He stroked himself as his eyes fell closed and he saw her above him, smiling and watching him move toward release.

Chapter Twelve

Sienna walked into Marc's Grille at five past six on Saturday evening. On her way, she saw the skinny stray cat again, only this time it had a companion, an equally skinny yellow and white one with a tail bent in the middle like it was broken. *Poor things.* Must be tough scrapping out a life when no one wanted you.

Inside the gorgeous, dark-wood interior of the upscale restaurant, she shook away the thoughts and looked around. Groups and couples sat at about half the tables, and it looked as though the maître d' had a long list in front of him. She hadn't thought to make a reservation. Had Mike? Maybe they were eating at the bar. Maybe they weren't even having dinner, but just drinks and appetizers while they watched whatever sporting event happened to be on television.

She slipped off her long black coat and dusted the snow from her hair. She'd chosen jeans, a body-skimming silver top, and tall black boots. Friends or not, every once in a while a girl liked to dress up for dinner. She spied Mike sitting at the bar, but as she walked over, he climbed off his stool and met her halfway.

The maître d', who'd followed her with menus in hand, directed them to a table in the back corner of the restaurant.

"This is a nice place," Sienna said. "Very fancy for Pine Point. Is it new?"

Mike nodded. "A couple of years old. This whole block is."

"It used to be farmland when we were kids, right?"

"Yep." He stared at his menu.

Sienna scanned the specials and decided on the pot roast with stuffing and asparagus. She needed something hearty on a winter night like this. She set her menu aside and surveyed the other tables. Mostly couples, a few businessmen eating together, and one family of six. A cute blond toddler sat in a high chair and waved her fist as her parents and grandparents oohed and aahed. An older brother, maybe six or seven, looked bored and played with his silverware.

The waiter came and took their order, and after their drinks arrived—martini for her, beer for him—Mike finally sat back in his chair and relaxed his tense posture. "So tell me about your first week of school."

"It's been challenging, that's for sure. I taught a special-ed class once, but now I'm remembering why I went back to grad school."

"Is it that hard?"

"I only have five kids, so I can't say it's *hard.* Emotionally trying, yes. Frustrating sometimes. They're all at different levels, and they all have different needs, and I have to try to meet them all at the same time, the best I can." She took a sip of her martini. "The resources are pretty limited too. I don't know how Lucy did it with just a chalkboard and one computer. We have a crooked table that barely seats them all and chairs that look like they're left over from the seventies. The books too. Well, they might be from the late nineties, but still. I ordered some new ones, and a bookshelf to put them on, but they won't get here for at least eight weeks." She was rattling on, but she didn't care. It was nice to have someone who listened to her besides Josie the waitress or Loni the school monitor.

"You know what I'd really love?" she continued.

"What?" A smile played on his face.

"Beanbag chairs." She laughed. "It sounds silly, right? But I had a teacher—I think it was in fourth grade—who had them all around the room. Whenever we finished our work early, or got a good grade on a test, we could sit in one and read."

"Let me guess." He tilted his head. "You spent a lot of time in those beanbag chairs, Miss Smarty-Pants."

She stuck out her tongue. She couldn't resist. "Why, yes, I did." She took another few sips of martini and welcomed the smooth heat that spread through her. *See, this was a good idea. We can be friends. We can joke around and not have it mean anything.* She just had to focus on something other than Mike's searing blue eyes, or strong arms and hands, or low chuckle that made her belly tighten in wonderful, sensual, not-so-friendly ways.

"You have Silas Turner in your class, don't you?" he asked as their salads arrived.

"I do. How did you know?"

"His father works out at the gym before work in the mornings. He mentioned it."

"Hope he had good things to say."

One corner of Mike's mouth lifted in a grin. "They weren't all bad."

"Terrific."

"Don't worry about it. I'm sure people know you're doing your best. It can't be easy to come in halfway through the year."

Sienna stabbed some lettuce and a cucumber. "I have a student who doesn't speak."

He looked up. "At all?"

"Not at school. It's not a medical or physical thing either. She has selective mutism. I've read through her file, and there's some history there…" She trailed off. She wasn't supposed to break confidence about things like possible past abuse or families' criminal records. "Anyway, it breaks my heart."

"Does she talk at home?"

"I don't know. I've called her foster parents twice, but they haven't gotten back to me."

"Shit." Mike scraped the last few pieces of carrot and radish from his salad plate and pushed it aside.

He wore a long-sleeved black button-down with the sleeves rolled up, and beneath one she could just see the tail end of a red and blue swirl.

"You have a lot of ink."

He flexed his hands. "Yeah, guess I do. I'm thinking about getting more."

"They all mean something? Or were they just…" She trailed off.

"Drunken whims?" He grinned. "I have a couple of those from when I was a lot younger. Probably oughta get them covered up or changed someday."

She cocked her head. "What's your favorite one?"

He rubbed the back of his neck. His dark blond hair caught the low light in the restaurant, and a jolt of desire hit Sienna. She knew what his hair felt like between her fingers. She knew how his mouth fit against hers. With effort, she tamped down her desire. *He just wants to be friends. You can't look at him that way.*

"I'd say I haven't gotten it yet," Mike said, and it took a minute for Sienna to realize they were still talking about tattoos. He turned his arms back and forth. "Haven't gotten a new one in a while though."

"What will it be?"

His gaze rested on hers, blue and serious. "Not sure."

She tore her gaze from his. "Any names?" she said lightly. "I always think of that Norman Rockwell painting with the sailor who has about eight or ten girls' names tattooed on his arm, and each one's crossed out except for the newest one."

He shook his head. "Just one name. My mom's." He touched his chest above his heart. "Right here. It's bad luck to put anyone's name on your skin except your mother or your child." He paused. "Can't trust that other people are going to stick around."

She spun the stem of her glass in her fingers and figured this was as good a time as any to ask. "You lived out in L.A. for a while?"

"Yep."

"Didn't like it?"

He shrugged. "Wasn't for me."

"How did you end up going out there in the first place?"

Their entrees arrived, and they ate in silence for a few minutes. The pot roast melted in Sienna's mouth, and she closed her eyes to savor it.

"I needed a change," Mike said abruptly. He sliced off a piece of filet. "After high school. An older brother of a friend of mine needed some help doing construction work. I went out there with him and lived in San Diego for a few years. Then I moved to Los Angeles." He chewed his filet and swallowed. "For a woman." A bitter laugh left his lips. "Stupidest decision I could have made."

Ah. That's where the distrust comes from. Sienna speared another piece of pot roast. "I'm sorry. Relationships can be damaging, especially when they don't work out."

"That's one way of putting it." Mike sliced into his filet again, scraping the plate with an ugly sound.

"But the gym seems like it's doing well," she said, wanting to change the subject.

He set his fork and knife on his empty plate and pushed it back. "It is. Thank God. Took a big risk with that."

"There aren't any other gyms in town?"

"Silver Valley has a Y. That's the next closest place to work out."

"So this was a smart decision, opening Springer Fitness."

He smiled for the first time in a long ten minutes. "You sound like you're trying to butter me up."

"Just trying to lighten the mood."

He sipped his beer. "I'm sorry. I've got a lot of shit in my past, that's all. Made some stupid decisions and I'm trying not to repeat them."

She finished her meal and concentrated on her martini. "I think everyone has a lot of shit in their pasts. Comes with being human."

"Yeah, maybe." He eyed her. "So what's yours?"

Pieces of memory flooded Sienna's mind. Her mother coming home late after cleaning other people's homes all day. Children at school whispering about Sienna's homemade clothes. The smell of Chinese food. The weight of heavy blankets covering her in the cold of winter. A doctor's kind face. A funeral on a hot, sticky August morning. Moving five states away to live with a father she barely knew.

"Sienna?"

She blinked. "I'm sorry."

"I know your mom died when you were in—what? Tenth grade?" He cracked his knuckles. "I'm sorry I don't remember you. From school, I mean."

"Don't be. I kept to myself. Didn't exactly travel in the popular circles." She took a deep breath. "My mom died the summer I was fifteen. I'd just finished tenth grade, yeah." She'd had her first job that summer, working at the concession stand over at Rockaway Beach. Every morning, she caught a ride with Marie Hadley, and every night she caught a ride back. Which meant when the call about her mother being taken to the Med Center had come, she'd had no way to get there until it was too late.

"I'm sorry," Mike said, breaking into her thoughts. "My mom's my rock. Can't imagine what I'd do without her."

"Thank you. It was, ah..." She picked up her fork with a trembling hand. She took one bite. Then another. "My mom was pretty strong too. Raised me all by herself."

"Were you born here?"

"No. My mom came over from Mexico when she was fourteen. She lived in Texas for a while and then moved to North Carolina with a cousin. She met my father there when she was seventeen, he knocked her up, and I arrived nine months later." She pressed one hand to her lap as her cheeks grew hot. She'd spent two years in a shrink's office during college. She'd worked through all her shit. Why this reaction?

"So how'd you end up in New York?"

"You know the Hadleys?"

"Of the four bleach-blond, blue-eyed, date-everything-in-sight sisters? Of course. Everyone in town does."

She smiled. "Their parents vacationed in North Carolina, and my mom got to know them. They offered her a job cleaning houses in Pine Point, so she took it. They gave her—us—a place to stay too, until my mom could afford her own."

"Huh." Mike finished his meal. "Never knew that. About the Hadleys, I mean. Most people around here just think they're stuck-up snobs with too much money."

Sienna didn't answer. *I'm sure there's a lot you don't know about people around here.*

"Hey, you want to get some air?" he asked.

Though she wasn't keen on walking around in the godforsaken cold, that sounded better than sitting in this too-warm restaurant while her head churned up more memories. "Yes."

He waved down the waiter.

"Let's split it," she said and reached for her purse.

"I've got it." But he passed her the bill. "You can leave the tip, how's that?"

She did, dropping almost thirty percent of the total on the table. Then she followed him out into the night.

"I'm sorry," he said as they walked up the block. "About your mom. And about bringing it up. Gotta be tough to talk about, especially being back here."

She took his arm as her boots slipped on the snow-covered sidewalk, and he squeezed his elbow to keep her hand secure. "Look at all these places," he said, pointing at the office buildings and boutiques along Park Place Run. Clothing shops. Gift shops. A pet-grooming service. "I never thought they'd make a go of it, but I guess Pine Point has more money than I thought."

"It's not exactly the same town I grew up in," she agreed.

They reached the end of the block. Suddenly, a pair of yellow eyes twinkled in the dark, and a moment later, a cat dashed across the sidewalk and almost tripped Sienna.

"Whoa." Mike tightened his hand on her elbow, and heat zoomed straight into Sienna's core. *Damn.* This friends-only dinner hadn't done anything to cool the chemistry between them. If anything, it had fueled it.

"Did you know there were stray cats around here?" She took a few steps off the pavement, but she couldn't go far on the uneven, frozen ground. "I've seen them a couple of times. They're way too skinny and matted to be anyone's pets."

"It doesn't surprise me. I'll tell Zane to mention it to Becca. Maybe she can bring some traps over from the animal shelter and get them." He rubbed his arms. "Pretty cold this time of year. Tough to survive."

"Look at that." Sienna pointed. "Maybe Becca's already been here." Three roughly made shelters sat close to the underbrush, large plastic tubs that had holes cut in the front and what looked like blankets inside. In front of each container sat a small dish of food.

"Huh." Mike bent down. "Maybe." As he straightened, another cat, smaller than either of the ones Sienna had seen before, bolted in front of him. It slipped into one of the tubs. A moment later, green eyes looked out at them. Mike chuckled. "Guess maybe we don't have to worry after all."

Sienna stared into the silent night. Evergreens took over where the sidewalk ended and stretched into the dark. If she remembered correctly, a ribbon of river ran along this side of Pine Point, all the way to the mountains outside of town. It never quite froze in winter. It ran deep enough that a current always slid along beneath the frosty surface, moving even in the dead of January.

"Where did you park?" he asked. "I'll walk you to your car."

She pointed down the block and around the corner.

"You're okay to drive home?"

The buzz from her martini had long since worn off. "Yes. Perfectly fine." They reached her Mazda in a matter of minutes, and she unlocked the door but didn't get inside. Mike leaned against the car, his blue gaze on hers.

"Thanks for dinner," she said. "It was nice to have a conversation with someone outside of school."

He inclined his head. "You're very welcome."

On impulse, she took his coat sleeve. "I meant that offer about us being friends. I'd really…" Her voice caught in her throat. "I'd really like someone to vent to or work out with. This would be nice to do, every once in a while. But nothing more. I understand. We'll keep a proper distance and all that."

"No kissing," he said.

"No kissing. Or touching." She withdrew her hand. "Or anything else that might be mistaken for, you know, romance or a relationship."

His Adam's apple moved up and down as she spoke. "I think that's probably for the best. All things considered." He held out his hand and Sienna took it. "Friends only."

"Friends only," she echoed. "It's a deal." And she made herself climb into her car and drive away without looking behind her, without wondering if Mike felt the same quiet sadness at their agreement as she did.

Chapter Thirteen

The following Wednesday, Mike dropped a set of keys into Hans's hand. "I'll be back around four. Text me if you need anything."

"Sure thing, boss."

A respite from snow the last few days had left Pine Point cold and gray, with dingy snow banks along Main Street rising almost as tall as Mike's waist. He eyed the sky. Didn't look like precipitation, but he had the tow trucks ready just in case. He hadn't had much action the last couple of weeks, and he could do with some cash flow from his side business. After L.A., he never wanted to be caught without extra savings again.

He climbed into his pickup and drove straight to Pine Point Elementary School. He glanced at the load in the bed of his truck a couple of times. *It's the kind of thing friends do for each other,* he told himself as he turned into the parking lot and found a visitor's spot near the door. But once there, he couldn't make himself get out of the truck.

Shit. I'm back at school. Didn't matter that he had decent memories of Pine Point Elementary. The bad stuff hadn't started until high school, when words swam on the pages of his textbooks and dates and places got all messed up inside his head. Eventually he decided skipping class was easier than going to it and getting Ds and Fs. He drummed his fingers on the steering wheel and stared at the squat brick building. The flag whipped in the wind above the courtyard, and Mike remembered on sunny days in the spring, the whole school used to go outside and say the Pledge of Allegiance before the day began.

You never think when you're that age anything bad will happen, he thought as he watched the stars and stripes ripple in the wind. *The hardest decision is where to sit at lunch or who to play ball with at recess.* He thought of the tattoos on his right and left calves, matching sides of the yin and yang. He'd gotten them when he was eighteen, first ones he could, back when he thought he knew when yin and yang stood for.

Good and bad. Light and dark. He figured getting one on each leg would balance him out, would somehow give him stability as he moved into adulthood. Mike killed the engine and made himself get out of the truck. Now he knew finding balance was tricky at best and elusive most of the time. He trudged across the shoveled sidewalks and swallowed away the lump in his throat. *Me at a school again. Who would've thought?*

Eva Hadley greeted him at the desk inside. "Mike Springer." She folded her fingers under her chin and flashed him a toothpaste smile. "This is a surprise."

"Uh huh." Mike scribbled his name on the visitors' log.

"What brings you here today?"

"Just dropping off some things for Sienna Cruz's class."

Eva's carefully plucked brows lifted. "Really? I didn't know…she didn't mention anything to me."

"She doesn't know." He clamped his mouth shut. That sounded idiotic. "I mean, she doesn't know I'd be here today," he added lamely.

Eva glanced down the hallway. "It's Room Eighteen. Down the center hall, all the way to the end on the right."

"Thanks. Think I'll go…" He gestured back outside and didn't bother to finish. Instead, he trotted to his truck and pulled around to the school's back entrance. He positioned the truck as close to the building as he could get it and then knocked on the small door marked *Custodial.*

A moment later, it opened, and Darryl Cobalt's wrinkled face peered out. Darryl lived down the road from Mike and his mom and had worked at the school as long as Mike could remember. The old man beamed and pushed open the door. "Michael Springer. My good man, what on earth are you doing sneaking around the back of my school?"

"Little special delivery for a friend." He gestured at his truck. "Do you have a minute? Do you think you could you help me? It's for Sienna Cruz's class."

Darryl's smile widened. "Ah, of course. She'll be thrilled."

Pleasure slid through Mike at the thought. *She needs a friend, she said so herself the other night.* Plus, his mother would be over the moon at the thought he'd done something nice for Sienna. He told himself that was the reason he was here, and not because he hadn't stopped thinking about her hand on his arm for the last five days.

Darryl produced a master key and unlocked the double doors that faced the playground as Mike lifted a brand new table from the back of his truck. Only three feet off the ground and painted with cartoon figures, it looked like something that might work for a class of eight-year-olds. He hoped. He blew out a long breath and carried the table inside.

Criminy. Did all elementary schools smell the same? Like paint and pizza and faint antiseptic? A cool sweat settled on his head and neck, and it took a long minute before he could make out the numbers on the doors. Room Eighteen. There. Right beside him. Before he knocked, he peeked through the window. Sienna sat in a rocking chair with one boy on her lap and three others sitting in front of her. She wore her hair down over a navy sweater and jeans. Silver hoops in her ears matched a long silver necklace that hung almost to her lap. The boys stared at her, rapt, as she turned the pages of a brightly illustrated book.

Mike knocked gently.

At once, the students turned. The tallest one jumped to his feet, pointed at Mike, and began talking rapid fire to Sienna. She put a finger to her lips and stood. The boy on her lap slid to his feet, and Mike could see it was Silas Turner.

Mike pushed open the door. "Hi, there."

When she looked up, the look of genuine pleasure on her face was worth every penny he'd spent. He set down the table just inside the door. "Surprise."

"Wow. Hello. I'd say it is. "

The boy who'd first jumped up took a few steps across the room and then stopped. "You're Mr. Springer. I met you once when my daddy took me to your gym."

Mike yanked at his collar. The kid didn't look familiar, but that didn't mean much. "Ah, yes, I am. Hello there." Four pairs of curious eyes settled on him, and he fought the urge to turn around and flee.

"Yes, Caleb, this is Mr. Springer," Sienna said. "How do you say hello to adults?"

The boy walked over and stuck his arm out stiffly. "My name is Caleb Arthur Williams. It's very nice to meet you." He spoke in clipped tones and looked at Mike's belt.

Mike took his hand and shook it. "It's very nice to meet you too, Caleb." His nerves settled a fraction.

"This is definitely a surprise," Sienna said again. "A very nice one." She ran her fingers over the table. "You shouldn't have. This must have cost a lot."

"Nah. Anyway, doesn't matter. That's what friends are for, right?" Without waiting for her response, he returned to his truck. The next gift took him two trips. When he was done, five brightly colored beanbag chairs sat on the floor of the classroom. Within minutes, the boys with identical faces had plopped themselves down on two of the bags.

Caleb remained standing and watched Mike from the middle of the room. "These are very nice," he said. He walked over and patted them each with a careful hand.

"Beanbag chairs," Sienna said in wonder. "You remembered."

Mike picked up the table. "Where would you like this?"

She shook her head. "I don't even know what to say."

"Say thank you and please put it over in that corner," Darryl offered.

Sienna smiled. "That sounds as good a place as any. They need a place to spread out when they're doing art projects."

"I'm pretty sure I can find some extra chairs to go with it," Darryl added.

"You are too much," she said, with a squeeze of the old man's arm. "Both of you."

Mike shuffled his feet, not sure what else to say or what to do with his hands. Caleb walked over to the table, next to the Turner boy, and the two of them stroked its smooth surface.

"Would you like to stay?" Sienna asked. "We were doing our afternoon read-along."

Caleb looked over in alarm. "Miss Cruz," he said, "we don't do read-along with anyone else. No strangers."

"You just met Mr. Springer," Sienna said. Her gaze never left Mike's face. "He isn't a stranger."

"I can't stay," Mike said. "I have to get back to the gym."

"Oh. Sure." She shoved her hands into the pockets of her jeans. Mike's traitorous mind took full notice of the way they hugged her hips.

"Maybe another time," he added. Yeah, right. He had no plans on spending extended periods of time inside a school. This was a one-time deal.

"We have Friday afternoons free," she said. "Drop in any time after two. Honestly, it would be good for the kids to interact with someone besides me."

He nodded noncommittally. He went to leave, but a motion to his right made him look over. Another student he hadn't noticed before, the lone girl in the room, began to walk. Backwards. Around the room she went, toe to heel, her gaze on Mike the entire time. She pinched her fingers together in a measured motion as she walked. *What the hell is she doing?* Her eyes held no expression, and her entire body had gone rigid.

"That's Dawn," Sienna said, and he remembered what she'd told him the other night at dinner. Selective mutism. She doesn't speak.

Hell, and I thought I had it rough. At least his troubles hadn't started until he hit junior high. How did an eight-year-old get so messed up that she dealt with the world by keeping her distance from it and staying silent?

"Nice seeing you," he said, and pushed open the door. "And nice meeting your kids. I hope everything comes in handy."

"It will. Thank you again. Really. It's more than you should have done." She reached for his hand, and Mike's heart flopped in his chest until he remembered their stupid agreement. *No touching.* But this wasn't going to be anything except a handshake, right? Her hand was almost inside his when a familiar voice called out his name.

"Mike Springer?"

Sienna froze. He turned. Harmony Donaldson, too made-up and too smiley, stood in the hall. A gaggle of kids stretched out in a long line behind her. "What are you doing here?" Her gaze moved from Mike to Sienna and back again.

"Just stopped in to say hello."

"Well, hello." The tips of Harmony's ears turned pink, and she motioned to the boy at the head of the line of students. "Brandon, you know where to go. Straight up the stairs and wait for me at the top." The boy nodded and skipped down the hall with the other students following in a meandering line.

Surely Harmony couldn't think he was here to see her. Yet the way she focused her gaze on first his mouth and then his chest, he wasn't sure.

"You know, the offer still stands," she said in a low voice. She took one step closer and gave him a look he couldn't mistake. "No strings attached."

He rubbed the back of his neck. "Yeah, well, okay," he stammered, knowing full well Harmony didn't have a snowball's chance in hell of spending the night with him, no matter how many times or how many ways she offered.

She reached out and patted his arm. Then she turned and followed her students, but not without one last wink in his direction.

I can only imagine her getting her claws into someone. Harmony Donaldson was someone to watch out for. Word around town was that she'd faked a pregnancy last year with a lawyer over in Silver Valley, and he'd almost popped the question before a phone call from the doctor's office set everyone straight.

Mike turned back to Room Eighteen, but Sienna had disappeared inside. He hoped she hadn't seen or heard that exchange with Harmony. He looked through the window. She had rejoined her students on the rug, but she looked up with a smile as he waved goodbye. *"Thank you again,"* she mouthed over the twins' heads. It took all he had not to let the movement of her lips turn into something wicked inside his head.

Friends. We're just friends. Mike repeated the words all the way back to the gym, through his workout with Zane, and later that night, when he stepped under the shower and found himself thinking of Sienna naked and wet and wishing for just an instant he hadn't screwed up his life royally in the past so that he could enjoy someone like her in his life and his bed without knowing how it would all end.

Chapter Fourteen

He brought me a table. And beanbag chairs.

Sienna couldn't stop staring at the new furniture in her classroom. Even the weird, flirtatious exchange between Mike and Harmony couldn't dim her pleasure.

Friends. We're just friends. She had to repeat the words to keep her feet on the ground. Still, it took a pretty solid friend to buy things out of his own pocket and deliver them here himself. "He's such a nice guy," she said aloud as she walked down the hall to check her mailbox after school.

"Yes, he is," Darryl the custodian said as he wheeled a mop bucket past her in the opposite direction. Then he winked. "Course, I don't see Mike Springer dropping off a special delivery to anyone else at this school. And he's friends with a lot of people."

Before Sienna could answer, the old man turned the corner. She trailed her fingers along the cool cinder-block wall. Drawings by the kindergartners and first-graders filled the display cases by the lobby, and she slowed to take a look. Words ran across the page in crooked lines below some of the drawings.

My favorite food is green beans.

My favorite color is black.

My favorite sport is baseball.

Sienna shivered in the frosty lobby air. What she wouldn't give to be sitting in a baseball stadium on a hot summer day, with peanuts and a hot dog and a beer in her hand as she watched the Yankees kick the crap out of the Red Sox.

"Hi, Hillary," she said as she fished next week's lunch menu and a book catalog from her mailbox. She checked the clock behind Hillary's gray braids. Three twenty-five. She still needed to ask Jenny a couple of questions about testing and the possibility of taking the students on a field trip in the spring. But the principal's door was tightly shut.

"She's busy again?" Sienna asked.

Hillary nodded.

"You know what, I'll wait." She plopped herself down on the vinyl couch and rolled her neck. She needed new worksheets for Caleb, and she needed to talk to the special ed consultant about Bailey's IEP. She also needed—

The principal's door opened at three thirty-two. Sienna stood before anyone else could zoom in ahead of her. "Do you have a minute?"

Jenny looked at her. For a moment, her eyes seemed cloudy, a little confused. Then she shook her head, and the cloudiness went away. "Of course. I've been meaning to check in with you. How's everything going?"

Sienna took a few steps toward Jenny's office, but instead, the principal motioned down the hall. "Mind if we walk? I told Mrs. Pennington I'd help her get ready for the book fair tomorrow." Before Sienna could answer, Jenny had pushed open the office door and begun walking in the direction of the library.

"Oh. Sure," Sienna said, though the only person who heard her was Hillary. She glanced back at the office. The other day, tears on the principal's face. Today, confusion. Sienna didn't know what Jenny did in there after the kids left each day, but she was beginning to wonder.

* * * * *

Jenny James, Elementary School Principal, Sienna wrote on her research list later that night. Above Jenny's name were a few lines about the two women Mike had told her about the other day. *Imagine finding out your one and only is someone else's too.* She whistled. She filled in the details she knew about Jenny's family background, then Googled her education and experience before taking over at Pine Point. She was ten years older than Sienna, still young to be running a school in Sienna's opinion, but every picture Sienna found online matched the image Jenny portrayed at school. Open, friendly, confident, a no-nonsense professional.

Closes herself in her office every day after the students leave, Sienna wrote at the bottom of the page. *WHY?* She underlined the word three times and stared at it for a minute. Then she tossed the notepad aside and walked into the kitchen.

She'd finally made it to the grocery store, but tonight the thought of actually cooking something held no appeal. She took out a container of yogurt, stared at it, and then put it back. "I need a drink." And a burger. She knew the perfect place to go for both.

Fifteen minutes later, Sienna pulled up outside Jimmy's Watering Hole. The local pub had opened shortly before Sienna left Pine Point the first time, and though it sat near the highway and had a view of nothing except a strip mall, people didn't go for the location. Sienna had discovered when she'd returned last month that Jimmy's had become known for, in this order, its burgers, its friendly bartenders, and its owners' zero-tolerance policy for fighting, swearing, or bullshit of any kind.

As a result, a mix of blue-collar workers and professionals gathered there on a regular basis, with the average age somewhere around thirty. No loud music to talk over. No college kids home on break, no drunks threatening each other over the pool table, and no sticky, suspicious spots on the bathroom floor.

Sienna hadn't expected much of a crowd on a Wednesday night, but the entire bar was filled, along with half the tables and booths. The karaoke stage in the corner was set up and ready to go, and a pool game already looked in full swing. A good-looking guy with long blond hair and a leather jacket stood up just as she squeezed her way to the bar.

"All yours," he said and motioned at his vacant stool. "Good timing."

"Perfect timing," she said.

"Gotta go home and give the kids their bath," he said, and then flipped his fingers at the bartender and left.

"Hiya," said the tall guy behind the bar. He tossed a coaster in front of

Sienna. "What's your poison?"

As tempting as a martini sounded, it would probably put her to sleep in a matter of minutes. "Just seltzer with lime, thanks. And a menu."

"You got it." A moment later, both appeared in front of her. The bartender gave her a wide smile and rested his arms on the bar. "Don't recall your name. Your face, yes, but…"

"Sienna Cruz. I just moved back to teach at Pine Point Elementary for a few months."

He snapped his fingers. "That's it." He reached out and shook her hand. "Nate Hunter. Well, kids used to call me Catfish back in school, stupid nickname, but no one calls me that anymore. I think we went to school together."

Sienna searched her memory.

"I know, it was a long time ago. But you were on the Red Team in middle school, right?"

"The Red Team? Wow. I haven't thought about that in ages."

He winked. "Who would?" He tossed his hair, long in the front and so blond it almost appeared white. "Middle school is something you're supposed to forget for good, isn't it?"

Before she could answer, someone at the other end of the bar called Nate's name, and he rapped his knuckles in goodbye and sauntered away. Sienna studied the menu for a few minutes and then turned to the crowd around her. She recognized a few faces, though she'd be hard pressed to put names with them.

She did remember Nate after thinking for a minute or two. Goofy kid, always skateboarding with his friends before and after school, or teasing his older sister Rachel. He'd shot up, though he hadn't filled out much, she noted. *Could benefit from some time at the gym.*

With that, her thoughts zoomed back to Mike. To the gifts he'd brought today, and the inadequate way she'd thanked him. She'd been so taken aback and hadn't known what to say. *I should text him. Just to say hi and thanks again.* She reached into her pocket, but someone jiggled her arm from behind, and her phone slipped from her hand and fell to the ground.

"Oops. So sorry."

Sienna turned at the familiar voice. Polly and Harmony stood behind her. Polly bent and retrieved Sienna's phone. "Hey, there. Sorry again. It's super crowded in here tonight."

"Yes, it is." She took a drink of her seltzer. "Didn't know you guys came here."

Harmony peeled off a tight ski jacket and draped it over one arm. "It's a pretty decent place on a Wednesday night." Her gaze roamed the room, pausing momentarily on each available-looking guy. Polly bent over her phone, her petite features drawn into a frown.

"What's wrong?" Harmony asked, reading over Polly's shoulder.

Polly shoved the phone into her pocket. "Nothing. And stop doing that."

"Please tell me you're not still—" Harmony looked at Sienna and stopped.

"It's none of your business," Polly said in a low voice. She finger-combed her hair from her face.

Nate returned and waved at the two teachers. "Hiya. Same as usual? Polly nodded, and he poured two glasses of white wine. Sienna passed them over. Polly held out a twenty, but Nate waved it away. "Already paid for," he said over the growing din in the bar. He pointed at Mac and Damian.

Polly flushed and put her twenty away.

"That was nice," Sienna said.

"They're nice guys," Polly answered.

"Not really what we're after," Harmony said, "but nice enough."

Sienna choked back a laugh. "What exactly are you after?"

Harmony shrugged. "Money. Isn't every girl?"

"Money's nice," Sienna agreed, "but I can't say it's everything." She took another sip of seltzer. "Besides, wouldn't you want to make your own money? So you don't have to rely on a guy to take care of you?"

Polly looked at her with genuine surprise. "I *want* a guy to take care of me," she said. "I don't want to have to worry about paying bills for the rest of my life.

I want to have kids and take care of them."

Sienna nodded, not sure what else to say.

"Not like I wouldn't keep myself busy in the meantime," Harmony said. Her gaze lighted on Nate. "I wonder what he's like in bed?"

Polly turned two shades of red. "God, Harmony, that's like all you think about." She pushed her way through the crowd. Harmony rolled her eyes at Sienna as if to say, "Do you believe her?" but she followed her friend.

Sienna ordered her burger and took some time to check out the rest of the crowd. She wondered if Mike would show up. Her watch read a little after eight. Wouldn't that be nice, if he walked in the door and bought her a drink and—

"Sienna? Sienna Cruz?" A wide-faced woman jumped in front of her. Sienna's hand jiggled, and she almost spilled half her seltzer down the front of her sweater.

"Ah, hello?" Another face she sort of recognized.

"It's Tanya Martin. Well, Tanya Jakubowski now. I heard you were back in town." She looked over her shoulder and waved at someone. "Marie! Come see who's here."

A blond with perfect makeup and hair emerged from the crowd, a near-mirror image of her older sisters Tara, Joyce, and Eva. "Oh. My. God." Before Sienna could say a thing, Marie Hadley flung her arms around Sienna's neck and hugged her. "You're back. I heard you were back, Eva told me, but still." She took a step back, then hugged Sienna again. "I'm so sorry I didn't text you."

A little rumpled and overwhelmed by the welcome, Sienna said, "You don't have my number."

"True, but still…" Marie pushed her hair behind her ears. "What's it been? Ten years?"

"Eleven, actually." Grittiness settled into Sienna's throat. "I'm sorry I never called you or anything after I left." The closest thing she'd had to a best friend in Pine Point, Marie had sent her two letters and a Christmas gift after Sienna had moved to North Carolina. She still had the tiny blue bear somewhere back home. "I was just kind of a mess."

Marie waved the words away. "Oh my God, of course you were." She leaned in and studied Sienna's face. "I missed you though. I always wondered where you ended up. And here you are, back home again."

"Temporarily."

"Right, right, of course. So how are you doing?"

"I'm okay."

Tanya wiggled her way to the bar and tried to catch Nate's attention. "You're filling in for Lucy Foster, right?" she asked as she waved him down.

Sienna nodded.

"That's so awesome," Marie said. "I'm glad you're back, even if it's just for a little while. We'll have to get together, have dinner or coffee or something."

A tall, broad set of shoulders appeared behind Marie, yet another face from Sienna's past, and the back of her neck went cold. "My word. Sienna Cruz?"

She blinked and tried to think of something to say.

"It's good to see you." The man's voice had grown a little deeper, and his hair a lot whiter, but she'd recognize Doc Halloran anywhere. He put a large hand on her shoulder and squeezed.

Sienna fought for air. "You too," she squeaked out. The last time she'd seen him had been at her mother's funeral. The last time before that, in the Med Center two nights before the funeral. Everything in between was a blur.

"Sienna, do you want to sit with us?" Marie was saying.

She managed to shake her head.

"Honey, you all right?" Doc Halloran bent closer, and she nodded. The anxiety went away after a moment, and she rubbed her knuckles on her glass to cool her skin and her racing thoughts.

"Sorry. It's just a little weird being back here and seeing familiar faces."

He nodded. "I'm sure it is." He squeezed her shoulder again, then took a large draft beer from Nate and turned to go. "I'm retired now," he said, "but anytime you want to stop in and say hello, you know where I live."

Oh, the kindness of small-town doctors. Sienna blinked away the wetness at the corners of her eyes. Doc had made a habit of dropping in every so often to check on her and her mother, as if knowing they couldn't afford the office fee. In fact, they'd seen him a few weeks before her mother had died. He'd brought her a book and a king-sized chocolate bar, sneaking them to her behind her mother's back. Now she wondered if he'd known something all those years ago, if he'd sensed some hidden risk factor in her mother's faulty heart.

Nate delivered her burger, and Sienna sank her teeth into it. Between Mike's surprise visit at school today and the reunions here tonight, her emotions were frayed to their last thread. She should probably go home and take notes with everything still fresh in her mind, but when she finally did open the door to her apartment, she left her notepads strewn on the floor and went straight to bed.

Chapter Fifteen

Sienna looked at the clock a half-dozen times Friday afternoon. The emotional chaos of Wednesday night had faded, and she'd woken on Thursday with fresh resolve to tackle the challenges of her research. Her kids had gotten through a whole day without a major meltdown, and she'd rewarded herself by going to the gym. She'd worked out on the machines and stayed for the kickboxing class, but she hadn't seen Mike at all.

"He had some meetings downtown," the thick-necked blond guy at the front desk said when she'd asked.

So she hadn't had a chance to remind him about her invitation to visit the class. Maybe he'd forgotten. Maybe he'd brushed it off. He didn't owe her anything, that was for sure. If anything, she owed him. Billy and Bailey hadn't left the comfort of the beanbag chairs in two days, except to go to lunch and the bathroom.

Silas still preferred his rocking chair, and Caleb had avoided the beanbag chairs entirely since Wednesday, proclaiming them too soft and pushy.

"Do you mean squooshy?" she'd asked him.

"No. Pushy. I can't get out of them. They're too tight," he said with an agitated motion of his hands, and she finally realized the way they conformed to the body made him feel claustrophobic.

I have to get his parents to agree to testing, she thought for the tenth time. *He's definitely on the autistic spectrum.* He was also bright as hell, way beyond his age for reading and writing and math. She suspected his IQ might lie in the near-genius range, but his parents so far steadfastly refused to believe he was anything except a little quirky.

She scratched Caleb's name on a notepad beside her computer. Caleb's father ran a dental practice in Silver Valley, and Caleb's mother was an interior designer whose work had been featured in a local magazine last month. Sienna bet a child with any kind of special needs didn't fit into the family, especially with an adorable, completely normal daughter two years younger than Caleb.

"Miss Cruz?" Caleb broke into her thoughts. "It's two minutes past read-along time."

"Ah, yes, it is. Thank you, Caleb." She looked around the room. Well, if Mike was coming, he'd have to join them mid-story. "Dawn, would you like to choose today's book?"

The girl stared at her from a beanbag chair that she'd pulled into the far corner of the room. She blinked a few times, and then she stood and walked to the bookcase. Her clothes, beautiful and impeccable as always, belied the terrified child trapped inside the body.

Just talk to me, Sienna wanted to say. *I can't read your mind.* But the girl remained silent no matter what strategies Sienna tried.

Dawn stood for a long minute in front of the bookcase and then chose *Where Are My Shoes?* and *Bears in Winter.* She turned and held them out.

"Those are perfect," Sienna said with another glance at the clock. Ten minutes after two. She settled herself in the rocker with Silas on her lap and began to read. Each time someone passed her door, she looked up, hopeful.

It was only when they'd finished both books, and Caleb announced they had ten minutes to pack up and walk to the buses, that Sienna's hopes fell. Mike wasn't coming by. Dropping off classroom supplies was one thing. Spending time with her and her students was something else altogether.

We're friends, she told herself as she fastened the boys' coats and wrapped a scarf around Dawn's neck. *Casual ones at best. Nothing more.* But that didn't stop the disappointment from hanging on her heart like a stone.

* * * * *

At one thirty, Mike started looking at the clock. *I could stop in for the last hour of school. She invited me. Said it would be good for the kids.* Plus, part of him wanted to see if they liked the beanbag chairs. "I'm going out around two," he said to Hans.

"Okay." The kid texted with a mad blur of his thumbs.

"Who the hell you talking to?"

"Liesel." Hans grinned and finally put his phone down. "She's amazing, man. So hot. So funny."

That could be a good combination, but Mike could've told Hans that women always seemed hot and funny when you first met them. Let them into your life, add them to your bank account, share some of your deepest fears, and see what happened then. He pulled up the membership numbers since the first of the year and was about to tweak the class schedule when Zane strode in the front door.

"Hey, man."

"Hey, yourself." Mike folded his arms on the desk. "Aren't you supposed to be at the Glen?"

"Working the four o'clock shift today." Zane winked. "Good thing too, since Becca stayed over last night. We slept in until almost noon. Well, didn't really *sleep*." He winked again.

"Shit, what's that make? How many nights in a row? When's she moving in?"

"Ah, not anytime soon. We're taking it slow."

"Good idea." Mike elbowed Hans. "Hear that? You can have a good time with a woman and still not get all wrapped up in her."

"Yeah, yeah," Hans muttered, bent over his phone again.

"I wanted to see if I could leave these here." Zane handed Mike a stack of red and white flyers. *Pet Me! Love Me! Take Me Home!* read block letters at the top. Red hearts emblazoned both sides of the page. Brightly colored photos of dogs and cats with pleading eyes lined the bottom.

"What's this?"

"Pine Point Paws is having a fundraiser," Zane explained. "It's next Saturday. Open visits and adoption fees waived during the day, and a dinner and dance and silent auction at night. Over at Villa Venezia in Silver Valley."

"Becca set all this up?'

Zane nodded. "She's been at it nonstop since she got back from Florida. Oh, and that reminds me. I'm supposed to ask if you'd be interested in donating a gym membership or a gift certificate for the auction."

"Sure." That was a no-brainer—tax write-off plus free advertising. "Do I get to come to the dinner and the dance?" he joked.

"Yeah, if you want." Zane took the flyers and arranged them on the desk. "Actually, Becca told me to ask if you and Sienna wanted to come."

It didn't matter how many times a day he thought her name. When someone else said it aloud, Mike's heart did a stutter step. "Yeah, I don't know…"

"You still doing that friends-only thing?"

Hans looked up with interest.

"Yes," Mike said, looking first at Zane and then at the kid. "So it might be kind of weird for me to ask her to go. Like it's a date."

Zane shrugged. "Whatever. Just thought I'd mention it."

Mike took a few flyers and stuffed them into his jacket pocket. "I'll put some on the desk out at the garage too."

"Thanks. It's a good cause and all that."

Mike grinned. Might be a good cause, but it looked as though his friend was already halfway to falling in love with Becca Ericksen, and feelings like that could make you leave flyers around town, ask for donations, or adopt stray animals in a heartbeat.

"I'll get that gift certificate to you next week," Mike said as Zane turned for the door.

"Thanks." With a touch of his hand to his forehead, he was gone, though not before bumping into a broad-shouldered guy walking into the gym at the same time Zane was walking out.

Mike almost didn't recognize him in the bulky winter coat and red watch cap. He wished a second later he hadn't, or that he'd left for the school ten minutes earlier. Because the absolute last person in the world he wanted to run into, the last person he thought would return to Pine Point, stood on the other side of the desk with a crooked grin.

"Hey, Mike. Long time no see."

Not long enough. Bile rose in the back of his throat, and he had to fight to keep his hands at his sides. The last time Mike had looked Al Halloran in the eye, the two of them had been on their way to serving time in the Los Angeles county jail.

Chapter Sixteen

Mike glanced at Hans and then walked around the desk and steered Al back toward the door. "What the hell are you doing here?"

Al unzipped his coat like he was planning to stay.

"When did you get back?"

"Last night." Al pulled off his watch cap. Gray peppered his dark, close-cut hair. He'd served fifteen months to Mike's eight, and the time had definitely worn him down. Wrinkles cut into the corners beside his eyes, and he needed a shave. Stubble covered his chin and throat.

Mike glanced over his shoulder. Most people in town probably remembered Al. His younger brother had moved away years ago, but his dad, Doc Halloran, had worked as Pine Point's family doctor for decades. Mrs. Halloran had split when the boys were still in grade school.

"What do you want?"

Al grinned, and Mike could see a missing eye tooth. Prison fight? Probably. "Looking for a job. Thought maybe you could help me out."

"Why don't you ask your father?"

Al sneered. "That fucker disowned me years ago."

"Can you blame him? Stealing prescriptions isn't exactly the way to get on Daddy's good side."

Al's breath hitched, and for a minute Mike thought he might throw a punch. Then he laughed. "Hell, guess you're right." He looked over Mike's shoulder. "I heard you opened a gym. Had no idea it was this fancy."

"It's not."

"Fancier than what I got going on."

"Getting off the drugs would help."

The front door opened, and two middle-aged moms walked inside. "Hi, Mike."

"Hi, Beth. Sherry. Have a good workout."

"We will."

Al waited until they'd checked in at the desk and walked toward the locker room before speaking again. "You can get yourself some tail here pretty much anytime you want, huh? Good plan."

Mike cracked his knuckles and didn't bother with a response. "I gotta get back to the desk." The clock on the wall read five minutes to two. So much for visiting Sienna's class.

"Do people here know?" Al asked.

"Know what? About L.A.?" Mike shook his head. "I don't think so. Like to keep it that way." He leaned closer to Al and lowered his voice, "I don't need you running your mouth. Telling people isn't gonna get you a job either." His arms tightened. He had twenty pounds of muscle and an inch or two on Al. If the guy knew what was good for him, he'd turn around and leave. Leave Springer Fitness, leave Pine Point, leave the whole damn country.

Except felons couldn't cross international boundaries.

Al twisted his hat in his hands. "Don't worry. I won't blow your secret. You think I want people here knowing what we did?" *Don't use the word* we. Mike's jaw clenched. Now the clock read two-oh-two. *The only thing I did was try to get back what was mine.*

"Just stopped in to say hello," Al said, "and ask if you knew of anyone hiring."

"I'm sure you can find a construction job when the weather warms up." *As long as you don't have to fill out an application.* Checking that box at the bottom to answer if you'd ever been convicted of a crime could be a major downer.

"Yeah, maybe." Al's gaze moved past Mike again, taking in the gym full of equipment, the locker rooms, the sleek wooden desk, and the smoothie bar behind it. "Keep me in mind."

Mike had no intention of doing anything of the kind. "Sure." He opened the door for Al. "See you around."

*****

Four hours later, Mike stormed up the front steps and into his mother's living room. He turned over his phone in his hand. He'd thought about texting Sienna a half-dozen times. But to say what? He hadn't promised to stop by her classroom. She'd probably forgotten she'd mentioned it to him at all. Besides, he was still so worked up over Al's reappearance that he'd probably say something stupid. The last thing he needed was Sienna finding out about the mistakes in his past.

"Mike?" His mother poked her head out from the bedroom. "I didn't expect you here."

"I know." He often stayed late at the gym on Fridays to close up, then went out for a burger and a beer. Not tonight.

The bedroom door closed and then opened again a few minutes later. His mother emerged wearing a pretty flowered top and blue jeans. She had hoop earrings in her ears and a silver watch around her thin wrist.

"You look nice." Mike sat up and put his phone away. "You going out?"

"Martha and I are having dinner at the diner. Nothing fancy."

"That's nice."

She nodded but looked concerned as she joined him on the couch. "Would you like me to stay home?" She patted his leg. "You look like you've had a rough day."

"It's that easy to see?"

"I'm your mother, sweetheart. Of course it is."

Mike hesitated. Ma knew everything that had happened in L.A. She'd written letters to the governor asking for his early release. She'd bought his plane ticket home. He could tell her all about Al's reappearance, and she'd know exactly what to say to make him feel better.

"Don't stay home for me," he said. No reason to bother her. With any luck, Al would take the next bus out of Pine Point. Doc would never let him live in his childhood home around the corner.

"You're sure?"

"I'm positive." He stood. "I'm going to take a hot shower, order a pizza, and watch the Knicks game."

"All right." She stood too and looped her purse over her shoulder. "I won't be late."

He kissed her cheek. "You be as late as you want."

She smiled as a horn beeped outside. "That's my ride."

Mike waved from the front window as the two women pulled away and drove down Cornwall Road. Actually, a shower and a pizza would be the perfect ending to this day. He headed upstairs, peeling off his jacket and shirt as he went.

But under the shower, his thoughts returned to Sienna. Had she waited for him today, looking up from her book as she read to her students? Had she thought of him at all? He shampooed, rinsed, and then soaped up from head to toe. He still didn't take the luxury of a long hot shower for granted. His hand closed around his cock, and he stroked it as he thought of her.

Was he a complete idiot for keeping his distance? His hand moved faster, harder. He rested one arm against the wall, the water moving over his shoulders and down his back as visions of a naked Sienna filled his head. He wanted to kiss her, He wanted to touch her, to feel her move underneath him. He wanted to fill her up with—

His orgasm shook him, and his legs wobbled as the release came. Mike let out a long breath. This was the situation he'd doomed himself to with that brilliant move of shaking hands over a friendship-only arrangement. Sure, Sienna was leaving town in a few months. Did that mean they couldn't enjoy each other's company in the meantime?

Mike rinsed and then toweled off. Yes, he was trying to start a new life in Pine Point. No, he didn't want to make the same mistakes he had in the past.

But he hadn't just met Sienna. He knew her last name and her goals, and he admired the hell out of her career. He wrapped the towel around his waist and walked out to the living room, where he picked up the clothes he'd dropped on his way in the door.

As he hung up his jacket, his fingers closed on the stack of papers he'd stuffed inside hours ago. He pulled them out and laid them on the kitchen table, smoothing the wrinkles.

Pet Me! Love Me! Take Me Home!

Boy, would he like to do that to Sienna. His cock stirred under the towel again.

"Fuck it." Life was too damn short to deny himself every pleasure. Maybe they'd be friends, maybe they'd be something more, but he was tired of sitting home alone when a woman he honest-to-God liked lived less than ten miles away.

Mike reached for his cell phone and dialed before he could talk himself out of it.

Chapter Seventeen

Sienna almost missed Mike's call. Hungry patrons filled Zeb's Diner, and the door kept opening and closing behind her, letting in a fresh gust of cold air each time. Above the noise of constant conversation, she didn't hear her phone buzz on the counter. Only when Josie pointed at it on one of her runs to the kitchen did Sienna see the incoming call.

Her heart skipped a beat as she scooped up the phone. "Hi."

Josie returned and set a coffee mug in front of Sienna. She was about to ask for decaf, but the waitress already had her hand on the pot with the orange neck.

"I'm sorry I didn't make it today," Mike said. "For your reading time."

She stared at the counter as her cheeks warmed. "It's okay. I'm sure you have a lot going on."

"I wanted to. Planned on it. Something came up."

"I understand. You don't have to apologize." Although it was awfully nice of him to say the words, she had to admit.

"Thought I might make it up to you," he went on. "There's a fundraiser next Saturday night. For Pine Point Paws."

"The animal shelter?"

"Yeah. Becca set it up. They're having a dinner and…" He cleared his throat. "And other stuff, like a silent auction. I wondered if you wanted to go."

She smiled. He might have missed read-along time with her students, but he still wanted to spend time with her. On a Saturday night. "Like a date?" she teased.

He didn't answer.

"Okay, not like a date. Like a friends' thing?"

"Yeah, I guess. Zane said Becca asked if you and I wanted to go. It seems like a good cause, and to be honest, I'd rather go with you than go alone, so…"

"I'd love to." She pointed at the pot-roast special and slid her menu over to Josie, who nodded and scribbled on an order slip. "Good cause and all that."

"It's over in Silver Valley, so I can drive if you want." A paper rustled in the background. "I'm not sure what time it starts. I'll ask Zane."

"Sounds good." Two older women walked into the diner, arm in arm. Sienna stared at them. *That one looks so familiar.* Former school teacher? A nurse from the hospital?

"Have a good weekend," Mike said. "I'll talk to you later."

Sienna hung up and tucked her phone into her purse. The women sat at a table nearby, and Sienna tried to figure out who she might be. For only being back in Pine Point a couple of weeks, she'd grown to know quite a few faces. Ella Ericksen sat in a back booth with a good-looking guy that Sienna guessed was probably the boyfriend of the month. They held hands and cooed at each other across the table. Two men from the maintenance crew at school sat at a table near the door, and a lanky bus driver had a family of five crammed into a booth beside them. People talked over each other, waved, got up to show pictures on their phones, and Sienna cataloged it all as best she could.

"Refill, honey?" Josie asked. She waved the coffee pot in front of Sienna with a bemused smile. "Or you busy taking in the Friday night sights?"

"Oh. Sorry. It's crowded in here."

"Every Friday at dinner time. Don't know why. Maybe people don't like to cook at the end of the week."

She looked again at the two older women, one about ten years older than the other, with dyed-red hair turning white at the roots and a broad laugh. The younger one had frosted hair and a wide smile.

That's it. The smile.

And the blue eyes, obviously passed down from mother to son. She couldn't believe she hadn't remembered Loretta Springer right away. "Hey, Josie?"

The waitress ambled over, clearing plates and topping off drinks as she did.

"That's Mike Springer's mom sitting over there, right?"

Josie's gaze shifted. "Yep. Want me to introduce you?"

"No, that's okay." Sienna took a long sip of coffee. She didn't need an introduction. She'd already met Loretta, eleven years ago in the waiting room of the Med Center. Heat moved over her, and she scratched the scar on her wrist. The kind woman had been the only person to talk to Sienna, besides Doc Halloran, the day her mother died. She couldn't believe she'd forgotten.

I should go over there. Say something. Thank her. But before Sienna could, the diner door opened, and all the color left Loretta's face. She blinked a few times, turned to her companion, and muttered something. Sienna couldn't hear the conversation, but it involved hushed tones and frowns. Sienna studied the man who'd just stepped inside. He didn't look out of the ordinary, other than needing a shave. He wore a red watch cap and a dark jacket that looked handed down a few times. He rubbed his bare hands together and looked around for an empty table.

"Well, would you look at what the cat dragged in." Josie set down her coffee pot and brushed her hands on her apron. "Didn't think we'd be seeing you again anytime soon." She pointed at the only empty stool at the counter, right beside Sienna. "Have a seat, Al, and tell us what the hell you've been up to."

He ducked his chin. "Evenin', Josie." He walked up to the counter, but he didn't sit. Instead, he ordered a cheeseburger to go and then disappeared into the restroom.

"You know Doc Halloran?" Josie asked. She slipped her order pad next to the cash register.

Sienna nodded.

"That's his oldest son. Albert." Josie looked around and then lowered her voice. "He moved away for a while, was workin' odd jobs and such, and no one heard from him. He got in some trouble with the law here, don't know if you heard, but he was takin' pills from his daddy's office, I guess. Back when he was still in high school." She snapped her gum and hollered across the diner, "I see ya wavin' your arm, Henry. I'll be there in a minute. Can't you see I'm havin' a conversation?"

She turned back to Sienna and shook her head. "Anyway, I'm surprised to see Al. His father threw him out after all that mess with the cops an' told him never to come back."

"Really? That's some pretty hardcore stuff to happen in Pine Point."

"Woo whee, tell me about it."

I'll have to find the old news articles. Sienna began a mental list. *See what he's been doing and where he's been living. And why he came back, and whether Doc's glad to see him.* Actually, it wouldn't be a bad idea to pick up the daily paper for her research. The police blotter, town meetings, and letters to the editor might give her more insight into the underbelly of Pine Point. She finished her burger in three large bites. This, finally, was the reason she'd come to town. She waited for Al to return, but he didn't. Ten minutes passed. Josie packaged up his burger and left it sitting on the counter.

"What happened to him?" Sienna asked after a while.

Josie shrugged. "Henry said he went out the back. He always was a strange duck." She carried a bucket of dirty dishes into the back. Sienna yawned. Time for some work and then some shut-eye. She fished out Josie's order pad and flipped through it, looking for hers so she could pay.

I long to be deep inside your soul,

Two hearts joined as one despite the…

My fingers and yours, ten then twenty.

Sienna dropped the pad as if it had caught fire in her hands. She recognized the large, loopy writing. Without a doubt, it belonged to Josie. But these weren't diner orders. Her gaze returned to the register, where another identical order pad rested. She blinked. *Josie writes love poems?* As fast as she could, Sienna shoved the pad in her hands back where she'd found it.

Josie reemerged from the kitchen. "Dessert tonight? We got homemade lemon meringue or store-bought cheesecake." She winked. "You know which one I'm recommending."

"Ah, no, I'm good, thanks." Sienna pulled out her wallet. "Just tell me what I owe you, and I'm on my way."

Josie narrowed her gaze. "You're in an awful hurry all of a sudden. You got a rendezvous with a guy somewhere?"

I long to be deep inside your soul.

Sienna almost choked as she paid the bill. "No," she managed to say. *But maybe you do, huh, Josie?* It certainly had been a strange day for secrets. She hurried upstairs as fast as she could.

* * * * *

"I thought he was still in jail." Early the following morning, Loretta sat stiffly at the kitchen table, one hand around a mug of coffee.

"Guess he finally got out." Mike poured coffee into a travel mug and added three packets of sugar.

"Is he going to cause trouble for you?" She tightened her hand around the mug.

"Ma, no. What can he do? It'll be fine." He had no idea if Al's reappearance in Pine Point was fine. He'd lain awake half the night thinking about different scenarios in which Al could bring more ruin to his life. *Guess who spent almost a year in county jail for felony theft? Yep, that owner of Springer Fitness you all love so much around here.*

Except ratting Mike out would also inevitably rat Al himself out, since he was the one who'd gotten Mike into the whole lousy situation to begin with. He supposed Al could come up with some way to blackmail Mike—*Give me a job at your gym or I'll tell everyone you were married before*—but he didn't think Al was that stupid either.

He screwed the lid on his travel mug and kissed the top of his mother's head. "Please don't worry about it. I have a feeling Al's only passing through. He doesn't have anywhere to go, so I don't think he'll stick around. His father won't take him back, that's for sure."

"He better not." Loretta shook her head. "Can you imagine him living right around the corner from us again?" She drank, then slammed her mug back on the table. "I hope Doc doesn't even consider it."

Mike cleared his throat. "You took me back when I screwed up."

Loretta got to her feet so fast the table shook. "You listen to me." She took his shirtfront in one hand and leveled him with a look that made him feel ten years old again. "You were set up. You were put in a position by someone you thought was your friend—" a dark expression twisted her face, "—and a horrible, money-hungry *whore*."

He flinched. "Ma." His mother never used words like that. Never.

"I don't care. She was, and she and Al ruined your life, and I will make it my mission to see that he never does anything like that to you again." She stood on her tiptoes and kissed his nose. "That no one does. You're a good boy, Mikey, and you're making a good life here." She patted his chest. "You've done your time and made your amends. That one—" she jutted her head in the direction of the street and the Halloran residence, "—I don't think he has. I saw him last night. He looked the same as always. Not sorry at all."

With that, she sat back down and returned to her coffee.

Mike pulled on his winter jacket. Leave it to him to end up with a guard dog five feet tall who weighed all of one hundred pounds. Still, there was something nice about knowing Ma had his back, no matter what. He touched his chest and the spot with her name tattooed across it. At least there was one woman in Pine Point he could trust. As he climbed into his truck, his thoughts turned to Sienna. Or maybe there would end up being two. He could only hope.

Chapter Eighteen

On Monday morning, Sienna hung a large poster on the wall of Room Eighteen. Across the top in brightly colored letters, it read *We're On Our Best Behavior!* As the students walked in from the bus, they clustered around it. Even Dawn stared at the banner instead of retreating to her usual beanbag chair in the corner.

Caleb was the first to touch the fuzzy raised letters that made up each of their names. "What is *this*, Miss Cruz?"

"This is a way we're going to keep track of all the good things that happen in this room." She touched each of their names and then pointed to the gold star pins lined up on the opposite side of the poster. "Each time you do something we all think is good behavior, you get a star next to your name. If everybody gets at least five stars every day in a week, we'll have a special celebration that Friday."

"I want a star, I want a star, I want a star!" Billy chanted. He hopped from foot to foot, leaving melted snow everywhere.

Sienna placed her hands on his shoulders. "Do you think calling out is good behavior?" she asked. Billy stopped hopping.

"I don't think it is," Caleb said with a serious frown. "But how do we decide what is?"

"I thought we could all talk about it together." She pointed across the room, to where she'd taped a long piece of construction paper to Mike's table.

Mike's table. She'd come to calling it that in her head. Silly, since all he'd done was buy it for them. But she smiled every time she thought of him carrying it into the classroom with an awkward look on his face.

"We can make a list together," she said.

"Okay," Billy agreed. He sat down, pulled off his snow boots and replaced them with his favorite blue and red sneakers. Bailey had matching ones.

Sienna helped Silas with his winter clothes, checked Dawn's backpack for notes from her foster mom, and remembered to take attendance and call in their lunch order without prompting from Caleb. Pretty good start to the week. She'd even managed to pack herself lunch today, which meant she wouldn't have to scavenge in the faculty room for lunch. Thanks to diner food and an endless supply of brownies, cookies, and coffee cake, she'd gained a few pounds since coming to Pine Point.

That means I need to get to the gym more often. And thinking of the gym meant thinking of Mike, which led into a lovely little fantasy that left her a little flushed by the time they finished their morning work.

"Miss Cruz, why is your face all red?" Caleb asked as they returned from the library.

Leave it to my child with Asperger's to point out the obvious. "I think the heat might be on a little high today," she said. Before Caleb could run over to the thermostat and check, she said, "How about we work on our list of good behaviors and give out a few stars?"

"Yippee!" Bailey clapped his hands together. His brother clapped too. Silas spun in a circle, his arms out straight like airplane propellers. Only Dawn seemed unaffected by the promise of stars and good behavior. She sank into her beanbag chair and pinched her fingers together.

"Billy should get one for doing his math without complaining," Caleb said.

"What about Dawn?" Sienna asked. The other students turned and looked at her. She ducked her head and played with the hem of her sweater. "Let's look at our list. I think Dawn definitely gets a star for being on time with her work this morning, right?"

The others nodded.

"And helping to clean up the book corner without being asked." She added another star next to the girl's name. Dawn lifted her head and stopped playing with her sweater.

Someone knocked at the door, and Sienna glanced up.

"It's Mr. Mike!" Caleb said with glee. "Miss Cruz, I didn't know he was coming to visit us today."

"Neither did I." And where had the name Mr. Mike come from? He'd introduced himself as Mr. Springer last week. But it didn't matter. Her pulse sped up as she opened the door. He smelled like the outdoors, like fresh snow and wind. "Hello there. This is a nice surprise. Again."

His smile washed over her, and that blue gaze caught and held hers for a moment before he stepped inside. "Hello, Caleb." He shook the boy's hand. "How are you today?"

"I'm fine." Caleb turned and pointed at the two posters hanging on the wall. "Look what we have."

"Wow." Mike walked over, put one hand under his chin, and studied them both. "This is very impressive." He glanced at Sienna. "Did you all make this? Or did Miss Cruz?"

"Miss Cruz did," Billy piped up. He tugged Mike's pant leg. "I'm Billy. That's my twin brother, Bailey. I'm older by six minutes."

Sienna stifled a laugh.

Mike crouched down so he was eye level with them. "Really? I don't have any brothers or sisters, so that makes you pretty lucky."

"I have a younger sister," Caleb said. "Her name is Dinah and she's in Miss Preston's class."

"All right, you chatterboxes," Sienna said. "It's time to get ready for lunch."

"Can Mr. Mike come with us?" Bailey asked.

"No, not this time." Sienna said and arched a brow at Mike.

"Will you come to read-along this Friday?" Caleb asked.

"I think I can. I will do my best to make it." His smile returned to Sienna, and heat zinged through her.

"Billy, you're line leader this week." Sienna waited as they arranged themselves in a haphazard group near the door, then she turned and beckoned to Dawn. The little girl hadn't moved from her beanbag chair. Her gaze moved from Sienna to Mike and stayed there. Sienna held her breath. Dawn didn't do well with strangers, especially the adult male variety. Sienna waited for the telltale signs of an anxiety attack—twitching fingers, burning cheeks, circling the room, vanishing into the closet. But nothing came. After a moment, Dawn got up and walked to the end of the line. She never stopped watching Mike with her huge brown eyes.

"She's freaking me out a little," he said under his breath.

"She's just being cautious."

"Hmm mmm." He stayed where he was, hands at his sides, as if Dawn was a wild animal and remaining motionless was his best approach to not scaring her off.

"Do you want to walk down with us?" Sienna asked. "I'm sorry, I didn't even ask why you came in today."

He peeled off his jacket and draped it over one arm. They followed the students down the long central hallway. "I wanted to give you this." He pulled a small envelope from his back pocket and took out a ticket. "It's for Saturday night." He flushed. "I thought you might want the details of the fundraiser. It has where and when and stuff on it."

"Oh." She took the red-and-white stub and peered at it. *Dinner. Silent Auction. Dancing.* "You didn't mention the dancing."

"I didn't?" Mike kept his eyes on Dawn's back.

Sienna smiled. "Are we still driving together, or since I have a ticket now, should I meet you there?"

"Oh. I didn't mean…" He rubbed the back of his neck. "Shit. I'm not good at this. Yes, I'd like to drive you there. I want to go together. I just thought you'd like this ahead of time."

They reached the cafeteria, and the students filed inside. Caleb looked back and waved. "Bye, Mr. Mike."

Mike waved too. "Cute kids."

"In a ten-minute time span, sure. Come back on Friday and stay a while."

His gaze locked with hers. "I'd like that."

"Well, then, ah, good. Anytime after two o'clock." They stood in the hallway, an awkward distance and an awkward silence between them.

Finally, Mike stuck out his hand. "I'll see you later."

Here we are again with the handshakes, Sienna thought as a pebble of disappointment lodged in her throat. But she took his hand and squeezed all the same. A jolt of attraction shot up to her shoulder. *Does he feel it too? Or is it just me?*

"See you later. And thanks for the ticket." She felt the warmth of his palm, and that amazing current of attraction, for the rest of the day.

Chapter Nineteen

The week passed without incident, mostly because Al Halloran didn't step foot inside Springer Fitness. The one time Mike did see him, Al was driving a rundown white truck and heading south toward Albany.

Good. Maybe he'll keep driving that way and never come back.

He saw Sienna briefly when she came in Wednesday night to work on the Nautilus machines and Thursday night to take the kickboxing class, and each time a dopey grin spread over his face before he could stop it. Each time though, she gave him a wide smile but nothing else. Didn't slow down at the desk, didn't stop to chat, nothing. Of course, he supposed he couldn't blame her. He'd sent her about a dozen mixed messages in the last couple of weeks. Sure, let's go out. Yes, I'll kiss you until neither of us can breathe normally. Nope, changed my mind. Let's just be friends. Oh, hey, would you like to go to a Saturday night fundraiser with me? No, not as my date. Just as…

Jesus, I'm like a goddamn indecisive, hormonal teenage girl.

Finally Friday rolled around. By eight he was at the gym, by noon he'd finished a workout and all his paperwork, and just before two, he pulled on his coat and hat. "I'll be back by four," he told Hans. The kid nodded, eyes fastened to his phone.

"Hey." Mike stopped and rapped his knuckles on the desk. "I'm not paying you to text your girlfriend. Put it away."

Hans looked up with a hurt expression. "Sorry, boss."

"Listen, I know how it is when you first meet someone," Mike said, softening. "But you can play a little hard to get too." Was that what he'd been doing with Sienna? It seemed so stupid now.

Hans grinned and put his phone into his pocket. "Tell Sienna I said hi."

"How'd you know?"

"'Cause you got that happy look on your face you only get when she comes in here."

Mike flipped him the bird and walked out into a brilliant day, complete with sunshine and blue skies.

"Back again?" Eva Hadley asked when he walked into the school a few minutes later.

"Yep." He scrawled his name on the visitors' log and made his way down the hall. Most of the doors were closed, including Sienna's. He took a moment to peek inside. She sat on the rocker with the Turner kid on her lap and the other three boys sitting on the rug in front of her. Hell, she looked at ease in that classroom. More than he would have guessed.

He knocked.

"Mr. Mike!" One of the twins jumped up and ran over to let him in. "You came to read-along."

"Yes, I did." He glanced at Sienna. She'd dropped the book to her lap and was marking her place with one finger. Her cheeks darkened. He hoped that meant she was happy to see him. She wore her dark hair down and loose, with a pink sweater and black jeans hugging her curves. Silver earrings dangled from her ears.

"We're glad you're here," she said. She motioned to the corner behind him, and when he turned he saw the silent little girl sitting in a beanbag chair.

The boy tugged at his hand. "Come over and sit with us."

"Ah, okay." He took off his jacket and looked around.

"You can hang it over there," said Caleb. He pointed at some hooks on the wall below the window.

Mike hung up his jacket and then joined the boys on the rug. Shit. He hadn't sat cross-legged in a long time. His knees and legs didn't work the way they had twenty years ago. He hoped he'd be able to get up later. He glanced at the girl again. She stared at him. He smiled, and she ducked her chin. *Oh, well.* He fastened his gaze on Sienna instead and listened to her read about a raccoon family that lived in the forest.

Hope there isn't a quiz on this, he thought absently, because his mind wandered after a few seconds. All he could focus on was the movement of Sienna's lips. He wanted to taste them. He wanted her tongue inside his mouth and her hands sliding down his back.

Mike shifted position on the rug. Getting an erection in an elementary school classroom was a sure way to get him thrown right back in jail. With effort, he returned his attention to the story.

"When one day, Mother Raccoon came home to find that Rocky had disappeared." Sienna raised her eyebrows and made a big O with her mouth. "What do you think happened to him?" she asked.

One of the twins shot up his hand.

"Yes, Billy? And thank you for raising your hand."

Billy beamed. "I think Rocky went to play with his friends even though his mother told him not to."

Sienna turned the page but kept the illustration hidden. "Should we find out?"

They all nodded. Sienna pointed to Billy's twin. "Bailey, it's your turn to read."

Mike's mind went into a tailspin again. Her fingers in his hair. Unzipping his jeans. Working their way down his bare abdomen until they reached—

Think about lost raccoons.

He forced himself to listen to Bailey read the next page in halting rhythm. It took the kid almost ten minutes to get through twenty words, but when he finished, Sienna gave him a high five.

"Good job! And you were right, Billy. Rocky went off to play with his friends without asking permission." She swept the room with a serious gaze. "Should you ever go off to play without asking permission from an adult? Do you think that's a smart thing to do?"

"No," they crowed in unison. Mike looked again at the girl. She hadn't spoken a word, but she looked rapt at the storytelling. This time when their eyes met, she didn't look away or duck her chin.

Sienna finished the last page and closed the book. "I think we have time for one more today," she said. "Who wants to choose?"

"I think Mr. Mike should choose," Caleb said.

Sienna smiled. "Oh, really?"

"Yes, yes," the other boys agreed. Even the Turner boy nodded and clapped his hands.

Sienna pointed at the bookcase. "It's all yours."

Well, shit. How had this happened? "Thought I'd just drop by and watch," he mumbled as he creaked to his feet. That extra set of squats and lunges was killing him right about now.

"Nope, we like to put visitors right to work," she said.

He ran his finger along the spines of the books. Many were so worn he could barely read the titles. A few looked brand new. Finally, he came to a title he recognized. *Mike Mulligan and His Steam Shovel.* "Aw, man," he said aloud. "My mom used to read me this one all the time." He wondered where his own dog-eared copy had ended up.

Sienna stood and patted the rocker. "It's all yours."

He arched a brow. "Thanks."

"My pleasure." Laughter touched her light brown eyes, and an unfamiliar feeling turned over inside Mike's chest. Not pure desire, but something else, something deeper.

He sat, opened the book, and read the opening lines. His voice sounded rough to his own ears. When had he read a kid's book aloud? Never. He glanced at his audience, who waited expectantly. Caleb folded his hands under his chin like he was listening to the president of the United States speak. *If these kids really knew my past…*

He forced the thoughts away. Blood crawled up Mike's cheeks, and his tongue felt thick inside his mouth. *C'mon, Springer, get it together.* He glued his eyes to the pages and kept them there. The minutes seemed interminably long, but somehow he reached the end of the book. His back and hands were damp with sweat.

"Is that your favorite book because your name is Mike too?" Caleb asked.

"Well, I think that's part of it."

Sienna stood. "That was wonderful, wasn't it?" She looked at the clock. "I'm not sure we have any more—" She stopped. Mike followed her gaze to the back of the room.

Dawn had gotten out of her beanbag chair and walked to the bookcase. She scanned the books with a furrowed brow and then pulled one off the bottom shelf. Carrying it in both hands like it was a serving platter, she walked over to Mike and held it out.

He didn't speak. Neither did she. *Am I supposed to read this one too?* He wasn't sure his nerves could handle it. But the girl was studying him with blue eyes so serious he didn't dare say no. "Ah, thank you," he said as he took the book. She scuttled back to her corner, but not before something that looked like a smile passed across her face.

"I can't believe it," Sienna said a few minutes later, when he'd finished reading. The room was filled with the chatter of voices and the sound of bags being packed up to take home. "Dawn's never done that. And I mean never. She barely interacts with me most days. I've never seen her come up to a stranger." She pushed her hair off her face, and Mike was about to take the one strand she'd missed and tuck it behind her ear when Caleb's thin voice piped up behind them.

"Miss Cruz! It's time for us to walk out to the buses."

"Ah, yes, so it is." She lowered her voice. "Can you wait around a few minutes? Or do you have to get back to work?"

"I can wait around." He stuffed his hands inside his pockets and tried to make it seem as though he was taking in the sights of the room as she shuffled the students out the door. But as soon as she was gone, he collapsed back in the rocker. *Teaching sure is one hell of a tough job.* He could understand why Sienna didn't want to do it long-term, even though she seemed good at it.

He rocked back and forth and wondered if she'd found what she was looking for when it came to her research. Small towns and personalities, something like that. Hell, she'd have a shit show to write about if she ever found out about Al and the things he and Mike had done together out west. He cracked his knuckles. *Have to make sure that never happens.*

Less than ten minutes later, she returned, cheeks pink and hair tousled from the winter wind.

"Still cold out there?"

She laughed. "Isn't it always?"

He stood. "I should go. I mean, since read-along time is officially over and all."

"You did a really good job." She crossed to her desk and straightened some papers.

"I thought I was going to pass out," he confessed.

She looked up in surprise. "Why?"

"I don't think I've ever read a book out loud in my life." He spread his arms wide. "I'm not exactly the intellectual type, in case you hadn't noticed."

"Hmm." She put one finger to her cheek and walked over to him.

Her proximity, her perfume, the way she fastened her eyes on his, sent his thoughts and hormones spinning.

"So what type are you?" she asked. One hand dropped inside his, as if to shake it. "The friend type?"

He cleared his throat, and she tightened her hand in his.

"Or the maybe-something-more-but-I'm-not-sure-how-to-say-it type?" She slipped her other hand to his waist, and before he knew it, one finger had teased its way inside the top of his jeans. "I know what you said before. I know what I agreed to. Friends only. And if you want, we'll keep it just like that."

He swallowed. If she moved her hand an inch or two lower, she'd know his answer.

"But I kind of think there's more going on here," she said. She took another step closer to him. "I like you. A lot."

At that, he bent and kissed her. He tugged the hair at the back of her neck, took that soft pink mouth he'd been staring at for the last hour and tasted it. His hands went to the small of her back, and he pulled her close and nestled himself against her. "I like you too," he whispered, "in case you couldn't tell."

She slipped her hands to his ass and began to rock against him in infinitely small motions as she kissed him again. Her tongue trailed from his mouth to his jawline to his ear and back again. Still she moved, making him harder with every passing moment, until finally, he pulled away.

"You're gonna make me come like a goddamn teenager," he said. He swiped a hand over his forehead.

"I'm sorry. I didn't mean…" Her gaze moved down his body. "I get a little carried away around you, Mike Springer."

He smiled, and pleasure lit every last inch of him. "Can you hold that thought until tomorrow night?"

She reached out and traced the bulge in his jeans. "As long as we can pick this up where we left off."

Chapter Twenty

Sienna changed her clothes three times on Saturday. At ten minutes to six, she was standing in her bathroom, bra and panties only, when her phone buzzed with a text.

"I'm outside. I know I'm early. Can I come up?"

Sienna fumbled with the phone and dropped it on the floor, where it slid under the vanity. "Oh, for God's sake…" She dropped to her hands and knees to fetch it.

"I'll meet you downstairs," she finally texted back a few moments later. *"Not quite ready."*

"I could help you with that," came Mike's response, followed by a winky face.

Oh, boy could he. Wicked thoughts whirled through Sienna's mind, all of them involving skin and tongue and her bedroom. She ran her thumb over the keyboard. Would it be the worst idea in the world to skip the fundraiser?

Mike texted again before she could answer, settling the debate between her head and her hormones. *"I'll go fill up the truck with gas. Be back in ten minutes."*

Sienna sighed and set her phone aside. Better this way. They still had this tenuous, maybe-we-should-just-be-friends thing going on. Jumping him ten minutes into their date might be a little presumptuous, despite yesterday's scorching-hot kiss.

Nine minutes later, she pulled on her winter coat and locked her door behind her. She'd gone back to her first outfit of the afternoon—black velvet jeans and a maroon sweater with a deep vee-neck. A long silver chain hung around her neck and matched the earrings that dangled to her shoulders. High-heeled black boots and a winter-white scarf and gloves completed the outfit. She'd never been to an animal shelter fundraiser before and hoped she wouldn't look entirely out of place.

The look in Mike's eyes when he jumped out of his truck to help her into the passenger side told her she'd chosen right. "Hi," he said. "You look great."

"Thanks. So do you." He wore a leather jacket, khaki pants, and what looked like a dark-blue button-down shirt and black tie underneath.

"One step up from gym attire, huh?" he asked as he climbed back in the driver's side.

"I'd say two or three steps up." She leaned ever so slightly toward him in case he wanted to kiss her, but he kept his eyes on the road as he pulled onto Main Street. Sienna pulled off her gloves instead and watched the shadows slide by outside. "Where is this place again?"

"Silver Valley. Villa Venezia. It's only a couple years old. Very fancy." They started to climb the long hill that would take them up and into Silver Valley.

"I think I saw your mom in Zeb's the other night," Sienna said.

"Probably. She goes there every chance she gets." He glanced over. "She says she remembers you from when you were a kid. She worked with your mom."

"Does she?" Sienna's voice grew husky. "She came to the hospital the day my mom died. I think she might have come there *with* my mom."

"That sounds right. She never told me much about it."

"She got me a soda from the machine in the waiting room. And she was there when Doc Halloran told me—" Sienna stopped. "Anyway, tell her thank you. I don't know if I ever did." She stared at the shadowy hills outside the truck.

"She was pretty young, right? Your mom?"

"Thirty-three. Way too young to have a heart attack." Even if she had been working fourteen-hour days. "She wasn't overweight. We didn't eat steak and eggs every night for dinner." *Some nights, we didn't eat much.*

Mike flipped on the high beams as two deer scampered along the shoulder. "There's no heart disease in your family?"

"Not that I know of. She never mentioned it. She was never sick either, not that I can remember. The only thing was that she started having back pain from working so much. Doc Halloran put her on meds, but she hated them. She didn't even like taking aspirin."

He reached over and squeezed her hand. "I'm sorry."

Me too, she wanted to say. Sorry she'd missed out on knowing her mother as an adult, on having a confidant through the lonely years of high school and college. "Thank you."

"What about the rest of your family? They all live in North Carolina?"

Sienna continued to stare into the darkness. Without a single streetlight or star above, the landscape outside resembled humpbacked ogres, dark lumps of hillside that rose into the air around them and swallowed the truck. "If you can call it family. It's not much of one, to be honest. My father's down there, yes, but we aren't that close. I have a half brother I met a couple of times. He lives in Texas with his wife."

Silence filled the truck, the only sound the crunch of snow under the tires. They crested the hill and began the long descent into Silver Valley. In the distance, Sienna could see the glimmer of lights, a pale blanket spread over the dark land. "What about your dad?" she asked. "Is he in the picture?"

Mike gave a wry chuckle. "Nope. He knocked up my mom and took off before I was born. Nice guy, huh?"

"So your mom did the single-mother thing too."

"She did her best. I wasn't an angel of a kid."

"Who is? We all do the best we can, right?"

"Right." He turned up the radio as a hard-rock song came on. The lights of Silver Valley spread out like a quilt in front of them. "Now what do you say we forget about everything else except having a good time tonight?"

"I say that sounds perfect."

* * * * *

Mike hadn't stopped thinking about their kiss in the classroom. Now, with Sienna beside him looking drop-dead gorgeous and smelling like something he wanted to eat in slow, deliberate bites, all he could think about was continuing that kiss. Later. In her apartment. And letting that kiss lead to something else. As they walked into Villa Venezia, he touched the small of her back.

"Wow. This place looks awesome." Sienna looked around the ballroom. Long tables lined two of the walls, and auction prizes covered them, fancy wrapped gift baskets and over-sized gift certificates mounted in frames. *Pet Me! Love Me! Take Me Home!* appeared everywhere Mike looked, which did nothing to ease the ache in his groin. *Have to tell Becca to choose a motto with less innuendo next year.*

"Hey, man, thanks for coming." Zane materialized from a group of men near the bar and shook Mike's hand. "Sienna, you're looking gorgeous as always."

"Thanks. You're not so bad yourself."

Zane tugged at his tie. "These things always choke me."

"I know how you feel," Mike agreed. "Want a drink?" he said into Sienna's ear.

"Sure. White wine would be perfect."

He followed Zane to the bar and watched as Sienna walked along the tables of prizes. She took her time, touching a few and smiling as she read the names of the donors. He wondered what she thought of all this. With the upscale decor, open bar, and band warming up in the corner, it was fancy by Pine Point terms, but he didn't know what kind of life Sienna lived down South. Maybe she attended things like this all the time. She'd scrapped her way through high school, that was for damn sure, but the way she carried herself now, she looked like someone who was used to the best. Educated. Intelligent. Classier than most women he knew, let alone dated.

Mike's hand jerked as the bartender slid over a glass of wine and a beer. What the hell did he have to offer her?

"So how's that friends-only thing working out?" Zane asked.

Mike gave him a lopsided grin and shrugged.

"Yeah, that's what I thought. You're both consenting adults. 'Long as you both know you're not heading down the aisle, what's the harm in having a little fun?"

Sienna looked over at him and smiled, and Mike's thoughts turned X-rated. She was classy, yes. Out of his league, probably. But she'd come here with him tonight, and that counted for something, right? He wasn't looking for a serious girlfriend. She wasn't looking for a serious boyfriend. "No harm at all."

Becca walked over and slipped her arm through Zane's. She looked like a little girl dressed up for her first ball, in heels that wobbled and a tight black dress. "Thanks for coming tonight, Mike. And thanks for the donation."

"No problem. Good luck. Hope you make lots of money." He took his beer and Sienna's wine and was about to walk away. Then he remembered and turned back. "Hey, those stray cats over on Park Place Run—are you feeding them?"

Alarm creased her face. "I didn't know about them. They're strays? You're sure? You've seen them?"

"A couple, yeah. They didn't look like they belonged to anybody. But someone put out shelters and food for 'em. Thought it was you."

"It wasn't. But thanks. I'll check it out first thing tomorrow."

"Maybe not first thing," Zane said and nuzzled her ear. Becca turned red.

"Get a room, you two," Mike muttered as he turned away.

Sienna offered him some appetizers from the plate in front of her. "Becca's done a great job. The shelter should make a lot of money tonight."

"Hope so."

The band started playing a fast rock tune, and Sienna jumped up. "Want to dance?"

"Ah, no. Sorry. I'm not the dancing type."

She rolled her eyes and tugged at his shirt sleeve. "Come on."

He grumbled but followed her to the dance floor. "I usually look like an idiot when I try this."

She began to move, all sinewy hips and arms and legs that sent his mind straight back to the bedroom. "Then you haven't had the right partner."

"Isn't that the truth." Hard, angry memories of Edie rushed in like waves. They'd never danced together. Drank, gotten high, gone skinny dipping, stolen from a 7-Eleven, gotten married on a whim out in Vegas, yes. But they'd never done this. He focused on Sienna, who worked her way closer to him, until her hands skimmed his hips every so often and he could smell her perfume.

Before he knew it, his feet began to move. His hips followed, not with any great style, but at least he wasn't standing like a statue in the middle of the dance floor. Enough people had joined them by now, and the lights had dimmed, so he hoped no one could see him.

"Ah, you do have a move or two," she said into his ear. She danced up to him and then away, teasing him with every movement, until finally he grabbed her hips and held her in place. Her brows lifted, and pleasure darkened her eyes.

The song slowed, and suddenly her arms were around his neck. Her entire body fused to his. Mike turned hard. *Oh, hell. If she feels that…*

She must have, because she leaned back far enough to give him a look. Then she circled her hips in tiny motions, the way she had when she'd kissed him in her classroom. God, he wanted her. Now. He didn't care who saw them. He didn't care what might happen tomorrow or the next day.

She moved one hand along his ear, tracing the ridge with a feather-light touch. A rumble grew in his throat, and he had to bite his lip to keep it in.

"Now this is more like it," she said against his cheek. Mike closed his eyes and rested his forehead to hers.

He was a goner, a dead goner, and he didn't even care. He hadn't touched a woman, held a woman close like this, in almost three years. The sensations swept over him, mixing with a faint dread in his gut that getting involved would be a bad idea.

She isn't Edie, he argued with himself. *She's not even close.*

The song ended too soon, and Sienna stepped out of his arms.

"While you're helping yourself to the buffet," Becca said from the podium at the front of the ballroom, "I want to thank all the sponsors tonight, as well as let you know…"

He didn't hear her. He didn't hear anything except his heart pounding as they filled their plates and joined Zane and a couple of bigwigs from Mountain Glen at a table near the back. Introductions went around, and Mike busied himself with finishing the chicken marsala and roasted potatoes and going back for seconds.

"How does Sienna like teaching?" Zane asked when everyone else had left to mingle.

Mike watched her talk to some women near the bar. "I guess she likes it all right. She's good with those kids."

Zane dipped his roll in some gravy and gave him a long look. "Heard Al's back in town."

Bile rose into Mike's throat. "Yeah."

"He staying?"

Mike shrugged. "Not if I can help it."

"He was in longer than you?"

Besides his mother, only Zane knew the truth about L.A. "He had weed on him when the cops pulled us over. Got an extra seven months." Wasn't long enough, not by a long shot, but at least it had bought Mike some time back in Pine Point to get his own life on track.

"You ever hear from your ex?"

"Fuck, no."

Zane finished his roll and took a long swig of beer. "She never got charged with anything?"

Mike shook his head. "Just smart enough to not get caught." He shoved back his chair, done with talking about the past. "Gotta get another drink."

"Hurry back," Zane said with a grin. "The auction's about to start."

But Mike wasn't interested in who might be buying or selling tonight. He'd put in his time. The only thing he wanted now was to get the hell home. He walked over and put one arm around Sienna's waist. "You want to get out of here?"

She looked up in surprise. Then her expression morphed into a grin. "Sure." She glanced at Becca, who was fiddling with the microphone. "Should we say goodbye?"

"Already did." He gave Zane a wave as they headed for the lobby. Outside, light snow fell, silhouetted by the lights. Mike tucked Sienna's hand into his as they waited for the coat-check attendant and the valet. Ten seconds with her skin against his, and all his desire from the dance floor returned. She hadn't said a word. He had no idea whether he was taking her back to his place or hers. All he knew was the magnetism drawing him to her.

She tugged on his hand.

"I think the attendant—" he started to say, but she crooked a finger and beckoned him across the lobby. With a quick glance left and right and then one lifted brow, she pulled him into the ladies' room.

"What the hell are you—?" he began, but the next thing he knew, her mouth was on his, and he stopped caring about anything else.

Chapter Twenty-One

"We're gonna get caught," he said as Sienna backed through the heavy gilt door.

"Maybe. Maybe not. All those animal lovers are probably in the ballroom right now outbidding each other to see who gets to take home the Springer Fitness gym membership." She took a quick survey of the restroom. Three stalls, three sinks, and a large sitting area with a fancy red loveseat and paintings hanging on the wall above it. She'd never done anything like this before, but she didn't want to wait any longer to touch him. Mike turned her on simply by grinning at her from across the room. She'd almost come in his arms on the dance floor.

She pulled his mouth to his and whispered, "While I get to take home Mr. Springer himself."

At that, he lifted her in his arms like she weighed nothing. Sienna wrapped her legs around his waist and felt every inch of his lean, hard body meet hers. She hadn't slept with a guy in almost six months. She hadn't seriously dated anyone in over a year. Yet a few short weeks back in Pine Point, and the tiny, tightly constructed wall inside her had started to crack. He kissed her, and she stopped thinking about everything else. His tongue moved inside her mouth, slow and deliberate. His hands cupped her ass as he braced her against the ledge of sinks. Everything inside her went hot, and she threaded her fingers through his hair, wanting him closer. He moved his lips to her neck and closed over the spot where her pulse jumped.

"You drive me crazy," he murmured.

She nodded, unable to form a coherent response.

He slid his hand down her arm, but when he reached her scar, he stopped. He brushed his thumb over her skin, tracing the white line. He looked at her without speaking.

"Sophomore year of college," she said, her voice rough. "Low point in my life."

He raised her wrist to his mouth and kissed the scar so sweetly she wanted to cry. "I've had a few of those low points," he whispered. "Glad it's just a scar now."

"Me too."

He slipped his palm beneath her sweater, and when he touched the bare skin of her belly, she jumped. The automatic faucet behind her turned on with the motion, and suddenly a spray of cold drenched her from behind.

"Oh, shit." She jumped. They wriggled away from the sinks.

"Hell, Sienna, I'm sorry. Let me see." He turned her around and ran the flat of his palm down her back. "You're pretty wet."

"Yeah," she managed to say. She braced both hands on the sink and savored the feel of his hand on her back, running from the damp hair at her neck to the curve of her hips. He did it again, then a third time, slower. By the time he slipped her sweater down her shoulder to kiss it, she'd almost come undone.

He began to move against her, one hand holding her hip, the other moving back around to tease beneath her sweater and cup one breast. *Oh dear God.* The rough lace pressed into her sensitive skin at his touch, and he squeezed just enough that she melted. Her eyes closed. He pulsed against her, and somehow it didn't matter that they were fully clothed, that he'd barely touched anything at all. The beginnings of an orgasm hummed through her, and the sensation both startled and scared her. She rarely came with a man. She rarely let down her guard that far. Messed up, maybe, but becoming vulnerable in the moment of release meant she trusted the guy. And she didn't trust. She couldn't. Too many people had hurt her in the past.

"Open your eyes," he said, his voice guttural with want.

She couldn't. She'd lose this moment, this feeling of perfect rhythm.

He tightened his hands. "Sienna. I want you to watch us."

With effort, she opened her eyes and stared into the mirror. She'd never done anything like this before, but the effect was nothing short of astounding. Her cheeks were flushed, her mouth slightly open. He panted with every thrust against her, and the sound and sight of them together, of them wanting each other, pushed her over the edge. Her hips pressed into the counter's sharp edge, her head dropped back, and everything inside her exploded. Her legs shook. Her arms shook. A whimper left her lips, and if someone had walked into the restroom at that moment, she couldn't have done anything except continue riding this wave.

When she opened her eyes again, Mike was watching her in the mirror. He brushed his lips against her cheek. "Now that's what I call foreplay."

She laughed, the sound breathless and echoey in the high-ceilinged room. It felt as though she'd walked a high wire all the way to the other side. Terrifying. Giddy. *You've crossed a line*, she told herself. *No going back now.*

Mike pressed a kiss to her temple. "What do you say we go back to my place and try that with clothes off next time?"

* * * * *

Mike couldn't keep his hands or eyes or anything else off Sienna. Their clothes landed in piles across his floor. He didn't turn on a single light. As soon as he'd pulled into the driveway, they'd rushed upstairs without words, felt their way to his bedroom, and fallen onto the bed with arms and legs entwined. Fragments of sentences started and stopped in the silence, like *Oh, God I…* And *I love when you…* But he didn't want to talk. He wanted to taste her, to feel her, to forget everything else except the pure pleasure of having Sienna in his bed. The faint moonlight through his window fell on her skin, dimpled with gooseflesh as she moved above him. She dropped kisses on his mouth, his jaw, his naked chest, then worked her way down until all he felt was her hair across his belly.

Mike groaned. So damn good. So damn long since he'd touched the skin of a woman's back. God, he loved the softest spots, the places that made her flinch when he stroked them, so he did it again. And again. He tried to keep track of how many times she came as he roamed his fingers and tongue over her body, but he couldn't. Only after he finally climaxed deep inside her did she stretch out beside him with a satisfied smile.

"Oh, honey," she said after a long moment. "That was amazing."

Still hard, still wet with sweat, with the covers tangled around one foot, he nodded. She crawled into the crook of his arm and lay there. *I've never had this.* Hot sex, yes. Hot, sober sex? Not in a long time. And never with someone like Sienna, a near-perfect package, and not because of her brains or killer body, but because in addition to all that, the scar tissue built up around her heart meant she'd struggled through life the same way he had.

He couldn't tell her about L.A. Of course not. But she might understand his reluctance. She might understand that his shit from the past needed to stay there.

As if reading his mind, she ran one hand down his bare chest. Her fingers tickled him, and he caught her hand in his. He pressed her fingers to his lips. "Want to stay?"

"Yes." She raised herself onto one elbow, still naked. "I guess that friends thing wasn't such a good idea after all."

"I don't know." He traced the bottom curve of her breast. "We are still friends, aren't we?"

She smiled. "Of course. Just with some added benefits." She pressed a kiss to his shoulder. "Tell me about you."

Mike shifted and stuck one arm behind his head. Shadows played on the ceiling as clouds drifted over the moon. "What do you want to know?"

She traced the outline of a red and black dragon that began on his shoulder and twisted down to his elbow. "When did you get this one?"

"I was twenty-one. And, no, it doesn't mean much except I liked the design." He stretched out his arm and turned it in the moonlight.

"Dragons are supposed to be powerful," she said.

He flexed, and the body of the dragon seemed to grow on his biceps. "Then that's why I got it." He leaned over and kissed the tip of her nose.

"What about that one?" She pointed to his other arm. A sunburst covered his shoulder. Small black footsteps walked away from it, down to his wrist.

"Twenty-three." He refused to entertain the memory of Edie picking it out. "It's a reminder to keep the sun at my back. Keep looking ahead, shit like that."

Sienna nodded. He could feel her gaze moving over the others. Before she could ask the meaning behind *Never Again*, he laced his fingers through hers. "No tattoos for you?"

She shook her head.

"Ever think about it?"

A curl fell over her nose, and she blew it out of the way. "Not really. They're too permanent. I think I'd choose the wrong one, and five or ten years later, I wouldn't like it anymore."

"There's always that possibility."

She put one bare leg over his, and desire stirred in him again. "What happened out in L.A.? If you don't mind my asking."

He minded. He minded so much it hurt, because if he told her the truth, she'd be halfway out the door before he could finish. He rubbed his nose. He watched the pattern of the light on the ceiling. "I made some bad decisions," he finally said.

"How long were you there?"

"Almost eight years. I left right after high school with the older buddy of a friend of mine. He had a lead on a construction job, said it would pay really well."

She dropped his hand and sat all the way up, cross-legged. Her eyes lit with curiosity. "So how'd you like California?"

"It was hot." He chuckled. "And crowded, at least where we mostly worked, in Anaheim."

"Eight years is a long time. I bet your mom was glad when you came back."

"She was."

"She ever go out and visit you?"

Once, the month after he went to prison. He did his best not to think about her drawn, white face looking at him under the supervision of an armed guard. "Nope. She's not really a traveler." He sat up and rolled Sienna so she lay on her back beneath him. Propped on his elbows, he ran his cheek along hers. She touched the small of his back and laughed.

"Tell me about you." he said. He lowered himself until he lay beside her. One hand rested on the gentle curve of her belly.

"What do you want to know?"

If she might change her mind about staying in Pine Point. If she thought about him half as much as he thought about her. "What's it like going to school for so long?" he asked instead.

She laughed, and her diaphragm rippled under his hand. "Sometimes it's exhausting. But it's also… I don't know. Exciting. I love school. Always did." She made a face. "Classes and my teachers, anyway. The other kids, not so much."

"No? School was the only place I sorta felt like I fit in."

"That's because you had tons of friends and a different girlfriend every other week."

He moved his hand north until it touched the underside of her breast. "Not tons. And not every other week. You used to eat in the library," he said with a smile. "I do remember that."

"You knew where the library was?" she teased.

He took her hand in his and drew her arm around his naked back. "I fantasized about having sex in that library," he whispered into her ear.

She leaned back to look at him. "You did not."

"Up against the book shelves." He moved his hand down her spine, curving around her belly until his fingers tickled the spots already turning wet again.

Yes, he'd had a good time in high school. Nothing mattered too much, and no one ever stabbed him in the back.

She wriggled closer. "I didn't feel like I fit in until I went to college," she went on. "I got my bachelor's degree in Exceptional Education and taught special ed for a year, but that wasn't really my thing. So I went back and took more classes."

"Tell me again what you're studying?"

"The psychology of personality development. It's a fancy way of studying how and why people develop the personalities they do. Kind of like the nature-versus-nurture debate."

"And you came back to Pine Point to do that." Mike withdrew his hand.

"Well, yes, but—" She rolled onto her side to face him. "What's wrong? Why does that bother you?"

He cleared his throat. "Are you studying me?"

She touched his face and didn't answer.

"Is that's what's going on here?" His voice grew gruff. Shit, he'd misread a situation yet again. He went to get up, but she took his arm.

"Mike. No." She squared her gaze on his. "I'm not here with you for any other reason except that I want to be."

He pulled in a breath. He wanted to believe her.

She dropped her hand to his thigh. "I want you." She crooked a smile. "I want this."

His eyes closed in pleasure. They didn't talk after that. He moved above her, taking it slow, making her cry out for his touch, and when it was over, they fell asleep in each other's arms. It was the first time he slept straight through to morning in over a year.

Chapter Twenty-Two

Sienna woke in stages, first with awareness of the arm around her, then of the sun streaming through the window above her head, and finally, the sensation of coziness under a blanket of just the right weight and softness. She'd stayed the night. She hadn't woken up once. Unbelievable. And scary as hell.

"Good morning," Mike murmured into her ear.

She turned over and smiled. "Good morning."

He ran one hand over her messy hair and down her bare shoulder. "You want some coffee?"

"I don't want anything." She snuggled closer to him and closed her eyes.

"I have to go to work," he said after a few minutes. "You could have breakfast with my mom if you want."

At that, she sat straight up. "You're kidding, right?"

He grinned. "Yeah. She'd love to see you though. I doubt she'd care you spent the night."

"Maybe next time." Was there going to be a next time? She bit her bottom lip and hoped she hadn't sounded presumptuous. Without looking at his expression, she climbed out of bed and gathered her clothes from around the apartment. Good Lord, how had her bra ended up in the kitchen? And she could only see one boot from the bed. He didn't bother to dress, and the naked view of him walking into the kitchen turned her on all over again. This wasn't what she'd had in mind when she'd returned to Pine Point for research, but...*damn.*

The smell of coffee filled the apartment a few minutes later, and then Sienna heard the shower run. For a long moment, she sat on the edge of the bed looking at her scar. *He asked me about it. And then he kissed it.* Most other guys she'd dated had avoided even looking at it. Wasn't hard to know that a scar like that came from drawing a razor blade deep into the skin, watching the blood flow and hoping for a quick release from the pain. But Mike had only looked at and then moved on, as if it meant nothing more than the color of her eyes or the shape of her chin. Her heart fluttered, and she put one hand to her bare chest. *I'm in a whole lot of trouble if I fall for him.*

She dressed, poured herself a cup of coffee, and then sneaked into the bathroom. With one finger, she pulled back the shower curtain.

He had his head under the spray, so he didn't see her at first. The water ran down his body, every inch of it muscle and nearly half of it covered in tattoos. He didn't have any scars that she could see, but then again, all the artwork would do a good job of hiding them. Her insides went warm all over again at the sight of his nakedness, and part of her wanted to strip and jump under the water with him.

"Hey, you." He flicked some water at her.

"Hey, yourself." She let the curtain drop back into place and walked into the living room. Cute place, if small, and distinctly a bachelor pad. A few fitness magazines, a laptop, an Xbox, and a huge flat-screen television hanging across from a well-worn recliner. She refilled her coffee and pulled open the refrigerator to see a jug of unsweetened iced tea and two containers of leftovers.

He came up behind her a few minutes later and slipped his arms around her waist. "Sure I can't interest you in some breakfast downstairs? Ma makes a mean French toast."

She flinched at the thought. Delicious sex with a bodybuilder? Yes, please. Domestic conversation with his mother the morning after? She already felt herself losing control around him, sliding down a slippery slope that involved emotions she hadn't felt in a long time. She set down her mug. "I think I'll take a raincheck."

One corner of his mouth curled. "Don't worry. I was kidding."

He's not rushing into anything, she reminded herself as she found her other boot by the door. Good. Because the last thing she needed was to get attached to anyone or anything in Pine Point. *Been there, done that.* She'd left this town a shattered shell of a person eleven years ago. She had no intention of it happening again.

*****

"I'll call you later," Mike said as he dropped her off at her apartment a half hour later. Sienna nodded and blew him a kiss. Upstairs, she showered and debated taking a nap, but her stomach growled and argued otherwise. She pulled on an old pair of jeans and her favorite UNC sweatshirt, grabbed a fresh yellow notepad, and headed downstairs to Zeb's instead.

"Hi, there," said the middle-aged waitress at the counter. "Coffee?"

"Yes, please." She looked around. "Josie's not working?"

"Nah. Never on Sundays." The woman poured a cup of coffee and pushed it across the counter. It sloshed over onto the saucer, and she sighed and handed Sienna a stack of napkins. "Sorry."

Sienna looked around. Two gray-haired men she didn't recognize sat at the opposite end of the counter. A mother and two toddlers with wild hair and Kool-Aid stains on their faces sat in a booth by the window. Other than that, the place was empty.

"I'll have the breakfast special," she said with a glance at the handwritten sheet inside the menu.

The waitress nodded and tromped off to the kitchen. Sienna bent over her notepad. She already had a nice collection of observations on the town, complete with a couple of affairs and sordid marriage secrets. Her gaze moved over the counter to the cash register and the stack of blank order slips beside it.

Diner waitress writes love poetry, she'd written last week. What was Josie's story? Unrequited love? Jilted at the altar? Sheer boredom? The waitress returned and plopped salt and pepper shakers in front of Sienna.

"Ah, Carol?" she asked, with a look at the woman's name tag.

"Yeah?"

"How long have you worked here?"

"'Bout two years. Used to work over at the Ponderosa, but that shithead of a boss cut my hours in half after I messed up my knee, so I left there." She shoved a stray lock of graying hair behind one ear. "Why?"

"I wondered how well you knew Josie."

Carol shrugged. "'Bout as well as anyone, I guess. She grew up here, course. I didn't." She said it with a certain amount of pride, as if Pine Point and Zeb's Diner were beneath her, and she was just biding her time until an offer to wait tables at the Waldorf Astoria came along.

"Oh, no?"

"Nope. I'm from jus' the other side of Albany. Small town called Troy. It's pretty famous. Got a girls' college there and everything."

"So how'd you end up here?"

Carol narrowed her gaze. "Got a lotta questions for a Sunday morning, don't you?"

Sienna resisted the urge to ask if her questions would be better taken on a Monday afternoon or Friday night. "I'm sorry. I didn't mean to pry."

Carol brightened again. "What d'ya want to know about Josie?"

Sienna put her notepad aside and tried to sound casual. "Just wondered what she does in her spare time. Seems like she's here all the time."

Carol whistled. "She is. But let's see now… I think she mostly goes to a quilt club over in Silver Valley. She's a damn good quilter."

"I didn't know that."

"Oh, sure. She usually wins first prize at the holiday fair each year. D'ya know, last year over fifty people entered the contest. Josie won, of course."

"Of course." Sienna smiled. So the diner waitress was not only a secret poetess, but an award-winning quilter as well. *Ah, the things my research is turning up.* She sighed and drank her coffee.

Carol delivered Sienna's order a few minutes later and then drifted back to the kitchen, where Sienna could hear her discussing her bad knee with one of the cooks. Sienna scanned Main Street as she ate. A few cars drove in both directions, but she didn't see a single pedestrian until she'd almost finished her meal. Ella Ericksen emerged from the apartment stairs, dressed, as always, like she was heading for a New York City fashion show. Today, she wore her bright-blue ski jacket, black jeans, and stiletto boots. A white hat with a pom pom matched fuzzy white gloves with smaller pom poms, and she carried a bulky paper bag in one hand.

"I don't know how those sisters ended up so different," Carol said from over Sienna's shoulder, echoing her own thoughts. "They're like night and day."

"They sure are." Sienna watched as Ella got into her SUV and drove out of town. She wondered if Becca was still sleeping after last night's fundraiser. Maybe she was soaking her feet after hours of wearing high heels. *Ella probably sleeps in them*, she thought with a grin. She paid the bill and walked back outside.

Down the street, St. Mary's Church had just finished its service, and bells rang as people poured from the front door and hurried to their cars. Sienna had thought about going to a service or two to help her research, but something about that seemed a little seedy. Now she stood on the sidewalk and watched families and couples and a few singles drive away. *Wonder who goes every single week? Wonder who goes only when they have something to atone for?* Her mother had prayed nightly in front of the porcelain Virgin Mary statue in their living room, but Sienna had never stepped foot in a church. Until the funeral anyway. Her mother had worked most Sundays, picking up extra shifts whenever she could.

Tears pricked her eyes as she walked along the sidewalk, but she told herself it was the wind and nothing else. The temperature had climbed overnight, and without a sharp bite in the air, being outside was almost pleasant. Sienna decided to walk off her breakfast. She pulled up her hood and headed north, out of town. *Might as well check on those stray cats,* she thought as she neared Park Place Run. Mike had said Becca didn't know about them, but someone did. Sienna slowed at Art's Mini-Mart on the block between her apartment and Park Place Run. On impulse, she ducked inside and bought three cans of cat food.

She turned the corner onto Park Place Run, a virtual ghost town on a Sunday morning. Closed signs hung in every window. Even Marc's Grille stated that it opened at five, for dinner only. She took a long inhale, savoring the air. One thing Pine Point had over Chapel Hill was the fresh evergreen scent that filled your lungs. No pollution here.

Halfway down the block, Sienna stopped. Looked as though she wasn't the only person bringing food to Park Place Run's resident strays this morning. She squinted into the morning sun. A few cars occupied private parking spots, designated for the second- and third-floor luxury apartments. An SUV sat in front of Divine Designs, the salon at the very end of the block.

An SUV Sienna knew well.

Her mouth dropped as Ella Ericksen climbed from the vehicle. She unrolled the paper bag she'd been carrying earlier, took out two cans of food, and spooned the contents into the bowls in front of the makeshift shelters. Then she returned to the SUV for blankets, got down on her hands and knees, and replaced the old ones in the plastic tubs. She sat back on her heels, pushed her hat back on her head, and whistled. To Sienna's utter amazement, three cats appeared from the bushes. They skittered by Ella, giving her a long look before gulping in the food. Apparently satisfied, Ella got up, tossed the dirty blankets into the back seat of her SUV, and drove away.

Sienna ducked into a doorway as she passed, hoping she hadn't been spied, but Ella looked straight ahead.

"Well, I'll be damned," she said under her breath. It might not be research-worthy, but finding out Ella Ericksen had a soft spot for animals was a pretty nice secret to discover on a Sunday morning. Sienna pursed her lips. Funny, but for the first time, it occurred to her that not all secrets might be bad. Maybe the different sides to a person, the secrets and the scars and all the past stories, could add up to something more complex than she could ever judge from the start.

Chapter Twenty-Three

All week long, the sun shined. Six more people signed up for gym memberships, and Pine Point got four inches of snow Wednesday night. That brief storm turned into a few hundred dollars in Mike's pocket after he spent a few hours plowing and pulling drivers out of snow banks. Friday morning, he caught himself whistling as he cleaned the blender and checked the protein powder supplies.

"Man, she's that good?" Hans asked with a grin.

Mike knew the kid probably meant in bed, but he nodded without saying anything. It wasn't just the way she turned him on. Having Sienna in Pine Point was like having the sun come out after weeks of cold and gray. Seeing her name on his phone when she texted or called made him feel like a teenager again, all thumbs as he fumbled to respond. They hadn't slept together since last weekend, between his long hours and her schoolwork and research, and they'd had dinner together only once at the diner. But they talked every night, and she came into the gym almost every afternoon.

Mike's chin twitched as he took a sidelong look at his office. He didn't spend much time in there, but she'd given him one hell of a blow job up against the desk yesterday evening, and he couldn't even glance that way today without getting hard. A stack of plastic cups slipped from his hands and tumbled across the ground.

"I got 'em," Hans said.

"Thanks." Mike rubbed the back of his neck and tried to keep his focus on the business. He spent the rest of the morning talking to the local cable station about a low-budget ad, training two clients, and counting the hours until he could leave. At ten minutes of two, he headed out the door. "Back by four," he called over his shoulder. Hans nodded, eyes on his phone as usual.

"Mr. Mike!" Caleb met him at the door of Room Eighteen. "Miss Cruz, you were right. Mr. Mike came for read-along time today."

Sienna smiled from across the room. She wore a plain blue button-down shirt with the tails out over blue and black print leggings. Chunky black ankle boots on her feet, and her hair up in a messy bun. Mike's fingers twitched. How he'd like to pull out whatever pins held it in place and let her hair fall around her face. Then he'd take her right on the desk. Or maybe the rocking chair. Or maybe both.

He wiped a hand over his face as one of the twins tugged at his hand. "You come over here." Obedient, he followed the boy to the rocking chair and sat.

"What am I reading today?"

The other twin carried over three books and dropped them in Mike's lap. "Here. We picked these out for you."

"Three?"

"They're short," Sienna said with a laugh. She sank into the chair at her desk and propped her chin on one hand.

Not short enough, he wanted to answer. Shit. He hoped they didn't have any tricky words in them. A sweat broke out across his forehead. *They're just kids*, he reminded himself. *They won't know if you screw up or skip a page.* But he'd never loved reading as a kid. He'd never even liked it. The irony of his reading to a group of kids in the hopes of impressing their teacher wasn't lost on him. Mike opened the cover of the first book.

"Sally Goes to the Store," he began. Well, that sounded easy enough. As long as Sally wasn't shopping for avocados or paprikash, he could make it through this one. He took his time, trying to make sure he held the book so the kids could see the pictures. About halfway through the story, Sally tried to sneak a carton of ice cream into her mother's shopping cart. The boys burst out laughing. Mike looked up, surprised.

"Look what she's doing!" crowed one of the twins. He kicked his feet and laughed again. His brother joined in. Silas clapped and laughed louder than both of them. Even Caleb smiled. Only Dawn remained silent in her beanbag on the other side of the room.

With a smile, Mike finished the story. The kids clapped, and before he knew it, one of the twins was leaning on his leg and pushing another book into his hands. "Read this one next."

"Billy, please be polite." Sienna said from her desk. "I don't think Mr. Mike wants you sitting on his lap."

"It's okay," Mike said. Sometime in the last twenty minutes, his anxiety had dissolved. Even the presence of sticky fingers and curious eyes didn't unnerve him as it once had. "So this one next, buddy?"

The boy nodded.

Before Mike had realized it, he'd finished all three books, and almost forty minutes had passed. Sienna stood. "Let's give Mr. Mike a big round of applause for reading to us today."

They smacked their hands together, and Silas whooped as he jumped up and down with glee.

"My gosh, that's more of a reception than I usually get," Sienna said to him.

Mike stood in the middle of the room, unsure of what to do or say. He'd never gotten a reception like that in his life. Amazing that a group of quirky eight-year-olds could make him feel better about himself than most people he'd known as an adult.

Sienna clapped her hands. "Fifteen minutes until we get ready for dismissal. That means Billy, Bailey, Caleb, and Dawn, you have bathroom time, and then please put your backpacks out so I can check what you're taking home." She put her hand on Silas's shoulder. "And you, my handsome man, need to finish coloring the last sheet in your packet." She directed him to the table. "Silas is our lover of all things having to do with baseball," she explained.

"Really?" Mike looked at the paper in front of the boy. Baseballs, gloves, bats, and containers of popcorn and peanuts covered the page. Silas caught his tongue between his teeth as he drew lines to match the pairs. "You know what?" Mike asked. Silas looked up. "I love baseball too."

A huge grin broke out on Silas's face.

"Maybe I could bring in a glove once the weather gets nice," Mike went on. "Throw around some balls." His face flushed. Everything he said around Sienna seemed to have a sexual connotation.

She lifted a brow and smiled. "I'd like that. I'm sure they would too. I wouldn't mind getting my hands on some balls either."

* * * * *

Sienna resisted the urge to grab Mike and give him a smokin' kiss in front of everyone as the buses pulled away. As it was, the heat between them drove her half-crazy, and she had to keep back a few feet or her hands would do things without consulting her brain. She waved goodbye and watched him walk to his truck. In three hours, she was meeting him for dinner. She could wait that long to jump his perfect body. She hoped.

She walked down to the library and picked out some new books for her students, looking for titles related to baseball. The boys would love playing catch with Mike. Billy, Bailey, and Silas already adored him, and Caleb was warming up in his own way. Dawn—well, Sienna hoped Dawn would come around. At least she didn't hide in the closet when Mike came by.

Sienna headed back through the lobby, empty except for Eva Hadley sitting at the visitors' desk. "Hey, Eva."

"Hey, Sienna."

"Have a good weekend."

"You too." She gave Sienna a curious look. "So, you and Mike?" she asked.

Sienna stopped walking. "Me and Mike what?"

"You're..." She flipped her manicured fingers in the air. "You're, like, together now?"

"We're spending some time together," Sienna said. She had no idea what *together* meant in Eva's world, and she wasn't about to analyze it in her own. "He's a good guy."

"Yeah, he is. Too bad he was married before."

Sienna's face flamed. "What?" *He wasn't. I would have known. He would have mentioned it.* Everything inside her dropped, and she wasn't sure which feeling hurt worse, the embarrassment that Eva had told her or the disappointment that Mike hadn't trusted her enough to tell her himself.

"Oh, yeah. You knew that, right?" Eva made a tsking sound. "I always try to keep my distance from divorced guys. You never know what went wrong the first time around."

Chapter Twenty-Four

"Hey, Ma?" Mike called from the driveway. Loretta bustled around the open garage, moving boxes from one shelf to another. He walked inside. "What are you doing?"

"Putting away the Christmas decorations." She turned and pointed. "Can you see on that top shelf? Are my Easter things up there?"

He strained to read the writing on a cardboard box. "I think so."

Loretta dragged over a step stool, but as she climbed up the first two steps, he took her around the waist and stopped her. "Ma. I'll get the boxes."

"I am perfectly capable of getting them myself."

"I know you are." He steered her to the floor. "But I'm your son, and you're letting me live here rent free. I like to earn my keep when I can."

She crossed her arms, but a smile worked its way onto her face. "Fine. I just want those two closest to the front."

"Okay." He climbed the step stool and retrieved them. "Where do you want them?" he asked, but Loretta didn't answer. When Mike looked over his shoulder, he saw that she'd walked out to the road. Without so much as a coat or a hat. Grumbling, he put down the boxes and went after her.

A sleek black Mercedes had slowed at the end of their driveway, and Doc Halloran rolled down the window. "Loretta, Mike, how you both doing?"

Mike backpedaled a step or two and lifted a hand. He knew Doc hadn't had any contact with Al in over a decade. He knew the retired doctor probably felt the same way about his son as Mike did. But still, seeing the same Halloran eyes and the same lazy grin made Mike's gut twist.

Loretta beamed. "It's good to see you. When are you going to stop by for dinner?"

"Well, now, I do have Rotary meetings on Tuesdays, and every other Thursday I..."

Mike watched the conversation with mild interest. *Is Ma flirting with Doc?* Huh. He'd wondered a few times if his mother might ever marry, but she'd never seemed interested in the idea. Her cheeks pinked as she talked to Doc though, and she rested a hand on the door close to the old man's.

Good for her. Good for both of them. Mike chuckled and turned to go when Doc called him over. "Got a gym question for you, my good man," he said with a wink at Loretta. She backed up the driveway, her eyes on Doc the whole time.

"Sure, what's up?" he asked. He'd never seen Doc step foot inside Springer Fitness. The sixty-year-old walked five miles a day and did pushups and crunches on his front porch in all kinds of weather. Someone like that didn't need a gym membership.

Doc lowered his voice. "I'm sure you've seen my son in town."

Mike froze, eyes on the ground. "Yeah. Once or twice." He took a deep breath and forced himself to look Doc in the eye. Wasn't the old man's fault Al had shot Mike's life to shit.

"He's not here on my asking," Doc said. "Just wanted you to know that. He called me up, said he wanted to make amends. I told him until I saw proof he'd been clean for a year, I wasn't interested in anything he had to say." The man talked in controlled tones, but the blood that rose into his cheeks belied his composure. Had to be tough as hell, turning his back on his own flesh and blood. Mike nodded.

"Now, I don't know all the details about what happened with the two of you out in California, and I'm not sure I want to. But I see what you've done here with that gym, and I know you're a good man with a good head on his shoulders. Just want you to know that." He peered into his rear view mirror. "If you see him around here, I'd appreciate a heads up. I told him he wasn't welcome, but if he's desperate for a place to sleep or something to eat, he might end up here."

"Will do." Mike cracked his knuckles. "How's Arthur doing?" At least the younger Halloran son had made a decent life for himself.

Doc's face brightened. "Just fine. Living down near New York City and working for a good law firm. His wife's about to have a baby, so I'll be heading down there as soon as she does."

"That's wonderful. Glad to hear it." Always nice when a little yin did balance out the yang. Mike waved goodbye as Doc rolled up his window and continued down the street.

Sure takes all kinds of people to make up the world, he thought as he walked to his apartment. Inside, he checked the clock on the stove. Only about ten minutes until Sienna arrived. He hadn't told his mother about them yet, but he thought tonight would be as good a time as any. He pulled off his shirt and turned on the shower. He was just about to drop his jeans and boxers when someone knocked at the door. He checked the peephole and grinned.

"You're early," he said as he pulled it open. *Want to join me in the shower?* he was about to add, but the disappointment on Sienna's face stopped him. "What's wrong? What happened?"

She didn't step inside. She didn't even take off her gloves. "Why didn't you tell me you'd been married?"

Damn. Why did Mike have to be half-naked? She swallowed hard and focused on his eyes, not a great choice considering they pierced through her and sent her thoughts spiraling into the bedroom, but that was better than the alternative of letting her gaze skate across his pecs and down his flat stomach.

"Sienna." He only said her name at first, and his mouth drew down. He reached for her hand. "Come inside."

She didn't take his hand, but she did step across the threshold. She could hear the shower running a few feet away.

"Hang on," he said, and went to shut off the water. When he returned, he pulled out a kitchen chair, sat, and folded his hands on the table. "I'm sorry I didn't tell you. It was one of the biggest mistakes of my life. I try not to think about it." He rubbed the back of his neck and stared at the table. "Her name was Edie, and Al introduced us."

She sat too. "Al Halloran?"

Mike nodded. "He had a big group of friends out there—" he snorted, "—if you can call 'em friends. Anyway, he knew a lot of people, put it that way. I'd been living out there about two years when I went to a party, and she was there."

"What was she like?" Part of Sienna didn't want to know. But she couldn't help asking. She'd never pictured Mike as the marrying type. Someone pretty special must have knocked his socks off.

He shrugged. "Long blond hair and a good body. Like everyone else living in L.A." He finally looked up at Sienna. "But we had some good conversations at the beginning. She wasn't from around there either. She grew up in the Midwest and was trying to make it as an actress." He raised one hand. "And before you say anything, yes, most of the women out there are. Not much else to say," he continued. "We started hanging out, one thing led to another, I was lonely, the lease was up on her apartment, so we drove to Vegas one weekend, and got hitched." He rolled his neck from side to side.

"How long were you with her?"

He blew out a breath. "We dated for about a year. We were married for three and a half."

Longer than she'd imagined. Slivers of jealousy moved through her, no matter how much she tried to tell herself it didn't matter and she didn't care. "So what happened?"

"What can I say? When you're young and dumb, you think things are gonna last forever. Found out about three years in that she was cheating on me with an old boyfriend. Maybe the whole time, I don't know and don't want to know." He waved a hand as if to dismiss Edie's infidelity, the marriage, this whole conversation. "Wasn't just that either. Would've been bad enough if it was, but she cleaned out my bank account and took my Mustang."

"What?" At that, all her earlier disappointment fled.

"Live and learn." His voice sounded casual, but his hands tightened. "I put her name on everything, so I couldn't do much legally." He started to say something else but stopped. "Like I said, live and learn. Last I heard, she'd gotten hooked hard on heroin, so it's just as well things didn't work out. People make bad choices, me included." His gaze flicked to hers. "I don't talk about my marriage because I'm embarrassed by it."

Sienna reached across the table. "I'm sorry. That's a pretty shitty story. I wouldn't tell people either."

"Does that mean you forgive me?"

She pulled off her hat and gloves. "It means I wish I'd known before Eva Hadley told me, but, yes, I forgive you."

He wound his fingers through hers. "Good."

"Do me a favor though."

"What's that?" He stroked the back of her hand with his thumb, sending tingles through her.

"If there are any other skeletons in your closet, do you think you could mention them to me before one of the Hadley sisters does?"

He paused only a half second before answering. "You got it."

Chapter Twenty-Five

He almost told her. Two or three times, Mike almost opened his mouth and told Sienna about the eight months he'd spent in prison. In the end though, he couldn't find the words. It was a leap to go from discussing the reasons behind his divorce to confessing he'd stolen enough money from his ex-wife to land a felony sentence. She'd never understand. The way Sienna looked at him, playful and sexy, put him over the moon. He didn't want that to change. Besides, he rationalized, she'd told him only to reveal any skeletons the Hadleys might tell her first, and no one knew about his prison sentence except Zane, Ma, Doc, and Al. The first three would never tell a soul. The last, he hoped, would be gone from Pine Point soon enough.

They went to dinner at a new Mexican place over in Silver Valley. He couldn't stop touching her over the table, under the table, any place he could get his hands on her.

"You're going to get us thrown out of here for indecent behavior," she said across a plate of nachos.

"I don't care." He just wanted to get as close to her as he could.

Later that night, they made love twice and then fell asleep until dawn. When the sun woke Mike, he wrapped one arm around Sienna and tucked his chin into the warmth of her neck.

"Is that a throw pillow, or are you happy to see me?" she said with a laugh. Her voice, low and sexy in the silence, turned him on all over again.

"What do you think?" He traced the length of her torso, from shoulder to hip. So gorgeous. So smart and put together. Never in his wildest dreams would he have thought someone like Sienna might wind up in his bed. In his life. Maybe the good was finally balancing out the bad after all.

I can't tell her about prison, he thought again as he snaked his arm between her legs. She moved against him and murmured. It would ruin everything. His lips went to her ear, then to her neck. He flipped her over and moved above her, sliding down the bed in slow degrees until he reached her belly. Then the soft skin inside her thigh. He ran one thumb along the crease of her leg, and her laughter turned to a quiet moan. His hands went to her thighs, pinning her against the sheets, and when she wriggled and cried out in pleasure, he smiled and took his time. This amazing experience, tasting her and feeling her come against him, he could do forever.

* * * * *

The guy's insatiable, Sienna thought as she waved goodbye to Mike and walked upstairs to her apartment. She ran her fingers over a raw spot on her neck. Not like that was a bad thing, but she hadn't come home with a hickey since college.

She unlocked her door and kicked off her boots. Then she frowned.

"This place is a disaster." Notepads, crumpled pieces of paper, jeans, socks, and scarves covered the floor. Her dirty coffee pot sat in the sink, and two towels in desperate need of washing hung over the shower rod. She'd spent so little time here the last couple of weeks, it looked like a neglected college dorm room. Sienna changed into sweats and a T-shirt, put up her hair, and spent the next hour cleaning.

Finally, she sat back on her heels and surveyed the apartment. Much better. She'd forgotten how the distraction of a new boyfriend could push everything else to the side.

Boyfriend.

Sienna stripped down and ran a hot shower. Is that what she was calling him now? She let her head fall back under the spray. They came from the same town, yes, but they lived in different worlds now. She wasn't staying in Pine Point, while he was putting down roots here. Still, the idea of having someone to call every night, to laugh with and have dinner with and, yes, have down-and-dirty, amazing sex with, came pretty close to the definition of a boyfriend. *I'll just be careful*, she decided as she toweled off and rubbed steam from the mirror. For both their sakes, she needed to.

She walked into the living room and glanced out the front window. Most weekends, you could throw a stone down the center of Main Street and not hit a thing. Pine Point residents apparently stayed tucked inside their homes on chilly weekends, not that she could blame them. She finger-combed her damp hair and considered her options for lunch. She did have some cold cuts in the fridge. She could order delivery from Gino's Pizzeria, two blocks down. Or she could venture downstairs to Zeb's.

As she weighed the pros and cons of putting on real clothes or enjoying pajamas for the rest of the day, a small red car drove into town. It slowed in front of the diner, but rather than park, the driver put on the flashers and pulled haphazardly to the curb. Sienna leaned closer to the window, but she couldn't make out the faces of the couple inside. The car looked vaguely familiar, but she couldn't place it either. A half-dozen people in town probably drove the same one. She was about to turn away when the passenger door opened, and a man stepped out. He said something to the driver, pounded a fist on the side of the door, and then scowled and walked into the diner. Sienna's eyes widened as he turned back to say something else, and she recognized the distinct face of Mac Herbert. *Wow. Really?* She couldn't imagine the laidback construction worker fighting with anyone. The car did a U-turn and pulled away, but not before she caught sight of a sticker on its back bumper.

Whoa.

Now she knew why the vehicle looked familiar. Sienna parked next to Polly Preston, and her *Vegan and Proud Of It* stickered red sedan, almost every day at work. She flattened one palm against the window. *Huh.* Mac and Polly. Driving together on a Saturday morning. Having some kind of quarrel, if Sienna had to put money on it. With a burst of new energy, she pulled on a pair of jeans and a long-sleeved shirt and headed downstairs. This looked like exactly the kind of juicy secret she'd been looking for.

"Morning, Josie," Sienna said as she walked into Zeb's a few minutes later. She pulled up a stool next to Mac. "Hi, Mac."

"Hey, Sienna." He didn't smile. Instead, he stared into his coffee.

"Surprised to see you here," Josie said as she poured a cup of decaf for Sienna. "You're not a lunch regular." She gave Mac a pointed look. "Neither are you, now that I think of it." She folded her arms on the counter. "There a full moon or something I don't know about?"

Sienna shrugged. "Just an empty refrigerator for me." She waited to hear what Mac's excuse might be.

But he didn't say anything. The only other person in the diner, one of Pine Point's local cops, sat at a table near the front door.

"I'll have a spinach and cheese omelet," Sienna said.

"BLT for me," Mac said. He hadn't looked up from his coffee.

"Hey, are you all right?" Sienna asked as Josie disappeared into the kitchen.

He shrugged.

Sienna elbowed him. "C'mon. What's going on?"

He rubbed a hand over his face. "Women."

Josie returned from the kitchen. "What about women?"

Mac looked up. "What d'ya got super-sonic hearing or something?"

"Of course. How else do you think I manage in this place? I got fourteen different people hollering at me they need water or a menu or some napkins or their burger isn't cooked right or where's the bathroom…" She stopped for a breath. "Of course I gotta hear 'em all." She folded her arms on the counter. "So what's your problem? This have anything to do with that woman who didn't want to see ya in public?"

The pieces fell together for Sienna before Mac answered. *He's been dating Polly. Or sleeping with Polly. And she doesn't want to give him the time of day or risk being seen together because she and Harmony are holding out for Mr. Rich and*

Right.

Mac nodded, a forlorn expression on his face. "Guess I gotta break it off, huh?" He spun his mug in a slow circle. "Thought she'd come around. Thought maybe—" He sneezed. "Doesn't matter. I don't think I'm good enough for her."

Josie's hand snaked across the counter. "You listen to me," she said as she squeezed his calloused palm. "You're a good man, Mac Herbert. Any woman who doesn't see that is a purebred idiot. She sounds like she's messed up in the head. I wouldn't be surprised if she has that mental illness after all. What's it called again?" she asked Sienna.

"Agoraphobia."

"Yep. That's the one." She patted Mac on the shoulder. "You keep your chin up. There's other women out there."

"Not in Pine Point," he grumbled.

She swatted him with a towel. "Ah, now you're just bein' fresh. There's plenty of women here." She walked back to the kitchen.

They sat in silence for a minute. "I'm sorry," Sienna said.

"Guess it's okay. I just really liked her, you know?"

Sienna thought of the look on Polly's face as she bent over her phone and the brusque retorts she gave Harmony from time to time. "I think she likes you too."

Mac looked over. "How do you know?"

Her face flushed. "I didn't mean…just like what Josie said. How could anyone not like you? Maybe there's more going on in her head than she's telling you."

"Why are all women like that? Why don't you just say what's on your mind, instead of making us try to figure it out?"

"I don't know," Sienna admitted. "I think men and women are wired differently, that's all."

"Well, it makes it damn hard to have a relationship."

They didn't say anything else. Mac ate his sandwich in about three bites, paid his bill, and left. The cop got an extra-large coffee to go and followed a few minutes later, and then Sienna sat alone in the diner. She pulled out her phone and made a few notes to transfer to her research, but the thrill of discovering Mac and Polly's secret had faded.

Josie scooped up Sienna's plate and empty coffee mug. "Anything else for ya?"

"No, thanks." She paused in her typing. "Do you know anything about Jenny James?" she asked on impulse. She'd written down the elementary school principal's name on her list weeks ago, but she'd added little since.

Josie unwrapped a stick of gum. "I know the family, sure. Been around Pine Point for generations."

"I just wondered how Jenny ended up working at the school. Because the rest of her family is in business, I mean."

Josie chewed with a thoughtful expression. "Well, she was the youngest of six, right?"

"That many?"

"Oh, yeah. And there was one after her that died young. Of that SIDS disease, I think. Where the baby just doesn't wake up? That happened when Jenny was five or six."

Sadness washed over Sienna. She'd had a professor in college lose a three-month-old baby girl the same way, and the grief on the man's face when he'd told the class had knifed through her.

"She was a few years behind me in school, but she always loved kids. If anyone needed a babysitter, they hired Jenny." Josie chewed some more. "She got married young, twenty-one or something like that."

"Does she have any children of her own?" Sienna realized she had no idea.

"Ah, that's the sad thing," Josie said. "She and her husband tried for years." Josie shook her head. "There's women gettin' pregnant left and right, can't even afford to feed 'em, but they got a pack of kids running along behind 'em at church or the grocery store or wherever. Then ya got someone like Jenny, who'd give her right arm to have just one, and she can't. Life ain't fair sometimes, that's for sure."

Sienna thought of Jenny's self-imposed sequestering each day at three o'clock. Did it have anything to do with her personal grief? With the ache of seeing kids run through her school each day and not having any of her own to go home to?

"The worst thing happened about a year ago," Josie went on.

"There's something worse?"

"She finally got pregnant. With twins. They'd done that fertilization thing, ya know. What's it called, where they put the fertilized egg right in ya?"

"In vitro?"

"Yeah. They went to doctors down in Albany, the whole nine yards. The day she walked in here and told me she was carryin' twins, I'd never seen her so happy. She was glowin'." Josie's face fell. "She carried 'em all the way to five months. She was at work an' miscarried. Ambulance had to come right to the school an' take her to the hospital." Josie lifted her shoulders. "Wasn't meant to be, I guess."

"That's terrible." Sienna reached for her wallet and pulled out a few bills as her omelet churned in her stomach. The principal's afternoon sadness and red eyes made sense now.

It's odd, Sienna thought as she flipped through her yellow notepads later that night. She'd never stopped to consider what turning up secrets might mean outside her dissertation. Ella feeding stray cats. Josie writing love poems. Mac and Polly sneaking around behind closed doors. Jenny mourning the loss of her unborn children. Mike marrying, divorcing, and building a new life. *There are people attached to secrets.* It seemed ludicrous she hadn't realized that before, but she hadn't. *People and feelings and motives we don't always understand from the outside.*

She put her notepad aside, curled up in the recliner, and watched as fresh snow began to fall outside.

Chapter Twenty-Six

For almost two weeks, Sienna didn't do one ounce of research. She set her notepads on the floor beside her recliner and focused instead on school. Her students. And Mike. He came to class each Friday at two, so punctual Caleb waited for him at the door and Billy and Bailey had his books picked out and waiting by the rocker.

"You're good with them," she said one Friday in early March. "They like you."

"I like them," he said as they watched the students prepare for dismissal. Silas trotted over with papers falling out of his backpack, and Mike straightened them and zipped up the pack before helping Silas slip the straps over his shoulders. "I didn't think I would," he added.

"Really? What's not to like about a bunch of eight-year-olds?"

"It's not them." He gestured at the chalkboard and her bulletin board. "It's school. I was never much good at it."

"You're good now."

"Reading picture books to kids who can't? I hope I am."

"They can read. Caleb and Dawn can anyway."

He caught her hand in his, behind the desk so the kids wouldn't see. "I didn't mean that."

"Good." Together they walked the class out to the buses and ignored Eva Hadley's stare as they passed the visitors' desk.

"See you tonight at six?" Sienna asked.

"Can't wait." He kissed her on the cheek, and she floated into the office six inches above the ground.

"He's been spending a lot of time here," Hillary said.

"Mike? Yes." She fished out a stack of progress reports she needed to complete over the weekend. "That isn't a problem, I hope?"

"It's no problem at all." Jenny James stood in her open office doorway. Her eyes watered, but she smiled. "It's nice to have people from the outside come and visit, especially our special needs kids."

Funny. Sienna hadn't thought about them that way in a while. Everyone had special needs of some kind, didn't they? "Oh, I wanted to ask you about taking them to the town park later on, when the weather warms up. Can we walk there?" she asked Jenny. "It's only a couple of blocks."

"As long as you get permission slips from all the parents, then, yes. I think that would be wonderful."

Sienna thought so too.

* * * * *

The following week, March surprised everyone with near-record temperatures. Mike checked the weather report three times before leaving the gym, and when it still predicted a high of sixty-five with zero precipitation, he grabbed two gloves and baseballs from his office before driving to Pine Point Elementary.

"Thought we might do a little preseason training," he said when he walked into Room Eighteen. He held up the gloves. Silas almost fell out of the rocking chair, and his eyes lit up. He ran to Mike and took one of the gloves, stroking the soft leather, and laying it next to his cheek.

"Mr. Mike, we always do read-alongs on Fridays at two o'clock," Caleb informed him with a worried expression. He turned to Sienna. "Miss Cruz, we always—"

"I know," she said. She put one hand on his shoulder and steered him to a seat at the table. "But since the weather's so nice today, how about we read two books instead of three, and then if there's time, we'll go outside and play catch."

Caleb eyed her with doubt, but he didn't say anything else. After Mike had finished *Where the Wild Things Are* and *I'm Going to the World Series!*, he picked up a glove again. "Who can tell me what this part is?" he asked as he ran his fingers over the inside.

"Pocket!" Silas called out. He clapped and beamed.

"You're right. That's where we always want to catch the ball." Mike picked up a ball in his other hand. "Now, does anyone know why baseballs have stitches on them?"

Silas grew sober. Caleb's face screwed up in concentration. No one answered.

"Well, one thing the stitches do is keep the inside part where it's supposed to be. There's a center of rubber inside this leather, but the rubber has to stay on the inside."

"Can you imagine if our insides were on the outside?" Sienna asked the class.

"Ewww!" said one of the twins.

"We don't have stitches, but what do we have?" she asked.

"Skin," Caleb answered. "Lots of it."

"Right." Mike said with a grin and tried not to think about Sienna's perfect skin, or how it tasted after a shower. "The second thing the stitches do is give the pitcher control when he's throwing the ball. He can hold the ball a certain way, and spin the ball a certain way, to make the stitches catch the air and move."

The boys stared without speaking.

"Too much?" Mike asked in a low voice.

Sienna smiled. "Maybe. Let's skip the mechanics for today and just take advantage of this sunshine." She clapped her hands three times. "I want everyone to put on their coats and line up at the door. We have fifteen minutes before dismissal, and Mr. Mike is going to go outside with us and show us how to throw and catch a baseball."

The boys tumbled over each other in their eagerness. Dawn moved at a slower pace. By the time she joined them at the door, the others had already inched their way into the hall and toward the back door.

They were the only ones on the playground, which made it easy to pair up and practice throwing. Silas took one glove, Mike kept the other, and the twins and Caleb took turns throwing the ball to them both.

"Not bad," Mike said. He struggled to keep from laughing every time a toss went wild. Billy had the least control of them all. Most of his throws ended up in the weeds or under a tree ten feet behind Mike. But no one seemed to care. Bailey retrieved them, and sometimes Caleb measured the distance of the errant throw by striding to the tree and back, doing calculations in his head.

"They're a funny bunch, aren't they?" he said to Sienna as she reined them in after ten minutes. "I don't mean funny bad." He wasn't sure what he meant.

"Yes, they are," she agreed. "But they're my funny bunch." She took his arm. "And yours too, now that you're spending so much time with them."

He smiled, the sun warm on his face. The boys lined up at the back door, waiting for Sienna to let them back inside. "Where's Dawn?" he asked suddenly. He looked around, but she'd disappeared.

Sienna puffed out a breath. "She does this a lot." She shaded her eyes. "Dawn! Honey, it's time for dismissal. Time to come inside."

Mike scanned the edge of the playground, the swings, the slides, the thick trees at the border. A chain-link fence circled the whole space, so she couldn't have wandered off completely. He stuck the gloves under one arm and dropped the balls to his feet. "Go ahead," he said to Sienna. "I'll look for her."

Sienna hesitated, but when Caleb tugged at her sleeve to inform her they had two minutes until dismissal, she hurried the boys inside.

"Dawn?" He traced a path from the open grassy area where they'd been playing to the edge of the school building. When he turned the corner, he saw her. "Hey, buddy."

She looked at him with huge brown eyes and said nothing.

"Whatcha doing over here?" Inside, the bell rang, and he could hear the roar of bus engines on the other side of the building. Dawn's gaze cut to the driveway, and fear flicked across her face.

Mike settled himself on the ground, thinking six feet of adult male might be a little intimidating for the little girl. "Ah, don't worry about the buses. You know Miss Cruz will make sure they wait for you." He had no idea if that was true. He hoped it was.

She dragged her fingers along the side of the brick building.

"You ever play baseball before?" he asked, more to hear himself talk than anything. "Or go to a baseball game? They're a lot of fun." An idea struck him. "Maybe we could all go to a game in the spring. There's a minor league team over in Silver Valley. The Panthers."

The back door opened, and Sienna stepped outside. She lifted her brows in a silent question, and Mike nodded. Sienna walked over to join them.

"Dawn, your bus driver is waiting for you. Are you ready to go home?"

Her gaze slid over Mike before she looked at Sienna and nodded. Sienna held out her hand, but the little girl didn't take it. She took a wide berth past both of them and walked back to the school on her own.

"Boy, she's a tough one, isn't she?" Mike said as he hauled himself up to stand.

"You have no idea. My biggest fear is she's going to do that, just disappear one day, and I won't be able to find her."

"You know why she does it?"

Sienna shook her head as they followed Dawn to Room Eighteen and watched her pack her backpack. "Maybe a safety thing? If no one can see her, no one can hurt her? It's my best guess. I have a meeting scheduled with her foster parents next week, but to be honest, they haven't shed much light on anything so far."

Mike rubbed the back of his neck. It made sense. He knew as well as anyone that trusting people could end in a world of hurt. It was just too bad an eight-year-old felt the same way. Dawn walked to the door and stopped.

"Honey, your bus is waiting," Sienna said. She gave Dawn a gentle nudge.

The little girl stood in the hallway for a long moment, studying Mike. She didn't say a word. Her expression didn't change. But she lifted a hand and waved at him in a stiff, awkward motion.

Then she was gone.

Chapter Twenty-Seven

"Can you believe it? I can't. She's never done that for anyone. Not me, not the principal, not Loni..." Sienna hadn't come down from the high of Dawn's brief wave at Mike.

Mike looked over from the driver's side of his pickup. "Clearly, she knows a good guy when she sees one."

"You *are* a good guy." Sienna leaned her head against the back of the seat. "I don't know what you did, or how, but you got to her." She reached over and took his hand. "You have no idea how big that is."

"I have kind of an idea. Since you've been talking about it nonstop since it happened."

She squeezed his fingers and stuck out her tongue.

He lifted a brow as he pulled into the parking lot behind Jimmy's. "Don't tease me."

She unfastened her seat belt and crawled onto his lap. "Are you sure? I thought you liked being teased." Her hand went to the button on his jeans while she ran her lips along his neck. He let out a sigh and curved one arm around her. He tugged her hair gently and slid one hand underneath her coat.

"I do," he murmured in the quiet chill. "I like teasing you even more."

She buried her face in the warmth of his jacket, which smelled like soap and faint cologne. She knew at least in part why Dawn had warmed to Mike. He made a girl feel safe. Cared for. Like he would take the world head-on if he needed to and rip it in half before it hurt anyone he cared about.

"We should probably get some dinner," he whispered into her hair.

She lifted her head. "Okay. But we're picking up where we left off when we get back in this truck." She slid her hand down his leg, and he grinned.

"It's a deal."

Nate Hunter waved them over to two stools at the bar when they walked in. He squeezed Mike's hand in hello and winked at Sienna. "Hello, beautiful. Good to see you." He tossed down coasters and produced two wrinkled paper menus. "Got a local band coming in at nine, if you like alternative rock."

"I'm hoping we'll be making our own kind of music by then," Mike murmured into Sienna's ear, and she smiled despite the corny comment. She felt shaken up, fizzy and fine and happy with everything.

Mike took their coats and carried them to the rack in the corner, stopping on his way back to talk to some guys Sienna didn't know. She studied the menu and sipped the martini Nate brought her. "Yum. This is perfect."

"Thank you." He turned his Yankees baseball cap backwards. "So I hear you're almost a professor."

"I don't know about that."

"You're working on your dissertation, right?"

She nodded. Nate took two empty beer mugs from a customer and sloshed them into a sink filled with soapy water. "What's it on? If you don't mind my asking?"

"Personality psychology."

He squinted in puzzlement.

"I'm trying to show how environment shapes the way people develop."

"Ah." He set the glasses on a drying rack and refilled the wine glass of the woman beside her. "And you're here because you think small-town environments shape people in significant ways? A case study on good ol' Pine Point?"

"Something like that."

Nate whistled. "You should stand on this side of the bar for a night. You'd find out everything you need to know about the people here and then some." He shook his head. "Half the stuff I hear and know, I don't want to."

Sienna could believe that. She scanned the pub, growing more crowded by the minute. Polly and Harmony stood near the door. No big surprise there. They hadn't even gotten their coats off, and Harmony was flirting with a guy with a graying beard and temples. Polly checked her phone and looked miserable.

"Nate, I'll have a plate of nachos to start," Sienna said. "I'll be back in a minute." She shrugged off her sweater and left it draped over her stool.

"Sure thing."

She wound her way through the crowd until she reached Polly and Harmony, surprised to see they'd dressed completely different from each other. Harmony wore winter-white jeans and a pale blue sweater cut halfway down to her navel, while Polly wore the same clothes she'd had on at school, maroon corduroys and a black T-shirt. Her mascara was smudged, and her bottom lip chapped. Sienna took her elbow and steered her away from her friend.

"Can I give you some advice?"

Polly looked startled. "About what?"

"Don't listen to your friend when it comes to men."

Polly crossed her arms. "I don't know what you're talking about."

Please. "Listen. We both know Harmony's got this whole I-have-to-find-the-perfect-rich-husband-or-I'll-die thing going on." She looked over her shoulder. Harmony tossed her hair and reapplied lipstick as she cooed up at whoever the guy of the night was.

"She doesn't really…" Polly trailed off.

Sienna gave her a look. "You and I both know there's no such thing as the perfect guy. Or that being rich means he'll be the perfect husband." She tried to figure out her next words without betraying Mac's confidence. "All I'm saying is, if you meet a guy you like, and he doesn't make a million dollars or own a yacht, don't immediately write him off."

One corner of Polly's mouth lifted. She swiped at the black smudges under her eyes with one thumb. "I guess a yacht wouldn't really be practical in Pine Point."

"But a pickup truck would be." Sienna winked. "As well as a guy who knows how to build your dream house from the ground up."

Polly's mouth dropped open. *You know?* her eyes seemed to ask. Sienna squeezed her arm and walked away. Some secrets, she decided, were meant to be kept.

*****

Mike couldn't wait to get out of there. More and more people filled Jimmy's in anticipation of the band, and by quarter to nine, he couldn't turn around without jostling someone's elbow or having someone step on his feet. He finally touched the small of Sienna's back. *"You ready to go?"* he mouthed, and she nodded.

"Too much of a crowd for me," he said as they walked to the truck.

"Me too. I'm glad for the place though. Nate'll make good tips tonight."

Mike nodded and helped her into the passenger side, letting his hands linger a little longer than necessary on her hips. His groin stirred. He couldn't wait to get her back to his place. Sienna must have had other ideas though, because as soon as he got into the truck, she had her hands in his hair and her mouth skating across his lips and neck.

"Whoa…" he began, but she nibbled his bottom lip before he could get anything else out. And why would he want to? If she wanted a little fun right here and now, he wasn't about to argue. He fumbled with the seat and managed to lay it back a few inches. She began unbuttoning his shirt, one slow movement at a time.

"You know this isn't the most private place," he said with a grin.

She tilted her head and continued to unbutton him, not stopping when she reached his jeans. "So?" She reached inside to take him in her hands.

Mike's eyes closed. *Ah, hell.* So good, the way she stroked him. His hips moved in rhythm with her motions, and though they had little room, the awkward close quarters of the truck, his elbow bumping the door and his knee pressed against the dashboard only turned him on more. When she sank down to take him into her mouth, it took less than a minute before he exploded.

"Ahhh—fuck!" His heart leaped out of his chest, and he looked down at her in wonder. "You didn't have to do that."

She licked her lips. "I know I didn't. I wanted to." She ran her hands along his thighs, still clad in jeans, then up the ridges of his pulsing cock. "Kind of fun, right?"

More than fun. He nodded, his breath unsteady. He stroked her hair, catching the curls in his rough callouses. "God, I could fall in love with you right now." The words came out before he knew it. Heat flooded his face. "Shit. I didn't—"

She sat up and pushed her hair behind her ears. Her eyes grew huge in the dim light from outside.

He pressed his lips together and did his best to tuck himself back into his boxers, not an easy feat while still hard. "I didn't mean that like—" He scrubbed his face with one hand. "Forget it."

She slid over to her side of the truck and took his fingers in his. "This is getting pretty intense, isn't it? Considering we were going to just be friends."

But he didn't want that anymore. He wanted more. He wanted all of this, seeing her at school and taking her to dinner and messing around in his truck like they were teenagers and had the world ahead of them. He cleared his throat. "Would you ever think about staying?"

"In Pine Point?" She took forever to answer. "I don't think so." She traced a random pattern on the window and looked away from him. "It's not my home."

"Of course it is. You grew up here. You came back here."

"My mother died here. I spent one hell of an unhappy childhood here."

He turned on the truck without another word and revved the engine.

"Please don't be mad."

"I'm not." Frustrated, yes. Disappointed, hell yes. But how could he be mad? He left the parking lot and turned up Main Street, away from his house. He didn't explain, and she didn't ask. When he parked in front of the diner a few minutes later, she leaned over and kissed him on the cheek.

"Talk tomorrow? After we both sleep on it?"

He nodded and pulled away without watching her go inside. He couldn't. As it was, he couldn't draw a breath without feeling like something inside him had broken.

Shouldn't have said that about falling in love with her. He pounded the steering wheel as he accelerated out of town, past Park Place Run and Mountain Glen and up the road that led to Silver Valley. At the top of the mountain, he glanced down and saw the speedometer needle hovering over ninety.

He screeched to a stop and then pulled to the shoulder of the road. Sweat broke out on his forehead, and he put down the window for some air. The warm day had turned to a mild night, and he drew in long, cooling breaths. *She's just a woman. Don't get so worked up about it. Doesn't matter. Nothing matters. You were never getting married again anyway.* He curled and uncurled his fingers around the steering wheel. He could lie to himself all he wanted. Sienna Cruz was far from just another woman, and every inch of him knew it. He did a U-turn and drove back down the mountain. So he could man up and talk to her about how he felt, or he could pretend he was twenty-two again and be the idiot who turned his back on something great.

He passed Jimmy's Watering Hole at almost ten. With his window still down, he could hear the band clear as day. Cars lined both sides of Main Street, and he had to slow as people dodged between them on their way to the bar. He dimmed his headlights and idled, waiting as a group passed in front of his truck. He was about to pull ahead when a single man stepped off the curb. He put up an arm to shield himself from Mike's headlights. Then he stopped and stared. A crooked smile broke out on his face, and Al Halloran walked over to Mike's open window.

"Fancy meeting you here."

Mike tasted something sour in the back of his mouth. "What the fuck are you still doing in town?" He glanced into the rearview mirror as headlights approached from behind.

"I live here."

"Where? You're not staying with your dad, I know that for a fact."

Al shrugged. "You're not the only one with friends in town."

Mike pushed the button to raise the window, but Al put a hand out before he could. "I wouldn't be such a dick to me if I were you."

"No?" Mike stared straight ahead. "Why's that?"

"Because from what I've heard, people here don't have a clue about why you really came back to Pine Point."

"I came back to open a gym and take care of my mom."

Al burst out laughing. "Sure you did."

Mike's ears burned, and before he knew it, he'd grabbed Al's collar and yanked him halfway through the window. "Listen to me. You say a word to anyone, and I'll make sure you never open your mouth again. You've got as much at stake as I do if people find out." That wasn't true, and they both knew it. But they also both knew Mike could make Al's life more miserable than it was if he ran his mouth.

Al wriggled free. The smile and the laugh disappeared. "Hey, I'm just trying to start over, same as you. Get myself a job, a place to live, maybe a cute little piece of ass like Sienna Cruz…"

Mike seethed but kept his mouth shut. A car pulled up behind him and beeped.

"'Course, maybe you two are meant for each other," Al went on. "Both got some history you don't want people knowing."

"What the hell are you talking about?" Mike put his truck into gear and raised a hand at the driver behind him. *Don't worry. I was just leaving.*

"Ask Sienna how her mother died."

"I know how her mother died." *And who the fuck are you to bring that up?*

Al shrugged and backed away. "She was awfully young to have a heart attack, right? Usually that only happens to people who are shooting or smoking or popping pills. They get so much shit in their blood that their heart either works overtime tryin' to keep up, or just slows down 'til it quits for good."

Mike stared at the spot in Al's mouth where a tooth belonged. His stomach churned.

"All I'm sayin' is, ask Sienna what was in her mom's system the day they brought her in. You might be surprised."

Chapter Twenty-Eight

I could fall in love with you right now…

Sienna tossed and turned all night. Mike couldn't have meant that. He'd been caught up in the excitement of the day, in the nice weather and baseball and the headiness of an orgasm. She stared at her ceiling. What if he *had* meant it? She had no plans to stay in Pine Point. She couldn't let herself get attached to him. Loving someone meant losing them, because no one stuck around forever. She threw one arm over her face and told herself the ache in her chest came from her earlier martini and the nachos, not from pushing her feelings down deep where they couldn't hurt her.

"Let's meet for lunch," he texted around seven the next morning. She ran her thumb over the screen and thought of a half-dozen responses. Finally, she typed, *"I have a ton of stuff to do. See you at the gym?"*

He replied with a thumbs-up, and she didn't hear from him again until late on Sunday.

"Tabata and meditation at five if you're interested."

Sienna picked up her phone from the floor. She'd spent almost the entire weekend on her research, organizing notes, making new ones, and drafting the first part of her dissertation. If she planned to finish by May, she needed to light a fire under herself. She stretched her arms overhead. Yes, a workout sounded good. Plus, she couldn't avoid Mike forever. She didn't want to. She changed into black workout pants and a baggy T-shirt and walked the mile and a half to Springer Fitness.

He sat behind the desk at his computer. When she walked in, he smiled.

"Wasn't sure you'd make it."

"I did."

They didn't say anything else for the next forty minutes. He pushed her harder than she'd pushed herself in weeks, until sweat dripped from her eyebrows and her elbows and everything in between. Before the last round, she pulled off her T-shirt and tossed it aside. "Sorry." She panted as she tugged her black and pink sports bra into place. "But I'm dying here."

"Don't be sorry." His gaze raked her torso, and she drank in his appreciation. She might not be falling in love with Mike, but she sure did like him a lot.

After they stretched and collapsed onto their mats for meditation, she closed her eyes and sighed. "I needed that."

"Good." He turned off the lights in the fitness room and sat beside her. He directed their first few breaths, but then he grew silent, and all she heard was the sound of their tandem inhalations.

She opened one eye after a couple minutes and caught Mike looking at her. "Hey. I thought we were meditating. It hasn't been ten minutes yet, has it?"

"Nope." He lifted both palms in a gesture of surrender. "I just couldn't help myself."

At that, she leaned over and kissed him. Salty and certain, his tongue slipped along hers. One hand went to the back of her head.

"I'm sorry I freaked out the other night," she said against his lips.

"It's okay. I came on a little strong." He ran his fingers down her cheek. "I don't want to lose you, for however long you're here."

She closed her eyes and rested her forehead on his shoulder. "I don't either."

He kissed her temple and then pulled her up. "What do you say I close up and we hit the showers?"

"Together?"

He gave her the wicked grin she loved, the one that curled her toes. "Of course together." He grabbed his mat and tossed it on the pile in the corner. "Race you there."

* * * * *

The students talked about Mike and baseball all week long. Even spats of mid-week rain couldn't keep them from practicing under the tiny pavilion with gloves Silas's father brought in for everyone.

"Miss Cruz, watch me!" Billy called.

"That's much better, honey," she said as only a few tosses went wild.

Caleb turned out to be the most accurate of them all, which didn't surprise her. He came in each morning telling her about the books he'd read at home the night before, about angles and speed and the difference between all the pitches.

"Mr. Mike is certainly going to be impressed," she told him. To her surprise, Caleb looked her straight in the eye as he responded.

"I'm glad he visits our class."

"Me too, honey." She looked at her brood, the whole funny bunch, as Mike called them. In weeks, they'd progressed more than she would have guessed. Now they talked to other students in the cafeteria and in the halls, and last week she'd caught Bailey playing tag with a group of fourth graders. Even Dawn stood with them under the pavilion, not throwing or catching, but holding a baseball in her hands. She turned it over and over, stroking the stitches with one thumb.

"Miss Cruz, Mr. Mike said he'd take us to a baseball game," Caleb said as they walked inside at the end of the day on Thursday. "There's a minor league team in Silver Valley, and they start their season on April sixth. He said we could go."

"Well, yes, but I'll have to make arrangements with the school and your parents," she said.

"I already told my parents," Caleb went on. "My dad said he would come with us if we needed a chaperon."

"You tell him thank you, and I'll give him a call to talk about it, okay?" She clapped her hands. "Five minutes to dismissal. That means everyone needs to pack up so I can check bags before you go."

"Miss Cruz, can we play baseball the whole time tomorrow instead of having read-along?" Bailey asked.

"I'm not sure, honey." She glanced at Caleb, who had frozen halfway through organizing his backpack. "Maybe just one book and then we'll play baseball. Fridays at two is always read-along, so we don't want to give that up entirely."

Caleb began to breathe again.

"We'll ask Mr. Mike what he thinks when he comes tomorrow, okay?"

"Okay."

But Mike didn't show up the following day. By one o'clock, the students had already chosen his book, *Forty-Two: Why We Remember Jackie Robinson*. Billy and Bailey were coloring pictures of famous baseball players, and Caleb was working on a math worksheet two grade levels up. Dawn kept looking at the door until Sienna steered her to a beanbag chair and gave her a book to read. At ten minutes to two, she gathered them all on the carpet. The last few days of rain had cleared for a glorious Friday, with sunshine and temperatures nearing sixty again. She couldn't wait to go outside. More than that, she couldn't wait to see Mike. They'd had a quick dinner Tuesday night and they talked every day, but he'd been busy with the gym, setting up spring advertising and hiring new instructors. Since the weekend, he'd also seemed oddly preoccupied.

"Everything okay?" she texted him last night.

"Yeah," he responded almost thirty minutes later. *"Just a lot on my mind."*

"Anything you want to talk about?"

"Not this time. Thanks though. XO"

At five after two, she checked her phone. It wasn't like him to be late.

At ten after two, Caleb left his seat and walked to the door. "Mr. Mike isn't here," he announced with concern. "He's eleven minutes late."

"I know, honey. But sometimes that happens. Maybe he got caught in traffic or at work." She sent him a quick text. *"Everything okay? Kids are waiting to play catch with you."* But she heard nothing in return.

At twenty after two, she stumbled her way through the Jackie Robinson story, despite the fact that no one was listening. She finally put the book aside and clapped her hands. "Let's go out to the playground for the last twenty minutes." She checked her phone again. No text or call. *What the hell had happened to him?*

"But Mr. Mike isn't here," Bailey said.

"I know." She forced a cheery tone into her voice. "But we can practice without him. That way we'll surprise him the next time he comes." With that, Sienna led her students outside and tried to ignore the niggling fear that something was very wrong.

Chapter Twenty-Nine

"Ma? Ma!" Mike took the front steps two at a time. "Where are—" He snapped off at the sight of Loretta sitting in a kitchen chair. Her right foot rested on a pillow, the ankle swollen to twice its normal size.

"I'm fine," she said, her face white.

Doc Halloran looked up as he dumped ice cubes into a plastic bag. "She's not fine. She has an ankle that's most likely broken and a wrist that might be sprained. She won't go to the Med Center with me or in an ambulance, so I'm hoping you can convince her otherwise."

Mike kneeled and touched the puffy skin of her ankle. "What happened?"

She waved a hand as if they were both overreacting. "I wanted to get some things out of storage."

"In the garage? And you fell. Didn't I tell you—"

"I didn't fall. The ladder shifted. I just missed the last step coming down and twisted my ankle."

He touched her right wrist, puffy as well.

"I caught myself with that hand," she said with a huff. "It's fine."

"Thanks for coming," Mike said to Doc as he stood.

"I'm glad I was driving by." Doc handed Mike the ice pack, who settled it onto his mother's ankle. She winced.

"Me too." Mike reached into his pocket for his cell phone. He'd missed his visit to Sienna's class by almost an hour. "Damn." He realized a moment later he'd left his phone charging in his office at the gym. He'd run out the front door the minute he'd gotten the call from Doc.

The doctor helped Loretta up. "Can you put any weight on the foot?"

She tried but shook her head. "And my…" She put a hand on her lower back. "I think I might have tweaked a muscle. I'll lie down on the couch and ice that too."

"Absolutely not." Mike put his arm around her waist. "We're going straight to the Med Center. And, no," he said before she could interrupt. "This is not negotiable."

Doc followed them outside. "Do you want to take my car? It'd be more comfortable."

Mike took one look at his own truck and nodded. "That'd be great. Thank you."

"No problem." Doc helped Loretta into the front seat and handed Mike the keys.

"Take my truck," Mike said.

Doc shook his head and ambled down the driveway. "I was on my way home." He tilted his face back to look at the sky. "It's a beautiful day for walking."

"Well, thanks again." Mike climbed into the sleek leather interior of the Mercedes and adjusted the seat and the mirrors. "How are you feeling?"

"Like an idiot." She rested her head against the seat and closed her eyes. "I'm sorry to pull you away from work."

"Don't be. Hans and the trainers have it under control."

"What about Sienna's class?" she asked as they drove toward the Med Center. "Weren't you supposed to visit them today?"

He checked the dashboard clock. Three-fifteen. "Yes, but she'll understand." Angst itched inside him at not being able to tell Sienna what had happened. His mother didn't have a cell phone, but he'd call Sienna from the Med Center as soon as he got Ma checked in. He patted her leg. "Stop worrying about everyone else. Let people take care of you for once."

They rode a few minutes in silence. As they neared the Med Center, Mike glanced over. "So was Doc really just driving by?"

"Of course." She narrowed her eyes. "What are you suggesting?"

"Nothing." He hid his smile at the blush that colored her cheeks. "Just glad he was there so fast after it happened, that's all." He slowed and put on his blinker. Traffic, heavy for Pine Point, stretched in the opposite direction. *Friday afternoon rush hour*, he thought as he drummed his thumbs on the steering wheel. Nothing compared to Los Angeles though. Thank God, not much here compared to Los Angeles, including the people and the women and his life now.

A gap appeared in the traffic, and he stepped on the gas ahead of a red sports car—Sienna's, he realized too late to beep or wave hello. Damn. He went to tap the horn, to get her attention somehow, but she followed the curve of road and was gone before he could.

Frustrated, he pulled into the Emergency entrance and left the car running. He hurried around and helped Loretta hobble inside. "Sit," he said as he found her a vacant seat. He gathered the required clipboard of paperwork from the receptionist, gave it to his mom, and then parked the car.

"You can go back to work," Loretta said as he joined her a minute later.

"Absolutely not. Let me just call Hans and let him know what's going on. I'll be right back." Funny how not having a cell phone could hamstring a person these days. The receptionist wouldn't let him use the desk phone, and the Med Center didn't seem to have a public one anywhere he could see. Finally, he found a gym member waiting with her sick daughter who let him use hers. He checked in with Hans, went to call Sienna, and realized he didn't know her number by heart. Another damn consequence of cell phones. He thought about calling Hans back and asking him to send Sienna a text from his phone, but that seemed awkward, especially since he'd spent the last month telling the kid not to get overly attached to a woman.

He dropped back next to Ma and folded his hands between his legs.

"Did you get ahold of Sienna?"

He shook his head. "It's okay. I will."

Loretta patted his leg. "She's a nice girl. Turned into a beautiful woman. I'm glad you're spending time with her."

Mike's cheeks flushed as he stared at the floor between his feet. I'm glad too. Yet he hadn't stopped thinking about Al's ugly accusations from almost a week ago. *"All I'm sayin' is, ask Sienna what was in her mother's system the day they brought her in..."*

"Honey?" Loretta stroked his back. "You're awfully quiet. Everything okay?"

He looked up. "You were with Sienna's mother the day she died, right?"

She blinked in surprise. "Well, yes, but where did that question come from?"

He cracked his knuckles. "I heard something the other day."

"You'll have to be a little more specific than that. Heard something about what? Elenita?"

He looked around the room. Most other people waiting were staring at their phones or slouched down in their chairs, eyes closed.

He lowered his voice. "Was there anything odd about her death?"

Loretta's eyes bored into him. She didn't answer.

Fingers of dread climbed up the back of Mike's neck. "Al Halloran told me the other night—I ran into him outside Jimmy's—he told me she had something in her system, drugs or something..." He couldn't stop himself from babbling. "Can't be right. Can it? Sienna's mom? She would've told me."

Or not. How quickly had Mike confessed his own dark past?

"You worked with her that summer," he went on. "You saw her almost every day, right?" He'd been out in California by then, so all he'd heard were a few words through the grapevine. Never drugs. Never the hint of any kind of wrongdoing.

After an interminable silence, her expression changed to sadness. "Elenita had terrible back pain that spring," she said. "Doc prescribed OxyContin for it."

He nodded. "Sienna told me that much. But she said it made her sick. She said her mom hated taking it."

"At first, yes. But it helped her pain, and after a while, she couldn't work without it."

Understanding dawned on him in slow degrees.

"She collapsed one afternoon when we were working together at one of the summer homes halfway to Silver Valley." Tears rose to her eyes. "I didn't know what had happened. I was upstairs, and she was in the kitchen. By the time I found her, by the time we got here, she hadn't been breathing for almost thirty minutes." Her gaze moved to the reception desk and the curtained room behind it. "Doc asked me to stay with Sienna when she arrived. She didn't have anyone else, no relatives close by." She pressed Mike's leg. "I was never going to tell that girl her mother had died of a drug overdose." She shook her head. "Besides, I don't know if that was the official cause. Elenita did have a heart attack on the table as they were trying to revive her. Doc told me that much. He said that would be recorded as the official cause of death."

Loretta took Mike's hand in hers. "I don't know how Al would have found out about the drugs, or why he'd be cruel enough to mention it to you."

He spent enough time sneaking through his father's office every time he came back east, Mike wanted to answer. Didn't surprise him at all. Drugs, confidential patient records, eavesdropped phone calls, whatever Al could put his hands on, he would have. As far as the cruelty, well, Mike had seen enough of Al's true colors to know the guy didn't have a decent bone in his body.

"Don't bring it up to her," Loretta said as a nurse came to help her into one of the treatment rooms. "There's no reason." She pinned him with the no-nonsense look he recalled from his childhood. "Michael Anthony, you keep that firmly in your head. Maybe Sienna knows, and maybe she doesn't. If she didn't tell you, she had her reasons. Some secrets need to be kept."

Chapter Thirty

Sienna stopped by Springer Fitness long enough for Hans to tell her Mike had rushed home because his mother had fallen and hurt herself. Then she jumped back into her car and headed to Cornwall Road as fast as she could. *Hope it's nothing serious.* She scanned the road for his truck as she drove, but she didn't pass it in the ten short miles out of town. When she pulled into the Springer driveway, it sat in front of the garage.

Thank God. They're still here. If it had been serious, he would have taken Loretta to the Med Center. She ran up the front steps and knocked.

No one answered. Sienna frowned, cupped her hands around her eyes, and peered through the window beside the door. Inside looked neat and tidy. She knocked again, but no one came to the door. She checked her phone. Still no response to the three texts and two voicemail messages she'd left. *If I were paranoid, I'd start to think he is avoiding me.* She stepped back and crossed her arms. Maybe they'd called an ambulance? New anxiety built inside her. He would have left his truck in that case. She pulled at her bottom lip.

"You looking for Mike?" An unfamiliar male voice came from behind her.

She turned. A white pickup, salt-stained and rusted around the wheels, idled at the bottom of the driveway. An arm waved from the window. She couldn't see the man's face. Sienna gave the Springer house one more look and then walked to the truck.

"I am, actually. You know where I could find him?"

The window rolled all the way down, and Sienna recognized the grizzled face of the man who'd come into the diner a few weeks earlier. She didn't recall his name. He stuck out his hand. "Al Halloran. Nice to meet you."

"Hi. Sienna Cruz."

He nodded. "You're teaching over at the school, right? Lucy Foster's class?"

"Yes." She hadn't thought of them as Lucy's class in a long time. *They're my class now.* "Anyway, it's no big deal. I can catch up with Mike later on."

"You're doin' research, right?" Al went on. "Heard that at Jimmy's the other night. You're studying Pine Point and the people who live here."

Sienna scraped one toe along the muddy ground. When he put it like that, it sounded as if she had a giant microscope up in the sky, and everyone down on the ground was an insignificant ant. "Kind of."

Al's gaze shifted over her shoulder. "You picked a good person to study."

Sienna frowned. "I don't follow."

"Most of the people who live here don't do much. Grow up here, go to school, get a job, have kids, die and get buried here."

She put on what she hoped was a gracious smile and took a step toward her car. The last thing she needed was to listen to a stranger babble on.

"At least people like Mike leave." He ran his tongue over his bottom lip. "'Course, then they make decisions that might not turn out to be the smartest. He tell you about his time living in L.A.?"

"Yes."

"And his ex-wife?"

She hated that word. She hated the darkness on Mike's face whenever he said it. "Yes, but—"

Al shook his head. "Can't believe someone as smart as you are would be spending time with Mike Springer, to be honest."

Sienna's hackles rose. "What's that supposed to mean?"

"You know he spent time in prison, right?"

All the blood left her body. She felt it run through her stomach, down her legs, and out her feet. "No." *I asked him to be honest with me.*

"Felony theft," Al added. "That's a pretty serious crime. Not like he ran a stop sign or forgot to pay a few parking tickets. Seems to me you could do a lot better than someone like that."

Sienna's throat closed. She hadn't studied law, but she was pretty sure felony theft meant Mike had stolen a large amount of money. Not a wallet. Not a hundred dollars. Thousands and maybe tens of thousands of dollars or property. Why would he do that? *Could* he have done that? *Al could be lying,* Sienna thought through her fog, but for what reason?

"Anyway," he went on, "I think I saw him driving my dad's car in the direction of the Med Center. Looked like his mom was in the passenger seat, so I'm thinking you might want to head over there."

He said something else, but Sienna didn't hear the rest of his words. "Thank you." On stiff legs, she walked to her car as Al rolled up his window and drove away.

You wanted secrets, a voice inside her whispered. She got into her car and sat there without moving. *You came here to prove this town had all kinds of darkness on the inside.* Sienna bent her head over the steering wheel and fought to keep her lunch where it belonged. *Yes, but I didn't think those secrets would belong to people I love.*

She mashed her lips together and turned the key in the ignition. *No.* She absolutely, positively, did not love Mike Springer. Tears rose in her eyes. Apparently, she didn't even know him.

An hour later, maybe more, maybe less, she had no idea, Sienna parked outside Zeb's Diner. She'd driven past the Pine Point Med Center three times. Each time, she'd broken out in a cold sweat. *Last time I was here was the day my mother died.* She didn't care that Mike and Loretta might be inside. She couldn't go in. She couldn't even stop in the parking lot. Finally, she drove toward Silver Valley just to get out of town. As her car climbed the mountain, the sun set, a ribbon of orange that lasted forever. At the peak, she pulled to an open spot marked with a blue Scenic Overlook sign and got out.

With the sun went the day's warmth, and she shivered and rubbed her hands together. She turned over Al's words, Mike's tight-lipped mention of his time in L.A., the last two months. A breeze lifted her hair from her neck, and she closed her eyes and breathed it in. The lights of Silver Valley twinkled in the valley below her. How many secrets did that town hold? How many people woke up, worked, went to bed, fell in love, and always kept their deepest thoughts and desires held tight to the chest? *You wanted to know*, came the voice again. Yes. She had. She stared into the dark for a long time. When she finally returned to the warmth of her car, three text messages waited for her.

"I'm so sorry. Mom fell at home & I had to take her to Med Ctr."

"Call me when you get these. Left my phone at work & couldn't text earlier."

"R u mad? Please don't be. Call me."

She wasn't mad. Or rather, she wasn't only mad. Sienna turned the car around and drove back to Pine Point. She was confused. Hurt. Worried too, because she liked Loretta. Mad was only part of it. She climbed out of her car and looked into the diner's brightly lit interior. Josie stood behind the counter. A handful of familiar faces filled the booths and tables, and Sienna knew if she walked inside, they'd greet her with smiles and hellos and stories about their day.

She didn't want to talk about her day. She didn't want to *think* about her day. Sienna locked her car and climbed the dark stairs to her apartment. She poured a glass of red wine, drank most of it, and dug out a box of microwave popcorn for dinner. Her phone buzzed with an incoming call, but she turned it off without looking at it. Instead, she refilled her glass, dumped the popcorn into a bowl, and carried it and the wine bottle into the living room with her.

"I'll call him tomorrow," she said aloud. She didn't want to talk to him tonight. She didn't want to talk to anyone.

Chapter Thirty-One

Mike slept on the couch downstairs, waking every few hours when the blanket slipped off or his mother rolled over in her squeaky bed down the hall.

Broken ankle and sprained wrist, revealed the X-rays. Crutches for a week, a walking boot for four more weeks after that, and a splint on her arm. The ER doctor gave her prescriptions for two different painkillers, but she folded them into tiny squares and threw them out when she got home. "Plain old ibuprofen will be just fine," she said.

Sometime around dawn, Mike gave up on sleep. He sat up and checked his phone for the hundredth time. Sienna hadn't called or texted. He ran one thumb over the screen. Was she mad? Or had something else happened? Maybe she'd left her phone at work. Maybe it had died and she'd misplaced the charger. He hated not hearing from her. It hadn't felt right, going to bed without the sound of her voice in his ear. *Shit, I've got it bad.* He set the phone aside. His mother's words echoed in his head, and he wondered what Sienna did know about her mother's death. Had she kept the truth a secret?

He scrubbed the sleep from his eyes. He'd tried to avoid falling for her, but in the end, it seemed stupid to deny the facts. She made him laugh. She turned him on. She listened, didn't judge, and trusted him with her students. He watched the sun rise over the mountain in the distance, a smudge of yellow over brown. She made him want to be a better person.

He got up and made a pot of coffee, then looked in the fridge. Fifteen minutes later, pancake mix sat in a bowl next to a plate of bacon and a dish of scrambled eggs.

"Are we feeding an army this morning?" Loretta said from the doorway. She wore a sweater and pajamas bottoms with cats printed on them.

"Ma! Why didn't you call me? I would've helped you get up."

"I am still capable of dressing myself, thank you very much." She hopped to a seat at the kitchen table and leaned her crutches against the wall.

Mike swirled pancake batter on the hot skillet and poured two cups of coffee. "How are you feeling?"

"Like I fell off a ladder and broke a few things." She shook her head. "You're right. I shouldn't have tried to do it by myself." She sighed and pushed her hair from her face. "I hate getting old, Mikey."

"Happens to all of us," he said as he flipped the pancakes. He added one to a plate of bacon and eggs and set it on the table. "What did Uncle Henry used to say? 'It's better than the alternative.'"

She smiled. "Yes, it is. He was right."

"Besides," he went on as he joined her, "there's someone who lives around the corner who doesn't think you're old at all. Seems like he might want to spend a little more time with you."

She looked up from pouring maple syrup on her pancake. "Are you getting fresh with me?"

"Not at all. I'm just saying that if you and Doc want to go out, you should. Call him up. Invite him to dinner."

She lifted one shoulder. "Maybe I will. We'll see." She rested her splinted arm on the table. "Speaking of calling people up, did you talk to Sienna?"

"No."

She tsked and took a long sip of coffee. "Well, you should. Don't let that one get away. She's the best thing to happen to you in a long time."

Mike grinned. He knew. Damn, but he knew.

An hour later, with the kitchen spotless and his mother on the couch in front of her favorite television channel, Mike changed into a pair of jeans and a Springer Fitness polo shirt. He'd told Hans he'd be in by ten, but he wanted to see Sienna first. He sent a quick text before pulling out of the driveway just in case she hadn't gotten up yet. Not like that would be a bad thing. He could think of little else he'd rather do than crawl under the covers and slide his hands along her naked curves.

"Good morning. Missed hearing from u. I'll swing by in 5. MB we can get coffee?"

He left his phone on the passenger seat, but she didn't text back. In a matter of minutes, he found an empty parking spot on Main Street and walked up the stairs to her apartment. He passed the Ericksen sisters' door with a grin. Sienna had told him her discovery about Ella secretly feeding the stray cats.

He knocked on her door and waited. Not a sound. He knocked again and checked the time. Almost eight thirty. Too early on a Saturday morning? This time, he pressed his ear against the door and heard movement inside. Just when he was about to knock a third time, she opened it.

"Hi there." She looked gorgeous, her hair still sleep-mussed and a robe tied loosely around her waist.

She met his gaze for a fraction of a second and then looked at his knees. She didn't open the door all the way or invite him in.

"Something wrong?" He held up his phone. "I texted you last night. I left my phone at work and we didn't get out of the Med Center until almost six. By the time I went back to the gym to get it—"

"How's your mom?"

"She's okay. Broke her ankle when she fell off the ladder."

Sienna put a hand over her mouth. "I'm so sorry," she said through her fingers.

"She'll be all right. On crutches and in a soft cast for a while. Maybe the upside is that she'll let me help her more often." He tried for another smile, but she didn't return it. "Are you mad?"

She turned and walked back into the foyer. She hadn't closed the door, so he followed her. "Hello? Earth to Sienna?"

She turned to face him and gripped the edge of her recliner. "Why didn't you tell me you spent time in prison?"

He had to hand it to her, she didn't pull any punches. Her face went white, and she bit her bottom lip. Everything inside him shattered. "How did you find out?"

"That's what you have to say? How did I find out?" She closed her eyes for a second. "I asked you to be honest. To tell me if there was anything else I should know."

"You think I was going to tell you about that? Shit, you'd never give me the time of day again. You'd look at me the way you're looking right now, angry and disappointed and like I'm a piece of gum you have to scrape off your shoe. You wouldn't care why or what happened."

"Felony theft? That's what your friend Al told me."

If he could have punched something in the room, he would have. As it was, it took everything Mike had not to put a hole through the wall. "He's not my friend," he choked out.

"I went by your house yesterday after Hans told me about your mom. I was knocking on your door when Al drove by."

I'll kill him. I'll fucking kill him. Mike's breath grew tight in his chest.

She sank into the chair. "Why didn't you just tell me?"

"Would you have gone out with me if I had?"

She didn't have to answer. Her face gave it away.

"That's why." He took a few steps into the living room. "It's a long story. It's the worst story of my life, and if I could live one hour of my life over again, it would be the hour I broke into Edie's apartment and tried to take back what was mine." Dullness settled over him, as if already the feelings were leaving him, the joy and comfort and natural high, the pure happiness he'd felt with Sienna over the last few weeks.

"You told me she cleaned out your bank accounts." Sienna ran one finger over a worn spot in the arm of the recliner. "So what, you tried to get the money back?"

"All I wanted was the title to my Mustang. I'd had that car since I was seventeen. Restored the whole thing the summer after I graduated from high school." He stared at a pile of yellow notepads sitting on an end table. "She moved in with her boyfriend after I kicked her out, so I knew where she was. Al and I went there one night when I thought she'd be working."

"You broke in?"

"Al did. He knew how to pick locks."

She wouldn't meet his gaze no matter how hard he tried. "Did you find it? The title?"

"Yeah. In the top drawer of a file cabinet in her bedroom." Along with a handful of naked photos that scumbag boyfriend must have taken of Edie. He'd actually gone into the bathroom and vomited into the toilet at the sight of them. The final time he saw her, he'd wanted to ask how long she'd been screwing someone else.

"If your name was on the title, they couldn't have prosecuted you for theft."

"They didn't. Not theft of the car anyway." He ran one hand over his forehead. "I was pissed. She had stacks of cash in that drawer too, under the envelope with the title."

"So you took the cash."

"She'd stolen almost ten grand out of our joint account, of which probably less than a thousand was money she'd actually earned. Yeah, I took it. Not all of it. Five grand. Figured that was compensation for the shit she put me through."

Sienna closed her eyes.

"She came home from wherever she was—not work, I found out that much, 'cause she'd lost her job six months earlier and never told me. Saw me and Al there and called the cops."

"Why didn't you just give her back the money?"

He shrugged. "I was stupid. I figured any judge would take one look at the situation and understand. Maybe even make her pay me back the whole amount."

She leaned back in the recliner and pushed herself with one toe, forward and back.

"I'm guessing that's not how it went down."

"I'm sorry. I should've told you. It's just a shitty part of my history, and I'm embarrassed as hell about it, and I'm hoping it doesn't matter now. I did my time." His legs went wobbly, and he sat in a straight-backed chair near the door. "Can you forgive me?"

She didn't answer right away. "It's a lot to forgive. I wish you'd told me the truth from the start."

He folded his hands between his legs. "You didn't tell me the truth about your mother."

"What are you talking about?" Her words were ice.

"The Oxy? The drugs in her system the day she died?" He glanced up, but before he finished, he could tell by her expression that she'd never known.

"Of course she had Oxy in her system. She was taking them for her back pain." Then realization flashed across her face. "You son of a bitch. Are you saying she—"

He didn't hear the rest of her sentence. Instead, his gaze snagged on a yellow notepad sitting on the table beside him.

Pine Point Blue Collar Workers, read the title at the top of the page. He reached down and flipped it over. *Local Professionals*, read the next. Below that title he saw his own name.

Owns a gym

Divorced

Lives with mom

Spent time out in CA? Came back why??

Mike grabbed the notepad in both hands and flipped to the next page. Then the next.

"Please put that down," Sienna said, her voice unsteady.

He didn't look up. On every page, he saw the names of people and places he knew. Arrows connecting them. Question marks. Theories about past mistakes and present connections and possible affairs. The blood climbed into his face.

"Mike, please don't read that."

"What is this? Your research?" He flipped back to the second page, the one with his name on it. "This was what you wanted? Dirt on me? Is that why you came back?"

"No."

"You must be damn happy you found out about me being in prison. Wow, that'll make your whole project, huh? Local guy hides great big secret from everyone except his mother and his former friend and the woman he's sleeping with." Agony tore at him. "*Was* sleeping with. You can be sure that's never happening again." Everything he'd told her, everything he'd shared with her, shot to shit. "Was that the plan all along? Get me to sleep with you and tell you everything I know about Pine Point? He whistled. "Man, sorry I held back." He shook the notepad so hard the top sheet ripped partway off. "I could tell you so much more," he said through clenched teeth. "Not like I would."

"Please, listen to me. I didn't go out with you or sleep with you as part of my research."

"Really? Because that's sure as hell how it looks." He got to his feet. She tried to reach for his hand, but he shook it off. "I didn't tell you about prison because I cared about you. I didn't want to ruin what we had." He tossed the notepad on the floor. "Thought maybe you cared about me too, but it looks like I was wrong."

"I do care. Please, don't go."

He shook his head and turned around. *You want secrets? Add your mother's drug addiction to the list.* But he wouldn't say those ugly words. He could never hurt her that way. Instead, he slammed the door behind him and walked to his truck, jaw and fists clenched so tightly that all the blood disappeared from them. Didn't matter. He didn't have much of a heart left anyway.

Chapter Thirty-Two

Somehow, Sienna got through the next few days. Only the nonstop needs of her students kept her from dwelling on her conversation with Mike and the look of betrayal on his face as he read the pages she'd written. It wasn't what it seemed like, she wanted to say, but she knew that wasn't true. All that work, all her research, did stem from the people she'd met over the past three months, the stories she'd heard, and the things she'd seen. A hundred times, she picked up her phone and tried to think of something to say to him. Then she thought of those words, the things he'd said about her mother, and she put her phone down again. Ridiculous. Impossible. Instead, she the spent nights curled in her recliner, flipping pages of her notepads, and painstakingly transferring the details to her laptop. The only person she didn't write about was Mike.

"Miss Cruz, is Mr. Mike coming to read-along this week?" Caleb asked on Monday.

"I don't think so," she answered. "He's very busy with his job."

"Maybe *we* could read to *him*," Billy offered. "Maybe he would like a break from doing all the reading."

He's taking a break, she thought, *but not from reading.*

"What about the baseball game?" Caleb asked on Thursday. "Mr. Mike said he would go to the Silver Valley Panthers' opening-day game with us. He said he'd sit behind home plate with us and tell us about all the players." He walked over to Sienna's desk and put his hand next to hers. "Opening day is April sixth. That's one week from Tuesday."

"I know, sweetheart." Sienna cleared her throat and looked at the hopeful faces of her students. Even Dawn waited with her hands clenched under her chin. "I don't know if Mr. Mike will be able to come along. But I'll call about tickets today, okay? If there are still some left, I'll ask Ms. James if we can take a field trip to the game."

"Yay!" Billy and Bailey danced around the rug. Caleb nodded. Silas rocked in his chair with a giant grin. Only Dawn didn't move or change expression, as if she knew Sienna was lying about Mike and the reasons he didn't come to see them anymore.

He lied to me, she thought at night, as she lay awake and stared at the ceiling. *He didn't really lie*, came the next thought. *He just didn't tell me about a pretty bad part of his past.* She tried to put herself in his position. Would she have confessed an arrest and jail time to someone she wanted to spend time with?

Probably not.

But that didn't change the heaviness in her heart. And when she let herself consider the possibility about her mother and the painkillers, everything turned darker. It couldn't be true. Elenita's death couldn't be connected to a drug addiction. Sienna blinked up into the dark. But what if it was? What else didn't she know?

* * * * *

That Friday, Mike pulled up a stool at the end of the bar next to Mac and Damian.

"Hey, look who the hell it is." Mac thumped him on the back. "Haven't seen you in a while."

"Keeping long hours at the gym." It was the only way to stop thinking about Sienna twenty-four seven, and even that strategy was barely working.

"Heard your mom took a tumble," Damian leaned across Mac to say. "She okay?"

Mike nodded and took the beer Nate poured him. "She gets rid of her crutches on Monday if the doctor gives her the green light. Then it's a month in a soft cast."

"She keeping you busy?"

"Not too much, believe it or not. Doc Halloran's been coming around and helping out."

"Oh, yeah? Some senior loving?" Mac asked.

"Something like that." He took a long drink of the cool amber beer. "I'm all for it, if it makes her happy." At least one Springer living in Pine Point deserved that.

"Sienna coming by tonight?" Damian asked as Nate dropped off three menus.

Mike trained his gaze on the TV behind the bar. "Don't think so. We're not really hanging out anymore." *She betrayed me. She betrayed all of us.* The names on the yellow paper swam in front of his eyes, and he had to drink again to banish them.

"Sorry to hear that."

Mike shrugged. Should've known he couldn't trust her. Couldn't trust any woman. They always found a way to hurt you.

Nate turned up the volume as the local sports broadcast came on. "You guys know what you want?"

They ordered, and then Mike found himself watching the scouting report for the Silver Valley Panthers.

"Hopes are high this year for the Panthers, who have newcomer Tommy Allen as a starting pitcher and the dazzling duo of Myers and Rivera at second and shortstop for another season…"

A lump caught in Mike's throat. *I told the kids we'd go to a Panthers game. Opening day.* He couldn't believe how much he'd looked forward to the idea of talking pitch counts with Caleb or helping Silas catch a fly ball. He couldn't believe how much those kids had gotten under his skin, period. He watched the highlight reels of the Panthers practicing in their home stadium and wondered if Sienna would take them to the game without him.

For the first time, his resolve faltered. He'd spent a long five days pissed beyond belief. He'd worked out until he could barely move, he'd snapped at his mother, and he'd gone for long drives, trying to make sense of someone who would exploit other people's private lives. He spun the beer mug in his hand. He couldn't forgive her with a snap of his fingers. But he wondered if he'd been too hasty in walking out of her apartment without letting her explain.

"Here you go," Nate said a few minutes later. He delivered burgers for Mac and Damian and a Reuben for Mike. He sank his teeth into the sandwich with gusto. For a few minutes, he forgot about Sienna. He ate every last bite, finished the fries on his plate, and declined another beer. "See you guys around," he said as he paid his bill.

"Taking off already?"

"My place is a pigsty. And I've got quarterly numbers to go over at the gym."

Mac and Damian waved goodbye, and Mike ambled to his truck, parked in the back lot. He tried not to think of the last time he'd parked here, when Sienna hadn't been able to keep her hands off him.

"How's yer girlfriend doin' these days?" Al Halloran appeared from the shadows, eyes bloodshot and words slurred.

Mike froze. *Count to ten*, he told himself. *Last thing you want to do is get into a fight with this asshole.* He didn't answer. Instead, he kept walking to his truck.

"Hey." Al cut him off partway there. "What, now you don't talk to an old friend?"

Old friend? Mike shoved by him. "We haven't been friends in a long time."

Al didn't take the hint. He followed Mike to his truck and reached for the handle.

"Get your fucking hand off my truck."

Al's eyes went dark and cold. "I'm blackballed in this town. Can't get a job to save my life."

"Could've told you that six weeks ago."

"Wasn't that hard for you."

"I don't spend my days stoned out of my mind."

Al shrugged and let go of the door handle. When Mike went to open it, he reached out and grabbed Mike's shirt instead. "You gotta help me. I helped you. When you needed a job, I gave you one. Gave you a place to live too, for a whole year when you came out to California. You forget about that?"

Mike wrenched away from Al's grimy grasp. "I've been thinking more about all the ways you screwed me since."

Al stuck both hands in his back pockets. "You took that money from Edie all on yer own, man."

Yes. He had. And he'd been paying for it ever since.

If Al hadn't told Sienna about prison, she wouldn't have ignored his texts that night. He wouldn't have gone over there the next morning. He wouldn't have seen all the things she'd written about people. One tiny pebble in the pond, and all the ripples spread.

Before he knew it, Mike took Al's shirt in his fist. He bent close enough to see the gap in Al's greasy smile and smell his terrible breath. "Why'd you tell her?" His fist tightened, and the fabric bunched around Al's neck. "Why'd you tell Sienna about me serving time?"

Al wriggled in his grasp and struggled for breath, but Mike didn't let go or loosen his grip. "It didn't have anything to do with you. You should've minded your own business." Al's eyes bulged in his face, and finally Mike dropped his hand. The Reuben and the beer churned in his stomach. "Get the fuck out of here. You make me sick."

He turned to go, but Al must be stupider than Mike remembered, because he punched Mike in the kidney as he went to unlock his truck. Pain shot through his back, and he staggered against the truck. "What the fu—" Another punch. This one took Mike almost to his knees.

With a roar, he spun. Red blurred his vision, and he swung out with both fists. *You ruined everything*, he thought as he made contact. Once. Then again. Then a third time. Bone splintered and drops of blood sprayed both their shirtfronts. Someone shouted from across the parking lot, and Mike backpedaled as his senses returned. Al crouched on the pavement, holding his face. Blood poured from between his fingers.

What the hell did I do?

Mike looked up to see Mac and Damian standing in the parking lot, wide-eyed. He grabbed Al's arm and pulled him to his feet. "Get out of here. You tell anyone I beat the piss outta you, and I'll send the cops to wherever you are so fast you won't have time to hide your stash." His hands trembled. In the blink of an eye, he'd returned to the punk he'd been years ago, fighting, cursing, letting someone else get the better of his temper. He swallowed back bile and hated himself.

Al staggered away without another word.

Mike drove straight home and took a long shower. He didn't want to be that person anymore. He'd come to town wanting to leave that guy far behind him. He closed his eyes and rinsed under the spray. Tiny spots of Al's blood covered one wrist, and he rubbed them until the skin went raw. *You have to be a better person.*

He toweled off and walked naked to his bedroom. He'd started to become a better person, first when he returned to Pine Point and then when he opened Springer Fitness. He'd learned from the past and left it behind him. He hadn't realized the missing part of his life until Sienna came to town. She'd changed him, her and her students. He stretched out on his bed and flipped on the TV. He wanted to be better. He wanted to be proud of the way he spent his days. Most of all, he wanted the feeling of deep-down happiness he'd discovered over the last three months.

But he had no idea had to get it back.

Chapter Thirty-Three

"Miss Cruz, look!" Caleb pointed at the Silver Valley Panthers pitchers warming up in the bullpen. The boy stopped and stared. Two young men, one a head taller than the other, wound up and let the ball fly in a steady rhythm Sienna knew fascinated Caleb to no end. The catchers squatted at the opposite end of the bullpen, returning the pitches and pounding their fists into their gloves.

"Keep moving, son," Caleb's father said with a pat on his son's shoulder. "We have to find our seats before the game starts."

Sienna held Silas by one hand and Bailey by the other. Billy walked beside Caleb's father with Dawn behind them. Every few feet, Sienna glanced over her shoulder to make sure Dawn hadn't disappeared. The sun beat down on the back of her neck, and a bright blue sky spread above them. Beautiful weather for opening day. She squeezed away her wish that Mike had come with them and relegated it to the place in her heart with other wishes, like *I wish we hadn't fought* and *I wish I'd explained things better* and *I wish we could get past all this.* Sometimes her whole body ached with wishing.

At the front gate, Sienna wrestled Bailey's sweaty hand from hers and dug into her purse for the tickets. Silas clutched his baseball glove in one hand, his eyes the size of saucers as he looked at the stadium.

"You excited, buddy?" she asked.

He nodded.

"Dawn, please come over here." The girl had wandered over to a kiosk selling programs, hats, and giant foam fingers. The guy behind the counter leaned down and asked her something, but she only stared and pinched her hands together. He frowned, made a comment, and then turned away. Dawn's face fell. Sienna walked over as the girl's bottom lip pushed out. She wanted to tell the idiot behind the counter he didn't have to be rude. Instead, she hugged Dawn for a half second before the girl ducked away and walked over to Caleb.

"Come on, come on," Billy called, almost delirious with excitement. They walked inside the gate, and he pointed at the enormous red signs hanging overhead. "We're in Row F," he shouted, and was about to dart away before Caleb's father plucked him by the sleeve.

"You've got your hands full, don't you?" he said to Sienna.

"You have no idea."

Together, they managed to find their seats along the first-base line—not behind home plate as Caleb had hoped, but in the third tier up. Still, they had a decent view, and if a foul ball made it this far, Silas might even have a chance at catching it. The crowd settled in around them, and soon the players trotted out for introductions.

Sienna sat on one end of the row with Caleb's father on the other. In between, the five students sat rapt with wonder. From the opening pitch to the third out of the fourth inning, they remained silent, only cheering when the Panthers scored two runs in the third. Caleb pressed his hand against her leg every so often, leaning forward in his seat to watch each play. Silas had his glove positioned against his chest, his gaze on every foul ball. Sometime in the fifth inning, Sienna finally relaxed. She'd spent two sleepless nights worrying about taking the students out of their familiar environment. Turned out she didn't need to. They looked like they were having the time of their lives.

This was a good idea. The sun warmed her face, and she slipped on her sunglasses. She tried not to dwell on the fact that it had been Mike's idea, and they wouldn't be here at all if he hadn't suggested it. The field, the players, the calls of strikes and balls faded. *I miss him.*

"Miss Cruz?" Caleb's father called down the row. "I'm going to take these two to the bathroom." He motioned to the twins squirming in their seats.

"Okay, sure."

"Want anything? Popcorn? Peanuts?"

Caleb jumped up and down. "Yes, please! Peanuts."

"Silas has a peanut allergy, so, no," she said as she sat him back down. "But some popcorn would be nice, thanks."

The man nodded and directed the twins ahead of him up the stairs. Sienna leaned over to ask Dawn if she needed to use the bathroom too, but at a loud crack from the field, a roar swept over the crowd. Everyone around them leaped to their feet. A Panther had hit a grand slam, and four players made their way around the bases, pumping their fists and waving to the crowd as they crossed home plate. *Six—zero*, read the flashing neon sign behind the outfield.

"Miss Cruz, did you see that?" Caleb asked, his cheeks flushed with excitement. "A grand slam is very uncommon in a minor league game. Last year the Panthers only had two, and they were both at away games."

"I did see it, and it was very exciting," she answered. She slipped up her sunglasses and scanned the row. Silas bounced on his tiptoes, the glove still cradled to his chest. Billy and Bailey were climbing back down the stairs with Caleb's father behind them. And Dawn—

Sienna's gaze lighted on the empty seat beside Silas. *Oh God. Oh, no.* She'd looked away for thirty seconds. Not even thirty. Her entire body went cold. "Caleb, did you see Dawn leave?"

He shook his head.

"Silas? Do you know where Dawn went?"

His face furrowed for a moment, and then he turned and pointed to a sign that read "Restrooms."

"Oh, God." Sienna pushed her way down the row. "You boys stay right here. Don't move." She grabbed Caleb's father's arm. "Did you see Dawn up there?"

He shook his head. "She's gone?"

Sienna nodded as panic closed her throat. "Maybe she just went to the bathroom." She tried to push away all the horrible news stories about abducted children and predators who waited outside public restrooms for children. *This is my worst nightmare.* She stumbled up the stairs. A stadium filled with two thousand fans and a little girl who didn't speak vanished among them. If anything happened to Dawn, Sienna would never forgive herself. Ever.

* * * * *

Mike parked at the far end of the lot and rolled down his window. At first, he'd thought Sienna might not take the kids to the game, but on his way to work, he'd passed the elementary school and watched them all climb into a small yellow bus. Silas held a baseball glove. Caleb wore a Yankees shirt. And against his better judgment, Mike had followed them over the mountain to the ballpark. The crowd inside the stadium erupted in cheers, and he drummed his fingers on the steering wheel. *Wish I could see their faces.* He pictured Caleb zeroing in on the pitchers' strategies, Silas arching up to reach for a foul ball, the twins wriggling in their seats. He wondered about Dawn's reaction, what she'd think of it all.

Probably be a little overwhelming for a kid like her.

He didn't get out of the truck. Instead, he rested his head against the seat and drank in the early spring day. A fuzz of green covered the ground and most of the trees, promising another rich, hot summer. Funny how spring could sneak up on you like that. Just when you thought winter would last forever, the sun came out and everything bloomed. Mike looked around the parking lot. He hadn't been to a game here in years. Looked like the place was about three-quarters full, not bad for early afternoon.

The wind shifted, and he could hear the umpire's call and the occasional crack of bat meeting ball. More applause. Then a groan. Then a crackle of the PA system.

"...little girl named Dawn Watson, please report..."

Mike sat straight up.

"Again, if there's a girl named Dawn Watson in the stadium, your teacher is asking you to please come to the concession stand behind the—"

He didn't hear the rest of the announcement. A knot lodged in his throat as he jumped from his truck and strode across the parking lot. *She's disappeared again. She's gotta be terrified. And Sienna's probably out of her mind with worry.* Halfway to the stadium, he broke into a run.

Chapter Thirty-Four

"Physical description?" asked a heavy-jowled security guard.

Sienna twisted her fingers in the hem of her shirt. "She's about four feet tall, blond hair in braids. She was wearing a blue T-shirt and jeans."

"Anything else we should know?"

Tears filled Sienna's eyes. She'd been up and down every floor of the stadium, in and out of every women's room. It was as if Dawn had virtually vanished. "She probably won't talk to whoever finds her."

His pen stopped moving on his notepad. "I'm sorry?"

"She's selectively mute. She doesn't usually talk."

He scratched the back of his thick neck. "Ah, okay." He shoved his notepad into his back pocket and repeated Dawn's description on his radio. "I'm going to notify the local police too."

Sienna nodded.

"I've got four men here. They'll scour the place." He patted Sienna on the arm. "Don't worry. We'll find her. She's probably just looking at stuffed animals in the souvenir shop."

Sienna tried to draw a full breath and failed. She'd already been through the souvenir shop twice. She glanced at her other students, who still sat and watched the game. Caleb's father looked up and caught her eye, but she shook her head at his questioning gaze.

I'm a failure. I lost a child.

She'd also ruined a relationship, hurt a good guy's feelings, and probably screwed up her research. Talk about striking out.

"Why don't you wait by concession stand in case she shows up?" the guard suggested.

Sienna nodded. What would she tell Dawn's foster parents? Or the principal, or the other students? Worse, what would she tell Dawn if they found her and she'd gotten hurt or scared and Sienna hadn't protected her the way she'd promised to? Her throat hitched. She laced her hands around the back of her neck and willed the ugly sobs to stay silent. *Don't get hysterical. You won't be any good to anyone if you can't hold it together.*

On wooden legs, she walked to the first-floor concession stand, the air ripe with the scents of popcorn and hot dogs and cotton candy. "Dawn!" She cupped her hands around her mouth and called until she was hoarse. She circled the entire stadium, checking every nook where a small, anxious girl might hide. Nothing. Back to the concession stand, where a lanky security guard shook his head with a grim expression when she asked.

"We'll find her, ma'am," he said.

She turned away without answering.

"Sienna?" Darryl Cobalt, the head custodian from work, walked over carrying a paper tray of hot dogs and fries.

"You're not at school?"

He winked. "I always take off opening day. Sixteen years and running." He frowned. "What's wrong?"

She pressed her lips together. "One of my students is missing."

He handed his food to a friend and took her in his arms for a quick, hard hug. "I heard the announcement. Didn't know that was one of yours."

Sienna nodded into his shirtfront.

"Let me help," he asked. "Where have you already looked?"

"I, ah…" She sniffled. "I've looked everywhere."

He patted her arm. "Gary," he called over his shoulder to a burly man in the beer line. "Come on over here."

Gary ambled over. "What's up?"

Darryl filled him in, and within minutes, a handful of other men had joined them. Darryl divided up his buddies, pointing each to a different section of the stadium and the grounds outside. "You want to stay here?" he asked Sienna. "In case she shows up?"

Sienna gulped. "I guess so."

A dark-haired woman with a snake tattoo covering one arm approached her. "Honey, you the one lost the little girl?"

"I hope I haven't lost her."

"No, no, that's not what I meant." The woman reached into a giant patchwork bag hanging from her shoulder and pulled out a bottle of water. "Here. You look a little peaked."

Sienna felt a little peaked, to be honest. "Thank you."

"Don't you worry. Kids wander off all the time. I got three of my own, half the time I don't even know where they are."

Sienna reserved judgment on that and instead drank more water.

"You want me to wait with you?" The woman pulled out a tube of bright pink lipstick and slathered it on. "I'm not a big fan of baseball. I'm only here 'cause my boyfriend loves it." She waved at an overweight guy wearing a Panthers T-shirt with cut-off sleeves. A matching snake tattoo covered his arm as well. "Dougie, this woman here is the one whose little girl wandered off."

"Aw, sorry to hear that." Dougie stifled a burp. "They just made another announcement about her. She ain't back yet?"

Sienna shook her head.

"You know what, hang on a minute." He grabbed his cell phone off the holster on his hip and sent a text. "My buddy's one of the assistant managers. I'll tell him to look down on the field too, and around the dugouts. Ya never know about kids, they can show up in the weirdest places."

"Oh, well, thanks." She felt a little overwhelmed by everyone's kindness.

"Sure, no problem." He patted her arm. "You want help looking around?"

"I think there's a lot of people already searching, but—"

"You got a picture of her?" Dougie's girlfriend asked. "Maybe they could put that up on the scoreboard."

Sienna flipped through the pictures on her phone. "I don't know." Once or twice last month, she'd snapped a few of them on the playground with Mike. She hadn't looked at them since. Seeing his smile now seared her heart all over again. "Here." Finally, she found one of Dawn standing next to the slides, eyes big, hands folded.

"Text it to me," Dougie directed. He gave her his number and then nodded as his phone pinged with the picture. "I'll have my buddy get it up on the screen. Picture's worth a thousand words, ain't it?"

Sienna nodded. Especially when it came to a mute child. That picture would be the *only* words.

"All right, honey, you hang in there," the woman said as she and Dougie turned for the hot dog line. "What's her name? Dawn? I'll see if I can't turn her up."

"Thank you so much." Sienna finished the last of her water. grateful down to her toes. She couldn't believe so many total strangers were trying to help her. She looked around for a place to sit. Her legs weren't going to hold her much longer.

Mike materialized from nowhere. "Where's the last place you saw her?" His blue eyes bored into hers. "Before she disappeared?"

She almost slipped right down to the ground. "What are you doing here?" Relief and want and sadness at the way he kept his distance washed over her in equal measures. "Row F." She pointed. "Third tier."

Without another word, he turned and walked away.

Sienna followed him as he traced the same paths she'd been over five times, from the restrooms to the seats and back. She watched Darryl do the same on the other side of the stadium. A moment later, Dawn's picture flashed onto the scoreboard with another announcement.

Mike stared at it, then at Sienna. "Wow, how'd you get that up there so fast?"

"A guy I don't know. He and his girlfriend stopped to help."

He turned in a slow circle. "If I were Dawn, where would I go?"

"I have no idea. I don't know why she disappeared in the first place."

"Too loud? Too many screaming fans? The world can be a scary place to regular people, let alone an eight-year-old girl who thinks she can't trust it." He caught her gaze. "Sometimes it's easier to just disappear and pretend the rest of the world doesn't exist."

The words fell heavy on her heart. *Tell me about it.*

The eighth inning finished with another run scored by the Panthers, and Sienna walked to the top of the stairs. The teams switched sides, and a few spectators began filing out, apparently confident in their home team's four-run advantage. Sienna flattened herself against the wall to let them pass and suddenly saw a small door marked *Private* she hadn't seen before. Its seams blended into the concrete blocks painted in the Panthers' team colors of red and blue.

"Where does that go?" She pointed.

Mike tried the handle. To her surprise, it creaked open. "I have no idea." He stuck his head inside. "Up to the next deck?"

"There isn't one."

"Are you sure? Must be access to the roof then."

The roof? Visions of baseball fans falling to their deaths filled her head. Her heart thumped an awful patter. "Do you think she went up there?"

"Dawn?" Mike said into the dark stairwell.

She isn't going to answer, Sienna almost said, but he already knew that. She wiped her forehead and realized she smelled of perspiration. Wonderful. She hadn't washed her hair in two days, she'd ripped out the bottom hem of her shirt, and she was dissolving into a certifiable wreck with every passing minute. She bit her bottom lip and walked over to the door.

"Yes, I know it is," he was saying.

Sienna froze. *Is he talking to her?*

"Miss Cruz is awfully worried about you. We need you to come down so we can all go back to school together."

In disbelief, Sienna stuck her head under his arm and looked up. Far at the top of the dark stairwell, a pair of eyes blinked down at them.

"Mr. Mike?" came Dawn's plaintive voice. It was the sweetest sound Sienna had ever heard.

"Yes, sweetheart. I'm right here." He glanced at Sienna. "And I'm not going anywhere. You're safe with me."

"Mr. Mike, I think I'm ready to go home now."

Chapter Thirty-Five

Loretta Springer hobbled out to the covered back porch, holding a bottle of champagne and four plastic glasses.

"Ma, what did I say? Sit down and let me get the rest." Mike jumped up from his seat next to Sienna on the porch swing. Doc Halloran sat in one of two cushioned chairs across from them. A spread of cheese and crackers, fruit, veggies and dip, and different kinds of breads and jams covered a glass-topped table.

"What? I've been keeping this bottle for years, waiting for the right time to open it." She lifted the champagne in the air. "Seems to me this is as good a night as any."

Sienna had to agree. As Mike popped the cork and filled the glasses, she watched his deft hands and imagined them feeling their way along her body. They hadn't talked much since the baseball game. But he hadn't left her side the whole way back to the school. He'd even parked his truck at the stadium and taken the bus with them. The boys had been thrilled to see him. Silas had practically climbed into his lap, and for one whole second, Caleb had let Mike drop one hand onto his shoulder as they watched the final out together.

"Dawn didn't stop talking after we found her," Mike was telling Doc. "It was like the dam finally burst or something."

Sienna welled up again at the thought. She'd met Dawn's foster parents for the first time at the school, and when she'd told them what had happened, both had choked out emotional thank yous as they'd taken Dawn in their arms. Good people. Reserved but caring. She rubbed her arms in the cool evening air. *I still can't believe she spoke.*

Mike rejoined her on the swing and looped one arm around her shoulders. "Maybe she was just waiting for the right person to come along," he said into her ear. "I know what that feels like."

Happiness and hope washed over Sienna. "I'm sorry about what happened between us," she murmured.

He moved her hair from her face. "Me too. We should talk about it."

She nodded. She had to talk about something else first. "I wanted to ask you all something." She glanced at Loretta and Doc, and nerves built in her stomach. "It's about my mom."

Loretta stopped arranging cheese and crackers and stole a quick glance at Doc. Suddenly Sienna knew. "It's true, isn't it? What Mike told me?" She felt as though all breath had left her body. "My mom overdosed the day she died." Saying it out loud sounded worse than inside her head. Raw sadness, anger, and disbelief washed over her. She felt turned upside down, unsteady, betrayed. Broken-hearted.

Doc coughed.

"Why didn't you tell me?" She dropped her gaze and focused on Mike's shirtfront. "I should have known."

"Wasn't something a fifteen-year-old needed to know," Loretta said, her voice firm. "You'd just lost your mother. Didn't matter how it happened."

Sienna shook her head. "I feel like a fool."

Mike took her hand and ran his thumb over her knuckles. "It doesn't make her a bad person."

"It doesn't make her a good one either." *Why, Mom?* Tears pricked her eyes. If not for some stupid pain pills, her mom might still be alive. They might still be living together in Pine Point, and everything from the last ten years would be different.

She looked at Mike's hand in hers. *Including this.*

Loretta leaned over the table and pointed at Sienna. "You listen to me. Your mother was a good woman, a hard worker who put her daughter first no matter what. She made a bad decision. So do we all. I don't want you to think on her memory for one minute with anything but happiness."

"Why didn't *you* tell me?" Sienna asked Doc. "I'm sure it was in whatever report you had to make."

He nodded, his gnarled fingers tight around the stem of his glass. "Like Loretta said, I didn't want to hurt you. None of us did. Thought the best thing was to protect your memory of your mother." He fixed his gaze on Sienna. "Her heart gave out at the end. That was the primary cause of death. The drugs?" He shrugged. "Did they contribute? Maybe. Probably. But the only thing you needed to know was that she loved you. She was working hard for you and a better life."

Sienna blinked away tears. *I can't believe this.* She'd spent so much time looking for other people's secrets, she hadn't even stopped to think she might discover some of her own.

"It's getting a little chilly out here," Loretta said, even though the temperature hadn't dropped a single degree. With a knowing look at Doc, she limped to the sliding door and waited for him to follow.

Sienna and Mike sat in silence for a few minutes. She sipped her champagne and watched the sun settle into the hills. *What comes next? Where do we go from here?* "I've been thinking," she finally began.

"Mmm?"

"I might change the focus of my research." Especially now, knowing the truth and trying to understand her place in it.

Mike's hand stopped moving along the back of her hair. "To what?"

She turned to look at him. "I always thought I wanted to prove that small towns had secrets."

"Yes, so you've said. Many times."

She elbowed him. "But I think I've had a change of heart. Or mind. Or something. It's not that I don't believe that anymore." She cocked her head. "It's true. You know that as well as I do."

"Yes, I do."

"But I don't think secrets necessarily tear a place apart. I think in a weird way, they might tie a place tighter together. If people know secrets about each other, maybe it makes them more likely to have each other's backs."

"You mean like blackmail? I'll keep your secret if you'll keep mine?"

"No. Well, not really. Not in a bad way. Just..." She sighed and leaned against him, loving the warmth of his chest that cradled her. "What your mom and Doc said. They kept my mother's secret to protect me, didn't they? They didn't judge my mom as this horrible person because of what she'd done. And when all those people helped me look for Dawn today, I don't think any of them judged me for losing track of her. They just wanted to help me find her."

He chuckled, and she could feel the vibrations. "There's judgment in small towns, don't get that wrong."

"But there's kindness too. And forgiveness, I think."

He kissed her temple.

"I understand why you came back here," she went on. "It feels safe, doesn't it? It's a place you can start over."

"Yes."

People make mistakes. Her mom's face appeared in her mind's eye, young and smiling. Sienna looked down at her own wrist, at the thin white line marking a mistake she'd almost made years ago. *It doesn't have to change everything good about them.* She turned and took Mike's face in her hands. "I didn't mean to hurt you." She ran her fingers over the faint stubble on his jaw. "I never wanted to. You were always more than a research subject. You have to know that."

"Ah, sweetheart, I do know that now. But it feels so good to hear you say it." He kissed her, and the kindness in his touch almost undid her. One hand went to the back of her head. The other slid down her arm, brushing her breast, and turning her skin to fire.

When he pulled back, the corners of his eyes crinkled as he grinned. "In the name of research, what do you say we take this celebration upstairs and do a little scientific experimentation? I think there's a position or two we haven't tried yet."

She smiled, and her sadness faded. "I hope there's more than one or two." She ran her hand up his thigh. "Because I have a feeling this experiment could take a long time."

"Maybe even past June?" He quirked a brow.

"I think almost definitely past June." She'd already thought about asking Jenny if her teaching position could continue into next year. She could write her dissertation anywhere in the country. Home seemed as good a place as any.

"I'm glad to hear that. Otherwise I was going to move Springer Fitness to North Carolina." He kissed her again, not slow nor gentle, and promising all kinds of wicked things. Then he took her hand and led her upstairs. At the top, he swept her into his arms and carried her inside his apartment.

I didn't know what I'd find here, she thought with wonder as Mike laid her on the bed and rained kisses on her neck. He took his time peeling off her shirt and stroking her bare skin, and she arched into his touch. *I thought I was doing a job. Finishing my studies. I didn't know I was coming home.* She hadn't had any inkling that the town where she'd grown up, the town she'd left with such heartache years ago, would be the same town to save her. To heal her.

To make her fall in love.

About the Author

Allie Boniface is a romance novelist and high school English teacher living with her husband in the northern New York City suburbs. She's had a soft spot for love stories and happy endings since the time she could read, and she's been caught scribbling story ideas on scrap paper (when she should have been paying attention to something else) too many times to count. When she's not writing, shoveling snow, or grading papers, she's traveling the United States and Europe in search of sunshine, back roads, and the perfect little pub.

Visit Allie's website at www.allieboniface.com to sign up for her newsletter, where you'll be the first to know about upcoming releases, giveaway and contests, review opportunities, in-person appearances, and more!

When a bad boy falls for an angel, the sparks could set the coldest season on fire.

Winter's Wonder

© 2015 Allie Boniface

Pine Point, Book 2

Pine Point hasn't changed much in the eight years Zane Andrews has been away. But Zane sure has. These days, this reformed bad boy has no problem resisting the bored housewives who flirt shamelessly with their gated community's security guard.

The only thorn in his side is the stray dog that keeps overturning the neighborhood's garbage cans, and the cute, crusading do-gooder who barks at him for trying to chase it off.

Becca Ericksen knows Zane is just doing his job, but his tactics are making her job—to rescue strays and bring them to Pine Point Paws—much harder. Clearly, they have nothing in common, yet when the legendary playboy asks her out, she finds herself saying yes.

With a sizzling kiss, something warm and unexpected beings to grow between them. Opposites can attract, but is attraction enough?

Warning: Contains a bad boy gone good, and a woman who's one good deed away from disaster. Cold noses and warm kisses—and that's just from the canines.

What if everything you knew about your past turns out to be…wrong?

Summer's Song

© 2009 Allie Boniface

Pine Point, Book 1

Ten years after leaving home, the last thing Summer Thompson expects is to inherit her estranged father's half-renovated mansion. And the last thing she wants is to face the memories of the night her brother died—sketchy as they may be. Now a San Francisco museum curator, she plans to stay east just long enough to settle the estate and get rid of the house. Until she finds it occupied by a hunky handyman who's strangely reluctant to talk about his past.

Damian Knight has something to hide: his mother and sister from a brutal stalker. They've found a measure of peace and carefully guarded safety in Pine Point. Yet when the lonely, haunted Summer steals his heart, he finds himself opening up to her in ways he should never risk. Especially to a woman who's planning to return to the west coast—after selling their refuge out from under them.

Summer's mounting flashbacks leave her confused—and more determined than ever to find out the truth behind her brother's death. But in a small town full of powerful secrets, confronting the past could cost her the man she loves. Even her life.

Warning: This title contains a hunky hero who can do anything with his hands, a heroine desperate to discover the truth, tons of summer heat, and a small town with so much charm you'll want to move there.

Can anything really change in 24 hours? Can everything?

One Night in Napa

A *One Night* Story

Journalist Grant Walker has one chance to salvage his job and his relationship with his domineering father. Terrorists have kidnapped a fading film star's son, and Grant has scored the first interview with the grieving mother. Even better, a new twist has just arrived on the scene—an illegitimate granddaughter who hasn't been heard from in seven long years.

It's the story of a lifetime, and all Grant has to do is deliver.

After discovering a terrible secret about her birth, Kira March left home vowing never to return. With her father kidnapped and her grandmother cracking under media pressure, it's up to her to find and destroy all evidence of that secret. Trouble is, a reporter has weaseled his way into the house looking for answers—and he isn't leaving until he gets them.

Yet as the hours pass, Kira finds herself falling for the very man who could destroy her. And when Grant comforts her in the wake of a midnight tragedy, he remembers why it's a bad idea to get emotionally involved with an interview subject. Especially when the family name is on the line.

Warning: This title contains a hunky hero who thinks he knows it all, an unconventional heroine who's out to prove him wrong, a ticking clock, family secrets, and enough sexual tension to heat every corner of an enormous mansion…especially when the power goes out.